THE WOMEN COULD FLY

A Novel

MEGAN GIDDINGS

AMISTAD

An Imprint of HarperCollins*Publishers*

THE WOMEN COULD FLY. Copyright © 2022 by Megan Giddings. All rights reserved. Printed in the United States of America. No part of this book may be used or reproduced in any manner whatsoever without written permission except in the case of brief quotations embodied in critical articles and reviews. For information, address HarperCollins Publishers, 195 Broadway, New York, NY 10007.

HarperCollins books may be purchased for educational, business, or sales promotional use. For information, please email the Special Markets Department at SPsales@harpercollins.com.

FIRST EDITION

Library of Congress Cataloging-in-Publication Data has been applied for.

ISBN 978-0-06-311699-3

22 23 24 25 26 LSC 10 9 8 7 6 5 4 3 2 1

THE
WOMEN
COULD
FLY

1.

On the day we all agreed that—yes, sure, okay, it's time—my mother was dead, I went to the storage unit where my dad kept all her stuff. I told myself if I wanted, I could burn it. Take all the boxes and clothes and loved things out into the parking lot. Kerosene, matches, patience, ash. Instead, I decided I would sort through it, choose a few things to save, clean the rest out and save my dad some time and money. I am a practical person.

The unit smelled like Black & Mild Jazzes, but I wasn't sure why. There were faint whiffs of her when I opened different boxes. Cedar. Mint. Rosemary. I want to be precise because every time I'm precise about her, she returns for a half-second. Her hands on the fork and spoon in a way where I can see the dirt beneath her fingernails, Saturday mornings that she spent spread out on the sofa, legs crossed and eyes on the ceiling, a forgotten book on her stomach. My mother's hand on my forearm, her skin shining brown and telling me I need to get lotion, she will not have her child walking around ashy. Her fingers pushing my hair away from my eyebrows and saying, Just because your forehead is big doesn't mean it isn't beautiful, look, there you are.

I said it aloud, again: "Yes, sure, she is, probably, no definitely dead. Say it again, like you believe it. My mother is dead." My voice was flat yet hesitant.

A box marked "hair care"—pomade, flat iron, a wig I had never seen her wear. Synthetic smell. Her books and research. My mother's biggest passion was researching our lineage. My great-great-great-great-great-grandaunt was burned for witchcraft: Birds that stilled, eyes that grew bright, their beaks and feathers following her as she spoke. A refusal to take a husband. The accounts about her disagreed.

The story my mother preferred: Our ancestor was just an ordinary woman. An ordinary woman in the wrong place, who upset the wrong man, and he used the laws of the day to teach her and all the other women in her village a lesson. Not a fun story, but an honest one.

The story my father, my grandmother, my aunt, everyone else in my life prefers to tell: My ancestor was a witch. Her burning took place on a beach, the heat from the fire so hot it turned sand into glass. My grandma has a bracelet made from the beads she swears came from that day that has been passed on from eldest daughter to eldest daughter. Our ancestress, when she couldn't handle the fire any longer, flew off the pillar and plunged her scorched feet into the sea. The smoke and steam sifted and became a weeklong fog. It crashed ships, blanketed the town, made the people who had tried to burn her afraid to leave their homes. My grandmother's records say this ancestor went on to the United States. Her older sister's records say this happened on Oak Island in South Carolina. My other great-aunt says no, this was New York.

In school like everyone else, like you, I was raised to believe that witches are still alive and living among us today—although most have died in the great eradications. My family was divided. My mother believed witches were a hoax still perpetuated today to keep women afraid and oppressed; my worst cousins, the ones who are loudest on the internet, believe that witchcraft is maybe an illness, like if you're in the wrong room at the wrong time, although for some it devolves into if you voted for the wrong person, you are a witch, if you vaccinate your children, you are a witch and are risking turning them into witches, and so on; and my uncles on my dad's side say shut up about witches and get back in the kitchen, dinner should be served every day at 5:30 sharp.

My mother pointed to the laws: how women are "encouraged" to be married by thirty; how unmarried women starting at twenty-eight have to do quarterly check-ins with the Bureau of Witchcraft to be tested. And what did being a witch have to do with being married? Didn't that seem suspicious? And what about how magic makes it tied to gender expression? How science can't even prove any links? Doesn't that seem a little too perfect? It seemed like that made it even easier to oppress two groups of people: women and anyone who did not conform to cisgender standards. She believed that most of what people believed was magic was actually just a way to wash out the accomplishments of women, make their hard work small.

All her books—medicine, gender, herbalism, art, protest—sitting in those wilting cardboard boxes, waiting for her hands to pick them up again, to flip the pages. Once one of my dad's brothers asked him if he was uncomfortable with "the way Tiana thought about things." Wasn't he afraid she would be accused of witchcraft? And worse, what did he think my mom's "nonsense" was doing to my brain? I love Jo's brain, my dad would say, and often that would be enough to change the subject. I picked one of the books up, one with a blue cover, flipped the pages, and did what I used to do when I was a teenager—pretended for just a moment that my hands were her hands.

At home, my mom would look at my schoolwork and roll her eyes. "The burnings that happened were a very bad thing. You should never accuse a woman of witchcraft unless you have a very good reason to, like she was actually hurting your family. And most witches don't even hurt people now! They are performers and artists. They stay away for all our safety." She never hung any of my A-pluses on the fridge, the way other moms did. Once I heard her whisper to my father, "I'm not celebrating lies."

I put the book down; it was a donate, not a keep. In my mother's research box, my dad had thrown in some papers of mine from high school. A paper that had gotten a D- on where I had argued—now I can see that I was simply echoing her, trying to keep her close—that everything we knew about "magic" was a lie. On the back page, a longer note about how my teacher understood I was upset about my family situation, that it was normal to be angry and "act out," but I had to write about actual, recorded—two underlines underneath the word "recorded"—history to do well in her class.

Below that, another essay I had written my freshman year, still grieving her, about a strange experience I'd had when I was eight years old. It was one of the rare times when my dad wasn't around. He was up north with his brothers, they were hunting, he was sitting in the blinds next to them refusing to shoot.

My mom was on the phone. I was half in reality, half in my made-up world, Marmillion. Everything there was made of potato chips and pretzels and popcorn and salt. Upstairs, in the attic, I heard what sounded like a horse's clip-clop. I wasn't scared, I was thinking of a Pegasus made entirely of mall pretzels with a horn made out of caramel corn. I would fly on it, then eat its horn. My mom was making a sound and I couldn't tell if she was laughing or crying.

I turned on the light to the attic. Sang to myself under my breath. Standing among the stacked cardboard boxes, the rolled-up area rug, was a deer. Its fur was bright white, its eyes shiny black. It was large, with a crown of shining antlers on its head. I took a step back. It took a step forward. My mouth was open, and it was so dry that my tongue felt like it was a piece of cut wood. The deer huffed at me. I could tell somehow that it was deeply annoyed.

"I'm sorry," I said, and walked backward downstairs. My mother was still on the phone. I tugged on her sweater. It was ugly—red, lime, black, stone-gray—and scratchy. I don't know why she ever wore it. She turned to me and tears were running down her cheeks. I had never seen her cry like that before. She was the type of mom who would tear up sometimes when watching TV: wiping her eyes when a dad told his daughter he loved her in a long-distance phone service commercial; a couple finally (re)uniting on a sitcom or in a movie; a beloved rapper-turned-actor wishing for his dad to love him like a father should love his son. Those tears were soft, gone within ten seconds with the help of the top of her T-shirt or a cardigan sleeve.

These tears scared me, made me wish I had stayed upstairs. Since I didn't know what to say, I took her hand. She dropped the phone and it dangled from its red cord, bounced in midair and then became a small bundle on the floor. I led her to the attic. Her shoulders were shaking. Some of her hair had fallen out of her ponytail and it was a dark squiggle on her shoulder. She looked taller and thinner, as if someone had grabbed her head and her feet and pulled them during the brief minutes when I had been upstairs.

My mother's feelings were always a sudden downpour to me. I was always soaked with the intensity of them. If she was upset, my teeth were clenching. If she was crying, my eyes were watering. No one else has ever made me feel that way. I could watch a boyfriend gesture furiously at that dumb motherfucker, the driver in the red van who had cut him off, that piece of shit, listen to a girlfriend ask me why I couldn't just take her side, why did I have to say well, they have a point, and didn't I know that a good partner always took their girlfriend's side, listen to my dad talk over and over about how he was so tired of people gossiping that he had killed Tiana, for the insurance money, how angry he was when he heard people saying things like a white man could never truly love a Black woman, so of course he had killed her, and I could empathize. Nod. But there was always an objectiveness that insulated me, always allowed me to stay cool and defuse the situation. It was better for everyone if I remained at least six inches distant. A space far enough for me to evaluate, assess, and then fix things.

But as my mother cried, I cried. I didn't know what was happening. I was sobbing and shaking. In the attic—the lights still on—the deer stood. My mother stopped crying. She said that it was a sign but did not explain of what. My mother wiped her face with her sleeve. The deer clomped on the ground. Huffed.

"Oh sweetie, don't be scared." My mom reached for my arm but paused, held her hand out in the air. There was an edge to her voice. An anger. I didn't put that in the essay, but I remember it still. I didn't wipe my face or nose, I let emotions coat my skin. She told me to go downstairs. For a moment, I didn't know why, I was sure she was going to kill the deer. I could see her treating it like a mouse, putting it into a box, dropping a brick on it with her eyes shut.

"No, I'm fine, I'll stay."

"Go. Josephine." She rarely called me by my full name. "Go."

The deer sat. It curled itself into a ball. I took that to mean, It's okay, I'll be fine.

In my essay, I wrote that no one could figure out how the deer got into our attic. My mother, the people from animal control who showed up, everyone who was involved in coaxing it safely out of the house, called it the impossible deer. In the two months that followed, other impossible things happened to my family. My mother bought a scratch-off lottery ticket and somehow won seventy thousand dollars, my father was hit by a car straight on and got only a small bruise on his thigh, and I won a statewide essay contest about what Martin Luther King Jr. meant to me, it would cover all my college tuition if I stayed in state for school. I wrote that this all happened because of the deer. Maybe, I suggested throughout the essay, it had been sent by a witch to repay a debt to our family. In her notes, my teacher wrote, "Good! But would be better if you supported this idea with pg 79 from *The History of Witches*. Look at the section about how a witch often brought her blessings by sending an animal familiar. Make it clear in your revisions that witchcraft should be feared."

What I did not say was how my mother chipped away at the details of my story. The deer went from being a buck, an eight-point with its antlers shining black under the low attic light bulbs, to a doe. Its fur transformed over time from perfect moonlight white to regular old tan. The last time she told the story, it was a small doe, maybe even a fawn, shivering. Very basic. There was no majesty to it; the animal thrashed around, hissed, and was deeply afraid of being in the attic.

When I revised my essay, I wrote that my mother was crying because she had learned her best friend had cancer. The deer was a sign her friend would live despite the odds. I ended the essay with a brief description of a recent meal with that friend. There were effects from her cancer treatment, stuff I plagiarized from YA romance novels called things like *You Will Always Have My Heart*. The friend's hair was now as white as the buck we'd seen, but she was alive. It was proof that the deer had been a blessing, I speculated, as if I knew anything real about magic. I was careful to make it clear that that magic came from no woman; it came rushing in and evaporated back into the air.

My mother was already gone, had been gone for years at the point I had written this. I never learned what she was actually talking to her friend about, why she was so upset on the phone. Later, I would try to connect the dots. Was the call what had set her on the path to leaving us?

For a while, everything I knew about her felt like a potential clue.

My teacher wrote me a long note that while this was an excellent personal essay, an essay was the truth. There had to be support for the claims I was making. Wasn't I doing the assigned reading? A good academic essay is an attempt toward gathering all the pieces past and present and creating something real and true. We spoke after class. I was a good student, my teacher said, and she was worried I was heading down the wrong path. Just because things are tough doesn't mean you can choose not to engage with the course texts. Her bright blue eyes were so sad beneath the ugly wire glasses she wore. I could tell in that moment that she thought in some way that she had failed me as an educator. In the class textbook was a chapter titled "The Protectors." It was all about how women needed men to guide them and help them stay on the path of light. Marriage is, yes, for love, but also a way to keep us all safe.

"What is truth?" I asked.

My teacher reached a hand out to me. Realized at the last second that she should not touch me. "Questions like that are dangerous, Jo."

Her lips were pulled flat. Her eyes were on the floor. Shoulders rigid.

"You're arguing in this essay that magic is good, Jo. There are some teachers who, given your family's history, would report you even for that implication."

I burst into tears. I told her I still felt so lost from my mother's absence. Nothing felt right. I cried and snotted and gulped at the air until she patted my shoulder and handed me a Kleenex.

"Don't worry, Jo," she said.

I blew my nose and didn't meet her eyes.

"I'll help you stay on the path," my teacher promised.

I nodded and reminded myself to never again be so stupid.

2.

The paper was better than the C-plus-I-am-clearly-still-worried-about-you I'd gotten for that revision. I put it on the concrete floor of the storage unit, smoothed it flat. I considered how I cared more now than I had back then about the grade I'd gotten. At fifteen, I had thought it was more important to express myself than to do what the teacher asked me. Now I was indignant on my teenaged behalf. At least I had something to say! I was going through a rough time! It didn't matter that my mom had been gone for only a year at that point. Everything was bad!

I stopped looking through the papers and shifted to sorting through her clothes. Blue high heels I'd never seen her wear. A shirt that read "I got cursed in Salem, that's why I have this dumb T-shirt!" I took her jean jacket, her wedding dress, a red dress that had been hers and my grandmother's before, and the cardigan she wore on Saturday mornings and put them in my car's passenger seat. Put as many boxes as I could fit in the backseat and the trunk to take to Goodwill in the morning. It was almost fall, and the darkness was coming like a sweater being slowly pulled over my head. A couple was bickering while lifting an ugly floral couch, a car was mumbling reasons why it should rest rather than start, music leaking from a truck grumbling its way down the street with its terrible transmission, and there was my own slight wheezing from the dust.

My dad had called me twice. Angie had texted me: beef and

bamboo? The man I slept with two to four times a month, whom I had in my phone only as Party City, texted me: scotch and eggplant emoji?

Kilkerran or Aberlour, I replied.

Cutty.

Eggplant yourself then.

I texted back to Angie: yes and fried dumplings, thanks for ordering dinner, know it's my night to cook. Going to be here for another hour.

Where is here? she asked.

Mom's storage unit.

Are you okay?

Even though my car was full, I was pulled back into the storage unit. In my mother's papers I found a yellowed newspaper account of her other obsession—the only witch story she loved, about an island in Lake Superior that appeared once every seven years. On this island, it was always harvest season: golden wheat fields, trailing vines of large black grapes, squashes, and pomegranate trees. The air smelled like bonfire and cold water. Hidden in a cave in the island's center was a vast treasure, riches collected and saved by generations and generations of witches. In her notes on the side, she had written, "Maybe it was witches or maybe it was wild rich people. What's the difference?"

I kept rummaging. An old atlas, road and property maps she had clearly stolen from our small town's public library, writings, a rune book, some tentative translations: a symbol that looked like a dying tree that meant transformation, a flare, a baseball cap with a flashlight installed in the brim, a bag filled with what looked like a perfectly preserved white lily and scraggly leaves.

I had liked that my mom was into this stuff. It made me sad

sometimes when I visited friends' houses and eavesdropped on their moms. They seemed to talk only about their kids, their husbands, what their houses needed. Anything interesting they had to say, they lowered their voices so it could barely be heard. My mom was always talking about her interests: exploration, survival, camping, red wine, genealogy, herbs. She was the only Black mom, and I wondered at times if it was a cultural thing. The white kids at school expected me to be able to dance well, rap, be interested in basketball and gangs. And I would think maybe what they couldn't know was that the Blackest thing about me was how I was fully, completely me, despite them trying to tell me what to do and who to be.

It seemed like a trait all the women in my family had. I rarely got to see them, but when my mother was with her sisters, she was barely interested in me. Instead, she wanted to know what was new with them, Look at this photo I found. Did you read this? They cooked, they sang, they said to each other over and over: let's watch a kung fu movie and have a beer. They would hand me a book and send me outside to the lawn while reminding me that I had to do my summer reading. This all took precedence over anything my father did, anything I had done during the school year.

My dad had complicated feelings about this. He was always disappointed when we would be somewhere and everyone else would be bragging about their kids and spouses—while my mother said nothing about him or me. Angie can speak Mandarin. My husband is researching bats. Meanwhile, my mother was to the brim with herself: she had made a new tea, yes, everything had been grown in her garden, and yes, of course, she had read that article, but had you read this one? Her tomatoes, the soil, the earthworm castings, the compost: those she could talk about for hours. And us: oh yeah, they're great. If we came up, we were side characters in her anecdotes.

Yet, when it was just my parents, I could tell he loved hearing her talk. My dad would lean in, ask thoughtful questions that showed he was deeply engaged with the full of her. He was always encouraging her to say more. Her sisters had taught him how to braid hair, and sometimes he would braid hers and she would talk and talk. Sometimes, the braids were too loose; he loved her too much to pull as tight as he needed to. But my mother's eyes would shut, and her face would relax as he separated and conditioned.

The dust in the storage unit was getting to me: I sneezed once, twice, three times. There were still two whole walls of things to sort through. I opened a shoebox; inside it were two soft dolls, the exact brown of my own skin. I lifted one up, and it looked like it was made to resemble me. Yarn hair turned into curls, a wide smile, my exact nose, small ears. I didn't remember having seen this before. The other had hair like mine but a mouth made out of white glass head pins in a close smile. The eyes were small stitched black X's. One ear was normal. The left was covered in a zigzag of red thread. Both were wearing a dress like I had worn in my second-grade photo: a big white-collared, black-and-white flowered dress.

"What the fuck, Mom?"

I put them both back in the box. It was probably one of her experiments, but she didn't have to use me for it. I scratched my right eyebrow. Told myself they were just poorly made dolls. Touched my ear, my mouth, rubbed my eyes. They were fine. I had been fine now for years. I put the box under my shoulder to take home and show the dolls to Angie. I knew they would make her laugh.

Had my mother been happy? It was a question I'd never wondered when she was around. Now, it was hard to tell because adult unhappiness is so much more compact, so much deeper than child unhappiness. There have been times when I've been laughing, my head bent over a martini, my favorite song playing in the bar, people dancing and flirting around me, and a small voice inside of me would whisper, "I would like to bite into this glass, chew myself dead."

Party City texted, Nikka Coffey malt?

My palms were gray and black from dust and dirt.

I texted Angie, more like two and a half hours.

* * *

I locked up and drove over to Party City's apartment. He was one of those irritating people who preferred that men call him by his last name and women by his first. I called him Party City to my friends because every time he fucked me it was fun, but somehow the next day felt cheap, a little embarrassing. His real name was Preston.

When I knocked on the door, he answered it by handing me a glass of whisky and leading me to the terrible black leather couch he owned. Every time I saw it, I thought oh, ick, because it was obviously bought to say, Look I have some money, look I am a desirable man as described in men's fashion magazines.

Our usual "date" routine was I would come over to his place. His apartment was always very clean, except for the entryway. In the two-feet-long, three-feet-wide space was a stack of magazines, multiple shoes, and a pile of coats: puffy, leather, tweed. I like men who like nice coats. Seeing his coats always made me feel a little kinder toward him. He would pour me a glass of Scotch or whisky or bourbon. Sometimes, he would tell me to guess the notes. Peat. Honey. Wildfire. Delicious dirt.

We disagreed and spent a half-hour going back and forth. No, this tastes like a deciduous tree. No, it tastes like sand blown into your mouth by a westerly wind, but in a good way. This tastes like organic supermarket cherries. No, it tastes like farmers market black raspberries. Please explain what the difference is other than you wanting to be right.

Sometimes, he would take a photo of me—especially if my cleavage looked good—while I drank. It was a mildly weird sex thing, but I didn't mind because all my friends laughed really hard when I told them about it. When I was done with my glass of Scotch, he would lead me to the bedroom. Above average foreplay. Very little kissing. Dark room. I liked how his hands felt on my wrists, I liked when I made eye contact and his eyes were soft, the look on his face that I always read as: Let me make you feel good.

Tonight he did not take a picture of me. He said, "You look tense," and rubbed the inside of my wrist. It seemed like he wanted to rub my back but I was uncomfortable with the intimacy of that and took his hands and kissed him hard on the mouth.

We kissed, he led me to his room. It smelled like someone said give me a scent that makes a person want to say the word "opulence." Leather and somehow butch roses. I stank of dust, dirt, and budget-friendly cigarettes.

* * *

I'd met Party City—Preston—on my twenty-seventh birthday. I knew my life was about to start changing again, and I wasn't pleased. There was something about being able to be dumb in a young way: drinking too much on a weekend, dating people not because I was that interested in falling in love, definitely not interested in a family, but because I liked the rush of someone new, the different ways that they tried to communicate love: staring at a phone in a bar while I drank and danced with my friends; writing me letters on monogrammed stationery; taking me to movies and asking me to tell them what I thought. It was the second most rewarding hobby of my adult life.

All day, people had wished me a happy birthday and then asked me when I was going to get serious. I had only a few more years of "complete personal sovereignty," as my dad put it in his email. And wouldn't I hate being monitored? "You love your freedom." I looked at the email, read it again, and then called him.

"Happy birthday." He sounded slightly stuffed up, like he had forgotten to take his allergy medication.

"I'll still have my freedom, Dad. I'll just have to take some tests every once in a while. An evaluation." That's what the pamphlets said. It's what I had heard since I was fourteen. I knew it couldn't be that easy, but it was my birthday and I didn't want to fight with him.

"We don't have to do this on your birthday."

"You're the one who brought it up."

He cleared his throat. "Jo, you're Black. And with our family history—"

"I know that, Dad."

I could tell he was gearing up to give me a lecture. One that would talk about my missing—dead—mother, about the way that my life was precious to me, that I should trust the government to have my best interests at heart. I knew it would make me furious to hear him say those things and wished I could say, Don't ruin my birthday. I reminded him I had plans with my friends. I complimented the cake he made me every year and told him I better be getting one soon. Strawberries and whipped cream and lemon. Every part of it homemade. When I went home that weekend for dinner, I knew it would be waiting for me, studded with too many candles.

I met Preston at a trendy restaurant's whisky night. He made me laugh, which I didn't expect. We talked briefly about family, about race. He identified as capital-M Mixed, his dad was "Korean-Adopted," his mom "your basic Midwestern White." I told him it was my mom who was Black, not my dad, and he said, "I thought you were just light-skinned."

He wanted to know why I didn't say I was mixed or biracial, why just Black. I'd had this conversation so many times with so many kinds of people. My mouth was still feeling the burn of the whisky, I was two steps away from being buzzed. A woman walked by, wearing a thin fall coat, her curls pulled by the wind. Mom, I thought for an excruciating second, then paused. Preston asked me a question; I didn't hear it. Instead of answering, I leaned forward, put my hand on his chest, looked into his eyes. Smiled. He smiled back. I kissed him.

"Do you want to leave?" he asked.

"Yes."

I'm from Clair de Lune, a small town in Michigan, where most of my former high school classmates had begun the cycle of cookin'-selling-and-going-to-jail (and repeat) or getting married and trying to sell me leggings or Jesus purses so they could afford daycare by the time we had all turned twenty-two. When I kissed Party City that first time, I felt the clean nothing scent, the pressure in the air, a type of winter day where a weatherman says a blizzard is on its way, but in the morning, probably, there would be only a light dusting of snow that always made me feel good. The snow would be melted in the afternoon. I wouldn't be inconvenienced.

We drank Johnnie Walker Blue. I said the name of it out loud three times. It felt like a character from a fairy tale: Little Johnnie Walker Blue walked into the sea, returned with a fish for his bride. She would have fins and scales of gold and diamond. Party City's hair was dark and the way it fell on his forehead made me lean forward, push it gently back.

The sex was better than I expected. He was the only man I had ever been with who took his time the first night. He told me to tell him if I didn't like anything. Asked me in a way that I found immeasurably sexy if I wanted to keep going after he went down on me. And then we just kept calling and texting, rarely going anywhere other than to his apartment. I liked that he was comfortable with me as a kind of sexual stray cat and him, the kind neighborhood man who was happy to let me come and go. I continued to call him Party City, though, because he seemed—with the leather couch, the whiskies, the job that I barely understood, the douchey friends, the NBA fantasy league—deeply suspicious. I was always waiting for him to confirm that deep down, there was nothing real beneath the surface.

3.

Party City's room was heavily air-conditioned. His mouth tasted like whisky and mints. His hands were warm and everywhere he touched me, it felt overwhelming. The hot, the cool, and I was making a noise that sounded like my mouth had forgotten how to say the word "shoes." When we were done, I turned on my side, wrapped myself close, and curled like a pill bug. I grasped myself and struggled not to burst into tears. I made a snuffly breathing sound, too close to a sob for him to ignore.

"Are you okay?"

I tried to curl even farther away from him and wished that he would do what a normal person would do—pretend that he hadn't noticed what was happening and go to the bathroom for an appropriate amount of time. I knew I felt this way because I hadn't told anyone—not even Angie—that we had finally declared my mother was dead. That still every time I thought about her for too long, an emotional hangover always followed. But knowing didn't make the feeling subside. Thinking about finally telling him about my mother made it worse.

"Did I hurt you?"

"No." My voice was muffled.

"Joey," he asked, "are you in love with me?"

It took all my willpower not to laugh. "What? Why?"

"You're crying."

Party City reached over, put one of his warm hands on my back.

His hands were always warm, but never moist. He breathed close to the nape of my neck.

"It's just been a long day," I said.

"You can tell me."

"I'm PMSing real bad."

"You can tell me." His voice plush soft.

I pulled the blanket over my head. Wanted to scream at my dumb eyes and feelings for welling up after seventeen minutes of sex. I took a deep breath. Another.

"It's just been a long day."

He patted me gently on the back, and it felt good, and it made tears well up again.

"You're married, right?" he said.

"No!"

"And the disgust and the shame are welling out of you. You can't take it anymore. And that's why you never tried to make this serious."

This time I laughed. "My husband thinks I'm at Meijer getting milk."

He laughed and stopped stroking my back.

I sniffed, put my head over my hands. "Oh, god, my kids will never forgive me!"

Party City stopped laughing. He told me that the last woman he was in a relationship with actually had been married. It had really fucked with him. They had broken up when she'd said that although he was fun, he couldn't compare to her husband. I could tell that he was no longer joking. I sat up. He was turned away from me in the bed.

The only light in the room was from the street, pushing in and around his dark gray curtains. "I thought," he said, "about telling her husband, but all it would do was make her hate me. And it still feels crazy to say, but I didn't hate her. I just felt bad for both of us."

I took his hand. He told me that the woman he had dated before the married woman refused to introduce him to her parents because he was half Korean. Her dad wouldn't like it. It was the most I had ever known about him emotionally.

"Are you okay?" I asked.

"I guess in a dumb way, I'm trying to tell you, it's okay if you're not okay. I feel it."

I paused. I squeezed his hand. It had been a strange, self-centered way to get there, but I still appreciated the sentiment.

"My mom disappeared when I was pretty young, and we decided today to finally stop hoping she would come home." My shoulders tensed as I said it.

"Is that a good thing or a bad thing?"

I let go of his hand. It hadn't hurt to say the words out loud. "I don't know yet."

We sat in silence. I listened to the white noise of the heat slipping through the vents, circulating through his apartment. The faint sound of his upstairs neighbor walking around—they sounded as if they were wearing cowboy boots. Laughter from the street floated up. He breathed, coughed, breathed. I willed all this to consume me, to be thoughtless. The words were inching toward my mouth: to describe what it was like to have her disappear, to confide in him that there was an episode of *Unsolved Mysteries* about her disappearance. My father and I had refused to cooperate with the TV producers, but we didn't stop it from happening; my dad was scared of anything that could potentially make him look bad. But some of her friends and my least favorite aunt had appeared in it.

My clothes were on the floor, except for my socks. Those were kicked to the foot of the bed. He sat up, took my cheeks in his large, warm hands, and kissed me. He was crying. It made me start again, but we continued kissing. I tried to pull away because my nose was running and he was sobbing a little, but he pushed his lips against mine.

When we were done kissing and crying, I gathered my clothes off the floor, went to the bathroom, peed, washed my hands and face. My eyes were puffy, my cheeks flushed. I pulled my hair into a ponytail and focused on getting every curl the right way. My heart was beating fast from the sex, the emotions.

The sudden emotional intimacy between us felt delicious and repulsive. I wanted to stay the night and kiss him goodbye in the morning. I wanted to drive away and block his number on my phone.

I put my clothes on. In the bathroom light, I could see how dirty my white T-shirt had gotten; a long dark line cut across my stomach, probably from carrying boxes to my car. I went to Party City's bedroom doorway, knew I probably looked like a shadow with the way the light from the hallway was hitting me.

"I'm going to take off," I said.

"This was." He sat up. He pushed his hair off his forehead.

"I know."

"You know." I watched the hair fall back down on his forehead as he spoke. "This could be something more."

"What do you mean?"

"I mean, we could know each other. We could build this into something."

"What do you mean by 'something'?"

"Come on, Jo. This could be a relationship. We like the same things. You think I'm funny. I want to spend more time with you."

"And I'm turning twenty-eight."

"It's not about beating a timer. I just like you." His voice was earnest. It made me more tense.

I tried to follow the line of his thinking, that a year of going to his apartment on and off for sex, the way we talked to each other before this night, the way all the emotional masonry I had set and bonded to keep myself distant had collapsed in one night. I couldn't remember the last time I had met a woman older than thirty who hadn't been married. I couldn't remember the last time someone had said to me, I like you.

"I'll think about it," I said.

In the kitchen, I picked up the bottle of Nikka Coffey, thought about taking it with me. I felt suddenly certain I would never see or hear from him again. Instead, I opened the bottle, smelled it one last time. It reminded me of the tea I used to drink before bed when I had a cold. I took a swig. Then, I put on my boots and left.

4.

When I was a child, my mother used to tell me a story she called "The Witch and the Garden of Life."

Once upon a time, there was a woman a witch loved very much. For her beloved, the witch created a garden. Every tree flourished with fruit. Golden berries for knowledge, ruby melons for fulfillment, onyx apples for respite, sapphire persimmons for passion.

When the garden was in full bloom, the witch led her beloved out among the soft grasses and through the hedges. "Most people will be able to eat only one kind of fruit," the witch said. "Some two, some none. But the chosen fruit shows their heart's truest desire. Choose your life." The witch gestured at the multicolored abundance, her face glowing with the pride of knowing she alone had made all this.

The lover walked around. Each fruit had its own wonderful perfume, but she couldn't choose a single one. Even the bees, the birds, the wind could choose, and the thought made her miserable. When the witch's back was turned, she went back into their cottage. Shuttered all the windows and sat in the dim firelight. It was better when making a decision, the woman felt, to see only the shape of things.

When I heard this story in school, it had a different ending. The witch and the woman weren't lovers, but just good-good friends. "Choose your life," the witch said in each version. The best friend walked around. She stopped and smelled each fruit and settled on amethyst grapes. They would mean a happy marriage, a house filled with children, a comfortable life.

This is how my mother ended the story the last time she told it: After reflecting in the darkness for three days, the lover woke up on the fourth day filled with certainty. She rummaged through the witch's pantry, overturning jars of herbs and black-as-night cauldrons, until she found a small sack of seeds.

The woman took them outside, dug at the earth with her nails and fingers until they bled. Her fingernails cracked. She wheezed and sighed and sweated. But when the lover was done, she had planted her own row. There could be grapes, there could be flowers, there could be thorns. It didn't matter. Whatever bloomed was hers.

5.

At work the next morning, I spent hours corresponding with witches and their representatives. Most of my emails were for our big Fall exhibition with a witch who called herself Blood Moon.

Like all other witches, she had agreed to give up public life, registering herself with her city and county so that everywhere she went could be tracked. No more going to large gatherings, no travel without approval by the local government to enter the city in question. Like most witches, she was allowed to send emails—although they all had to have the standard disclosure at the bottom: This email was sent by a registered witch. I verify that there are no curses or malicious intent attached to this message. I agree to be held accountable for any supernatural circumstances that might occur as a result of this correspondence. All her communications came through either her gallery or her assistant. The gallery called her Moon, the assistant called her Blood, and I wasn't sure why. I spent too much time trying to figure out what to call her and settled with "We can't wait to celebrate your work at The Museum of Cursed Art of Southern Michigan."

Her art was very social media friendly. Cursed Object #54 was the most popular piece on the tour. It was a small staircase with thirteen steps. Each step except for the fifth was painted a flat matte black. In the show catalog, Blood Moon explained that she got that level of flatness in her work by adding the ash of bat skeletons. Up close, the steps smelled strongly of artificial black cherry. It reminded me of scratch-and-sniff stickers that I used to put on the walls of my bedroom closet, where my mom wouldn't mind them. The fifth step was painted faded-silk-camisole pink. Patrons who looked at the staircase from the back saw a large resin object filled with a preserved bouquet of wild roses. There were two placards on the walls. One read that repeated exposure to this art may make the viewer long to contact childhood loves; the other read For sale price, a secret.

I did not see how this piece was cursed. My work at the museum had made me feel certain that most of today's witches were just people who refused to conform, who saw tradition as the shackles and bonds it was. It pushed me closer to my mother's thinking. I thought the art by Blood Moon was definitely worth the fuss. We had spent weeks working overtime to set everything up, dealing with her sudden layout changes via email, and her inability to come to Michigan for any fund-raising events. We knew people would want to take pictures for social media, and big crowds would please our donors. But I also thought, hoped, that the artist knew her work would be treated more seriously and would be more valuable if she were an untouchable art witch, someone who could tell the world about itself because she was not a person and could see things as an outsider. Some people argued it was easier to be thought of as a witch in the art world. That there was no way that meaningful art could come from a woman who had a husband who signed off on her life and sanctioned her art.

The closest we got to magic was on the holidays when we brought out some of the mummified remains of witches. The most famous holding was a witch who died in the 1750s. It was courtesy of an anonymous donor who admitted to buying it at a "definitely, absolutely illegal auction." The witch's body showed no signs of decomposition, her dark hair still growing. Her face was brown but with an ashy tinge, her lips a mix of gray and pink. She was brought out last year at the solstice, and a little white kid kept knocking on the glass of her casket and saying, "Wake up. It's time for breakfast."

It was lucky she was completely intact. Most witch bodies were stolen, turned into powders, and snorted by rich people in the 1920s and 1930s. Prosperity, fertility, bigger dicks, and great overall health were the promised results. I still get angry thinking about the desecration of those bodies, but there's also something hilarious to me about being so rich that you can arrange to have a body stolen and cremated, to be so completely stupid-desperate that you think this corpse powder can fix all your problems.

After work each day, after helping install one of the "cursed" objects, I either went out for a drink with friends or worked on a dance-art-comedy thing with Angie. We used a robot voice and software and had gotten a friend to make dance beats for us. The songs' lyrics were us reading break-up texts, transcripts, and emails. "My mom did think you were weird." "You never let me in, Jo." "Angie, you cheated on me. At least, you emotionally did." "You were a bad girlfriend." For the video we were going to make, we couldn't agree whether we should dance or whether we should slowly spray each other with cheap champagne while the song played. What if we made it look like we were spontaneously combusting? And when it ended, we were just two fireballs getting low? We had made so many of these, I guess the only way to describe them is as comedy videos.

We disagreed about whether to put them online. What if my mother were out there somewhere, maybe with amnesia, and she was flipping around on YouTube? And there I was being hilarious or smart and she remembered, I have a daughter. Sometimes, I lay awake at night thinking about my career. What did it mean to "make it" if the only thing I considered "success" was something that brought my mom back into my life?

How embarrassing, this fantasy soap opera idea, that all I had to do to cure her amnesia was something funny or interesting or great. Something attention-worthy. Something that would put pictures of me all over the world. I would be smiling—sometimes I thought my smile should be mysterious because it would make me feel more like a genius to be described as unknowable. Sometimes I thought my smile should be radiantly happy so my mother would see that her absence hadn't ruined an inch of me. She would see me, see the glowing words people wrote about my work, and she would drop a wine glass, be flooded with images of me and my father, and run back to us.

Often when I couldn't sleep, if I wasn't thinking about my mom or Preston, I would think of another of Blood Moon's pieces. This one consisted of six small black-and-white televisions in a row showing footage of the same young woman eating. She cries while eating a large, luxurious salad. It's an incredible salad: glistening lettuce, big flakes of pepper, white crumbly cheese, tomato. The woman sets down the salad, then laughs and picks up a terracotta pot. She takes a bite of it. Another. The video flickers throughout that segment, but she laughs and laughs. Her mouth appears bloodier and bloodier. When she's done eating the pot down to the last shard, she sprays some canned whipped cream into her mouth. The scarlet and black of her lips and teeth make the cream look extra white. "It's my cheat day," she says, and the screen fades to black. Then the video plays in reverse on all the screens.

The first time I saw it, I covered my own mouth, had to look away. Seeing it for weeks and weeks, the images sat in my brain, refusing to wash away.

At work, I was reading about Cursed Object #92—a black velvet high-back chair, a sterling silver blade engraved with all the moon's phases, a small TV made in 1987 painted a shade described as "gumball lavender"—when my father called.

"What's wrong?" I asked.

He was quiet.

"Are you there?" I sat up, pushed my chair away from my desk, went out into the hallway. I didn't want my boss to overhear. She was always trying to treat me not like her colleague, but her daughter. An emotional phone call would lead her to call me into her office—Kleenex box strategically placed on her desk—shut the door gently, and say in a soft television-mom voice, "Tell me." Something about her made me sure that when she talked about me to people who didn't work with us, she referred to me as "you know, my young African-American friend." Somehow, I could hear the hyphen, the capitalized A's.

Since my mom died—as if "died" is the right word; for years, I used "left," "vanished," "disappeared," "dipped," if I talked about it at all—anyway, since she died, so many people have tried to become my de facto therapists. My friends' moms, putting a baked good on the table in front of me. My friends late at night at slumber parties, after the talk of boys, after the gossip, when they thought everyone else was asleep, "Is it hard?" My ex-girlfriend, who told me the reason why I was so closed off was that my mother wasn't around when I came out. "We could go to her grave," she'd said. "You can say it to the headstone." I had told her twice before, there was no grave. And her idea sounded so much like something from a movie. I bring some flowers, I say, "Mom, I'm bi," and a ray of light comes down from a cloudy sky or maybe a bird lands on the headstone and sings. I laughed thinking about it, and that was the beginning of the end of that relationship.

It was worse for a while after the TV episode about her came out. My mom had kept her last name, Marshall, so that was a small buffer against everyone immediately knowing it was about my family. The episode was forty-eight minutes long. There were reenactments of what my mother did on her last day. A blurry brown me as a teen that Angie had freeze-framed, and we agreed the resemblance was terrible; I joked about making it my social media profile picture. The host speculated that my mother had been abducted and killed in a supernatural ritual in the great Michigan wilds. I'm not sure what those are; I assume they're the three hours it takes to go "up north" and stay in a mouse-infested cabin by a lake heavy with rot-smell.

There was speculation my dad had been having an affair. He or his mistress had my mom killed. Or my mom was in the wrong place, wrong time, and a serial killer just got lucky. They showed footage of a serial killer who had been in the Midwest around the time of her disappearance—a young white man with a patchy beard and skin that had the texture of peach fuzz—who had murdered several Black women. He claimed, while leaning back in a chair, hideously relaxed, that they were the easiest pickings. You could find them anywhere, and most people didn't give a shit as long as you didn't leave a mess.

I had to turn off the episode after that even though there were twenty-two minutes to go. I didn't want to watch the hosts speculate about whether she was a witch; I felt sick enough already.

Usually, when my dad called me during the day, it was because he had read too much internet or felt that in some way someone referenced the allegations against him. I could tell by the sound of his voice when he was anxious or spiraling. It happened rarely, but I could guess when he needed to talk to someone who likes him, who trusts him. The slowness of his responses made me automatically assume someone else—Grandma, Aunt Rob—had died.

"I'm there. I mean, I'm here," he said.

"Are you okay?"

"Josephine, I'm fine. Sorry. I don't mean to scare you."

Most of the time, I'm happy to be there for him. My dad stayed. He was at the big events. He made the dinners and drove me to school. But there were always times when I thought about how he was never emotionally there for me. I couldn't tell him about the way kids told me my mother was a witch. That I was disgusting and evil like her. He never noticed or seemed to acknowledge that I, too, was depressed. And how he never said anything to make me feel better about the Bureau of Witchcraft investigation that happened after my mother's disappearance. I alternated between feeling like a terrible person and daughter for holding these grudges and thinking, No, I deserve to be angry about these things. There is nothing wrong with knowing you've been treated poorly for no good reason and wanting to be treated better.

"Oh." I breathed. "So. Hey, what's up?"

My office was on the second floor of the museum. The hallway's right side was all glass, looking out at the university across the street. Students were walking and talking on the tree-lined paths, the leaves between green and red and gold, the tops of the students' heads overgrown brown and blond and black. Along the left side, some students—either art or witch studies majors—were sitting in the oversized gray chairs. Because of the number of people I've seen crying or breaking up in those chairs, I've wondered if more curses soaked into their fabric and arms and legs than in the art we exhibited.

"We finally found the most up-to-date version of your mom's will," he said.

"Do you want me to drive up tonight? We could talk about this in person." The only people at work who knew about my mother were my bosses and the HR staff. My file had a flag in it because of my mother. A vanished woman always had to be investigated for witchcraft. And if your mother was a witch, well, the odds are much higher that you are too.

A student below with hair dyed green and wearing bright headphones watched me pace.

"The thing is, your mom left you a lot of money."

"How?" I cleared my throat, knowing what I had attempted to say had been unintelligible to him. "How?"

"She invested most of her lotto ticket earnings."

I could not tell what the problem was. Every other word that came out of his mouth was hesitant. Usually when he spoke about her, it was a flood of emotions. Rage to nostalgia to hope to sorrow. He was reacting to something else. Was he having a hard time financially? Did he want the money? He could have it. I wasn't rich, but I was fine. I knew no matter the amount of money, I would feel immediately conflicted about receiving it. That my impulse would be to probably pay off credit card or car debt, but I would end up feeling so weird about it that I might end up donating all of it to a nature preserve or some sort of environmental group that centered Black women. I viscerally knew that I did not want anything tangible bought with that money.

"You know how she was," he said.

I turned and faced the window. The wind picked up, pushed some of the leaves free from their branches into the air.

"She wants me to do something, doesn't she?"

He sighed.

I couldn't imagine what my mom would want from me. She believed in cremation. Wanted a small gathering of her favorite people around to gossip and say their favorite things about her. I couldn't imagine her wanting me to do something trendy like a pilgrimage to an ancestor's grave, a ceremony for prosperity, or burning sage and cedar every night for six weeks to help her soul be purified as it was weighed for judgment.

My dad told me there was a small island in Lake Superior.

"Like the one in the story?" I asked.

"What?"

"The one she was always talking about. It appears every seven years. A treasure at the heart of it, placed there by witches or eccentric rich people."

"I don't remember her telling any stories like that. There was the one about the island near South Carolina, the one that turned out to be a large whale in love with a witch. I remember you loving that one." When I didn't try to disagree with him, he coughed and told me I would have to be on a small island in Lake Superior on one of four very specific dates. The closest one was in four days. The next, seven years from now. The third was in fourteen years, and so on.

"Can't I just lie and say I went there?"

In the story my mother used to tell, a special tree grew only on the island. Its leaves were purple, and so were the apples that grew on it. The will stipulated that I was supposed to gather some apples and bring them back to show her lawyer. It would also make life easier for everyone if I took a picture of myself that was time-stamped in some way while harvesting the fruit.

He told me that there were two dolls in the storage unit; I had to take one to the island with me. I thought again of the X's sewn in that were supposed to be eyes. They had made me so uncomfortable; I had shoved the doll and the box it was in to the very back of my closet. Put heavy books on top of it, even though I knew the doll was inanimate.

"Is she making you do anything like this?" I asked him.

"I'm supposed to drink a one-hundred-dollar bottle of wine and think of her fondly."

"Let's trade."

We laughed.

"No one else was like her." I meant it as a compliment but heard the judgment in my voice.

"Truly."

I scratched the side of my face. It would be cold in the Upper Peninsula near the lake.

"Did she give any instructions as to how I'm supposed to get to this island?"

I imagined myself in a kayak on Lake Superior. Even if I didn't capsize and die, I would be deeply miserable. One last grounding from beyond the grave. Thanks, Mom.

She had loved the lakes. Michigan was for luxury, Erie was for mourning, Ontario was for Canadians, Huron was for daydreaming. And Superior was for mystery. The lake that kept its secrets. For a second, I could almost hear her singing what I called the shipwreck song, as we drove up to Marquette for a family vacation.

"If you say yes, apparently arrangements will be made," Dad said. "Her lawyer will call you tomorrow morning."

"Do you know how much money it is?"

"The estimation was $133,740."

Her lucky numbers: 33, 7, 4, 13, 3.

I wanted to bite my fingernails like I was a child again and everything was different. A small voice inside me wanted to say no, but deep down I knew I had to do it. I wanted this. It wasn't about money; it would be an adventure. For a few days, I would be living the type of life my mother had envisioned for me.

6.

I went to my boss's office and asked if we could talk. Her office was small, navy chairs and a gray desk, sharp-white walls that seemed to amplify the brightness of the overhead fluorescent lights. I used my softest confiding voice, held a tissue, told her the circumstances, talked about my mother and her will, made the details as ambiguous as possible—and she told me I could take a week off. The moment made me think that it was possible we could be friends. Then I remembered the only bumper sticker she had on her Prius: Abstinence Lets You Finish Your Education.

"We need to talk about something else, though," she said before I could stand up.

My brain went to emails missed, my unwillingness to join in the staff fitness challenges, whether I was dressed professionally enough. I was wearing a striped T-shirt beneath a blazer, red high-tops like I always did when I had a no-meeting day. Stacked layers of gold rings on my fingers were meant to communicate that I, too, was artistic and interesting.

"You turn twenty-eight soon. I got my reminder from the state about you this morning."

I sat up straighter, crossed my legs at the ankles.

I thought about joking, swallowed it, tried to look relaxed. "I'll finish my registration tonight."

"The state won't allow you to continue your work here if you don't."

"Sometimes, these laws seem so ridiculous to me." I knew I was making a mistake as soon as I said it. When would I stop getting myself in trouble? "What am I going to do? Start accidentally cursing people? Fly here instead of walk?"

"If you don't comply, you can't continue to remain employed." My boss tried to make her face soft. "We would hate to lose you over something like this."

I nodded.

"I should remind you that a lot of the museum board members and donors are pretty conservative." She paused, pushed her wire frames up her nose. Her engagement ring was a large emerald surrounded by two obnoxious diamonds. She wore a bright gold wedding band that was too big to be attractive. "I haven't heard you talk about anyone special in your life for a while."

"I'm seeing someone." I hated how quickly I said it, but she was speaking in the tone of someone who was ready to send another "concerned" email about me and my future to her superiors. My boss seemed like she could be easily convinced someone was a witch. She liked high collars, had a long narrow nose that her square-framed glasses relished sliding down, an heirloom china complexion, eyes that never changed even when her thin lips were curved up into a small smile. If penalties weren't in place now for falsely accusing someone of being a witch, she would be the first person who would say, "I saw Josephine Thomas point at a woman, and thirty minutes later that woman slipped on the ice and died. She has always pushed me closer toward embracing evil. Josephine Thomas is a witch."

"Oh, you're seeing someone. That's perfect. What are they like?"

I knew the "they" my boss used was a trap, not an invitation. I smiled.

"He." And I saw her face relax, the relief dissolve away some of her tension. "It's intense between us, at the moment. I guess."

Party City's last text message to me was: how are you last night was intense.

I had not responded.

"Well, that's great. Excellent news. You should keep working on that too. Josephine, I felt so relieved when my husband proposed to me. Happy, too. I could see the map of my life in front of me. Safety, security, a career. I want that for you."

"That sounds wonderful," I said in the most neutral way I could. I couldn't imagine being pleased about any of those things. I'd read an article once that claimed the average man became 50 percent happier when he was married. The average woman became 33 percent more discontent than when she was single. I knew my boss would say that for women, happiness was not important. She would say something a lot of older women liked to say: women bring people together, that we do the intricate embroidery of living—childcare, cleaning, emotions, caretaking—because society wouldn't exist without our doing it. And we're better suited for it. They would talk about men's roles, the big things they do like work and organizing and (insert a giggle if they're trying to be cute) opening jars.

"You'll see. Once you're married, that's when you'll start to thrive." She smiled. "Women need structure."

Next to her keyboard was a picture of my boss, her husband, and their two kids. All of them blond and smiling in a way where I could tell the photographer had said something confusing. They were wearing crisp white button-downs and unfashionable blue jeans that made them all look as if they were trying to be cool youth pastors. I couldn't imagine anything could make me want a life like theirs. I would rather be in a plane crash and have to figure out how to survive on airplane peanuts and two vodka shooters than pose for a family photo like that.

Because I couldn't think of anything to say, I thanked my boss for the advice.

I gathered my things and went up to the third floor, the place I went most often when I needed to be alone. Rarely did anyone go there. I walked through the exhibit of items classified by the state as cursed: a pair of dress boots from the 1860s that had supposedly caused three different men to dance themselves to death at parties. A necklace that, when you stood in front of it, you could hear your heart beating louder, louder, until it was deafening. The recommended skin-on-object exposure time to these objects was only forty-five seconds. We have to use gloves, heavy-duty welding masks, and tools made out of silver when we move the pearls or analyze ancient leather for possible restoration.

Those objects are on the small list of things I think are actually, truly magical. I can't explain the necklace. It's hundreds of years old, there is no technology, no trick. I wore it once and I had a headache for two days afterward.

It's not that I don't think magic could be real. I'm not my mother. Even if she were around to show these objects, Tiana would have found ways to explain how they were based on science or tricks. But I think how people understand and interact with magic has been diminished over the centuries. Maybe before, it truly was something people practiced and performed. Then people, as they do with everything strange and beautiful and inexplicable, found a way to destroy it.

The third floor always makes me daydream about being a woman a thousand years ago, standing along a shore and imbibing a potion I made that will allow me to explore the oceans' depths.

And now, you might pay two thousand dollars a ticket to go to a show where witches change themselves into stone, water, and moss while dancing and singing. But you can't tell truly if it's real or you're watching some elaborate and in its own way magical combination of stage design, technique, and performance. You might go to a museum like this and feel deliciously uncomfortable while looking at a pair of worn-out boots and reading an accompanying short essay about Tobias Leon Bourne, who two-stepped himself into the grave because he didn't take curses seriously. But all the magic in these museums is the magic of the dead—corpses and curses and in its own way reminding women if there is anything inexplicable in the world, it is dangerous.

Women start receiving pamphlets from the state at age eighteen. We are told starting at fourteen to monitor ourselves for signs of magical expression. Floating while sleeping, lights consistently flickering as we walk beneath them, unconsciously repeating ourselves three times, having a desire to eat raw meat, hearing voices others can't hear, wanting to teach other people cruel lessons. At school, we are separated from the boys for classes about menstruation, our changing bodies, and what we should do if we ever feel like we are being swayed toward the dark one's path. Our parents could opt us out of health classes, but no one could miss any of the classes about checking ourselves and our peers for witchcraft.

When I felt calm enough to be around other people, I went up to the fourth floor. I peeked into the new exhibit to see how things were going. A necessary sign was posted outside the doorway: No Children Allowed in This Room. The object looked like a giant glass bubble. Bright red. As I walked closer, I could see faint tremors rippling across its surface. I stopped when I was close enough that I could see my own reflection distorted in it—left eye large, the right spread down my cheek, mouth obliterated. There was a small fence around the lower third of the object; the wires looked sharp.

"Any compulsions you might feel should diminish as you leave the room," the docent said to me.

I asked what she meant by compulsions. She had only recently become a docent, and I wanted to hear how she would talk to a patron.

"You might feel the urge to self-soothe. Some men react violently. A lot of people really want to lick the object."

"I get that. It's like a lollipop the doctor gives you. But sinister."

She pushed her white hair off her forehead, looked at me for a long moment. "Oh, you're joking."

I nodded, then walked a slow circle around the object. It was called *Self-Portrait #69 (NICE!)*. I laughed at the name but it was also annoying. Something about it took away all the magic. It made me want to look for the mechanism that was causing it to move. It made me think about Blood Moon the person, not the art she had labored over.

Self-Portrait trembled again. The base it was mounted on was very thin. The placard said nothing about a motor or metal. It listed only resin. My left hand was gently scratching my scalp over and over. I tried to remember the list of objects in the exhibit, the assembly emails about this one. The more I looked, the more my brain kept asking my tongue, Strawberry or watermelon? Or maybe it was the flavor some candy has that tastes only slightly like something called wild berry.

The thing about the human brain is a person can be smart, they can know what's happening around them, and still on a subconscious level—vanity, desire, a little dent in their personality—they want to be fooled. It wasn't magic making me want to lick the object in the room. It wasn't.

When I left, everything in my sight was tinged red. Birds on a branch, the couple arguing about where to go to dinner, the police officers walking the sidewalk, the ice cream store painted to look like layers of a hot fudge sundae: the top, cherry and whipped-cream white; the middle, warm chocolatey; the bottom, cone-toned. I was still occasionally scratching my head; it felt nice to feel my fingers on my scalp, blink at the bright warm air. Every woman I saw was wearing an engagement ring or a wedding band. The world slowly lightened, from deep coral to strawberry-cream pink to, finally, everyday brown and blue and white.

I walked to the nearest outdoor apparel store and started planning for my trip. New waterproof hiking boots. Moose brown with bright pink laces. A lavender jacket that was a little too warm in the store. Even though I was still wearing my modest office slacks, for a moment in the mirror, I looked like my mother on a Saturday morning. She would put on an outfit like this with jeans ripped at the knees and walk the woods where hunters weren't allowed.

She would come home with wild asparagus, a trillium that was illegal to pick but she needed to use it for something important. The flower was so white and beautiful, I wouldn't have been able to resist picking it either. Morels. Herbs. Grasses. Once, she came home with a giant puffball mushroom. It looked like a button mushroom you could buy at the store that had somehow become the Godzilla of mushrooms—about the size of one of our throw pillows, but firm, and a little taller. In the kitchen, she handed me a butcher knife and had me cut it lengthwise. It was one of the most satisfying things I'd ever done in my life. My mother showed me how to check to see whether it was edible, how to examine its flesh for spores. When it was deemed safe, we cut it into large slices, putting some in the refrigerator in a plastic bag. Those we would take to a doctor if something went wrong. Then my mom pulled out a cast iron skillet and fried us each a slice in salt, pepper, and butter.

Other mushrooms—chanterelles and morels—taste better, but there was something so wonderful about a mushroom slice as big as our dinner plates. It made me never want to eat any other type of mushroom again.

Next to the apparel store was Inner Witch. It was filled with dried herbs, crystals, brightly colored books filled with spells and observations, blank books, capes, brooms, tea leaves and sets. A room in the back offered classes like How to Understand the Letters of Dreams; The History of Witches: A Story of Oppression; The Beasts of Your Souls. Even though the store stood for so many things I'm against—women have been burned for witchcraft, are regularly oppressed for even a hint of it, but here are these stores making money off "witchy vibes"—I still wanted to touch expensive velvet and seemingly reasonably priced amethyst. I lingered over a red cape embroidered with white daisies.

A lot of people don't know Inner Witch is actually a chain store. They rename the stores based on location—like The West Wind, Heart Source, Little Miss Cauldron—so they're better suited to the surrounding community. The chain is owned by a CEO who makes huge contributions to anti-choice organizations. His family contributes a disgusting amount of money to lobby for the age of either being married or registering with the state to begin at twenty-five rather than thirty. They successfully lobbied to keep unmarried women from getting credit cards without a trusted male cosigner. If there's a politician actively working against gay communities, trans people, Black people, the family has donated to them. Various members of the CEO's family have argued there should be no penalties for false accusations of witchcraft; Americans deserve to be safe. They've poured a ton of money into keeping burning laws on the books. They're trash people with too much money.

About two years ago, I was at a protest we organized when the

CEO was invited to speak at the local university. Our group had coordinated it well; we were all dressed in black and holding signs that read either "Why are you afraid of women?" or "Why are women more regulated than guns?" A few people had shown up holding their ideas of witty or jokey signs, but they were shuffled to the back and sides.

The CEO had decided to make a show of walking past us. He was surrounded by three large security officers; all of them were wearing the type of big sunglasses I associated with celebrity women. The CEO was sweating, and the glasses were sliding down his nose. It made me feel powerful to see him pushing them back up, the nervous dweebishness of the gesture. During his talk, he referenced our protest. He said: "I love women. But magic is very dangerous. Just like we regulate cars and guns and anything that can hurt other people, we have to be strict for the sake of our community's health."

I waved at the salesclerk and said in my fakest friendly voice, "How are you?" I let the salesclerk talk at me about candles and tea that could help with menstruation. I said, like I did every time, "I just want one month where I'm not eating a whole family-sized bag of chips, you know?" And when her back was turned, I slipped into my purse the brightest crystal within reach. I wasn't about to pay for something that gave that asshole and his corporation more money.

When I got home, Angie was on the couch, wearing her pajamas and typing something.

"Textbook or social media?"

"Sketch script."

She typed a little more and then looked up. "You're home late."

I told her about my mother's request, showed her the things I'd bought. After I was done, Angie pulled her vape pen out of the mug full of pens and pencils we kept on the coffee table. She took a hit. It lingered in the air.

She handed me the pen. I took a hit.

"Maybe this is a good thing for you," Angie said.

"What makes it a good thing?"

"Do you ever think sometimes that Ti just left your dad and did it in a real asshole way? I loved your mom, but she was also a little bit of a jerk."

Angie took another hit. She reminded me about the time one of our classmates sent me an earnest message about how he was sure he had seen my mother eating at a Wendy's in Toledo, Ohio. How my mother had chitchatted with him and acted like nothing was wrong. This was five years ago. I was grateful Angie didn't bring up the TV show, the resulting social media threads.

"That kid was probably being a little racist. He probably cornered some nice Black lady and treated her like he knew her, and she was nice because she didn't want to upset some big white guy."

Angie nodded. Over the years, she had seen so many white people—waitresses, cashiers, people at bars—do the same thing to me. I've been Keisha, Dani, Addy, Cassie, all those Black girls whose white acquaintances' brains think all Black women with the same skin tone and similar hair texture are them.

"Look, don't get offended. But I think sometimes about the way she just destroyed you, and even if she's dead, I'm angry for you."

My immediate instinct was to tell Angie I was fine. To say using the word "destroyed" was a little melodramatic. I'm twenty-seven years old. I have a job, no kids, I'm still best friends with my childhood best friend, I'm creative, and sometimes people think I'm interesting and funny.

It wasn't like I was thirteen again, like my dad had also disappeared because he was looking for her, or at work, or talking to the police, or trying to do all the things my mom had done to keep us both alive. I wasn't fifteen, drinking a full bottle of wine while taking a forty-minute bath. I wasn't in love with obliteration. I was no longer writing the word "bullshit" in bubble letters in my notebook over and over again in an empty house. I wasn't eating most of a tub of ice cream just because I could. I didn't think I saw her every time I left the house, only once in a great while, and I didn't feel nearly as depressed as I used to. I wasn't thinking nearly as often that there was no point in being alive because we were all going to die anyway and sentience was the only true fucking curse, and I would have been blessed to be a beloved houseplant with green-and-pink leaves. I wasn't seventeen, taking molly and leaving a party to walk around a graveyard and calling that immersion therapy.

But Angie had seen all this. She had cleaned my puke, made me breakfast. She had seen me, and unlike most people, it brought us closer. I liked that she could see me ugly, see me beautiful, see me boring, and still just like me.

"What are you thinking?" she asked.

"You said something very complicated, and honestly, I don't know what to say."

"I'm sorry."

"Don't apologize. It's a good thing. Maybe?"

We laughed, but it was mostly to clear out the cobwebs of the conversation, to move forward. We talked for a while about the sketch Angie was writing. It was about a very cute white girl—Angie wearing a blond wig—who is getting her makeup done by one of the people at Sephora and learns she can get away with anything if she tells a man that she's on her period. And it keeps escalating. It starts with getting him to bring her a blanket on the couch, and escalates to cheating on him, to his giving her a check for ten thousand dollars. Drunk on power, the character goes to a bank and tries to hold it up by saying, "I'm on my period." And we were stuck there.

I paced around the room. "What if she goes up to a teller, thinking they're an old man, says it, and then they turn around. Surprise: the teller is an old woman with a short haircut. And she says something like, 'I conquered that bitch thirty years ago.'"

Angie paused. I could tell she was barely listening to me. She was still stuck on her idea—she wanted the bank to get robbed but couldn't figure out how to make it feel unquestionably feminist. It needed to be funny, the joke needed to be about how most people acted about women's periods, not that women got away with stuff by claiming they were menstruating. We made some tea. We talked more.

Then I went up to my room. I took the stolen crystal out of my bag and put it on my dresser next to nine others. I pulled out my computer, the three letters I'd gotten in the mail from the state, reminding me I had to register by my twenty-eighth birthday, and started typing the answers to the required survey.

In the past thirty days had I: Menstruated? Floated in the air? Felt punitive urges? Conversed with a goat? Felt powerful under the light of the full moon? Felt suddenly sure an object was powerful? Been inexplicably confused? Heard voices? Wept uncontrollably for no reason? Seen someone else looking at me in the mirror besides my own reflection? Felt compelled to be in nature? Wanted to eat mud? Felt transmuted into a vapor? Felt certain words were powerful? Repeated myself three times? Set a dark intention?

The next part of the survey was about where I worked, who I associated with, whether I was in a relationship that could be registered with the state. The name of a trusted man (father, romantic partner, family friend, uncle, work supervisor) who could be my power of attorney if I was infected with magic. On the top and bottom of each survey page were the words "Your honest answers are required by law. Those in violation could face imprisonment."

In high school, a woman had come and spoken to all the girls in my school. She had talked about being drawn toward power. She heard voices encouraging her to burn down her own high school. The woman had clearly dressed in a way that she thought made her look relatable to teens: her hair in a high cheerleader pony, a sweatshirt with our school mascot Mr. Moon on it, and iridescent sneakers. The only reason why she was still here, now, the woman said in a wavering voice, was because her boyfriend, Brad, had stood up against evil and reported her before it was too late. The greatest love a man can show you, she said, was through interventions like this. While most of the other girls had smiled or nodded as if they were learning a great lesson, I had rolled my eyes. I knew most of what she was saying had to be lies.

At the end of the assembly, we all took self-quizzes. Have you ever felt as if you were possessed by a spirit of justice? Have you ever lost time? Have you ever seen any of your friends levitating?

"This is bullshit," I muttered to myself, but I kept filling out the survey. I couldn't afford to lose my job. I felt certain that to ignore this or to continue to disengage would only make my life harder. But I also kept thinking of every man I had ever known. The ones from high school who were now in jail or had DUIs or posted pictures on social media of their assault rifles. The men I would see at campus parties where at least two women would discreetly point to them and say, "Watch your drink when he's around." The men who would walk too close behind me when I was going home alone at night, who made me grip my keys in my hand, made me reach in my purse and pretend I had a canister of pepper spray in my palm. None of them had to sacrifice their privacy like this.

I was so tired of people suspecting me, so tired of always having to follow arbitrary rules. How could I live the rest of my life like this? I was almost twenty-eight and exhausted already. I reminded myself that throughout history women had endured far worse things. I had the internet, a job, access to pizza, money, no kids; no one had tried to burn me at the stake yet; I had not had to flee in the night to freedom. All I had to do was shut the fuck up, get married, and try to be good. All I wanted was to live a life where I knew I wanted to do those things, not because that was how I could survive or because it was expected of me, but because I wanted them.

7.

I know only one married couple I feel sure are in love. Luis and Gwen. I met them both when I was an undergrad; we were all part of Equality Now! It was a group that protested for women to receive equal rights, for the government to recognize same-sex marriages, for there to be actual state recognition of transgender people, that spoke out against the tax credits for arranged marriages and against state-sanctioned witch burnings. We raised money for queer rights. Organized teach-ins about the histories of queer people, Black people, and Indigenous people whose lives were rarely taught in textbooks or classes because they had been tried and found to be witches. We would gather in different houses and write postcards to legislators, come up with fundraising ideas, and try to think deeply about how to change the world. We would also drink and fuck each other and make each other miserable and then hold hands and smoke weed late at night in basements and often I wondered if I was the only one who thought things would never change and asked myself why I was letting cops yell at me and teargas me, nuns pray at me, and counterprotestors throw things at me. Once a man grabbed my wrist and said, "You fucking bitch, I'll see you burn."

In meetings, my eyes would be on Luis's hands. His fingers were long and tanned, his fingernails a pink that felt momentous only because of the attention I gave them, and his palms were square, and I was sure a little rough. We ran into each other on a July Saturday. He was walking around and smoking a cigarette. He handed me one, even though I smoked only when I was drinking. We decided to have coffee. There had always been a feeling of maybe between us. He leaned close to light the cigarette, our foreheads almost touching.

"I felt so lonely this morning," he said. It was summer and everything was panting and leaking from the humidity.

"People always say animals don't feel loneliness. I think that's a lie," I said. I was trying to be deep, to impress him. "I think the reason why people like dogs is because they get lonely, too."

He told me he had a dream he was walking in a warehouse filled with boxes. Dream-Luis was compelled to open the boxes, grabbed a chainsaw that appeared in his arms. He opened a box and in it was him. Inside each box was another him. I took his hand. He put his fingers between mine. We understood suddenly that there was a way for us to both be less lonely. His hands were, indeed, rough. I could feel on his fingertips the hours he spent playing guitar, on his palms, the volunteer work he did for Habitat for Humanity.

Gwen's hands were soft, she loved touching people. Her hand on my hand. Her hand on my cheek. Her hand on my neck. Her hand inside me one morning after we spent a night together dancing, drinking, and kissing in a crowded basement. I liked to put her fingers in my mouth, suck on them like hard candy. I could taste the expensive lotion she used to keep them soft: hinoki, a word I loved saying after she taught it to me.

We were never in love. I knew because when she and Luis became a "we" I didn't feel anything but weirdness that these two people, of everyone I knew, would become a couple. I told Angie and she laughed and laughed. "What if they got married and you gave a speech? And it, like, scandalized everyone? And what if the minister said if there's anyone here who has been 'intimate' with the bride and groom, well, speak now or forever hold your peace?

You should at least write to an advice column asking what the social norms are for going to a wedding like this; it'll go viral." Each idea made me laugh and laugh. "You wear messiness well," Angie said to me.

"My mom always told me the only way a woman can survive is to have a good sense of humor."

Angie paused. "What if they've never told each other about you?"

I closed my eyes. "I would love it if they found out from each other twenty years later and their minds were just blown. Both of us? Whoa!"

Luis and Gwen were certainly in love. I saw them all the time, talking to each other and laughing. They never made a big show of it. Didn't even put it on social media. They were just clearly together. What I couldn't figure out, though, is how they could do it so easily. How could two people who could articulate so well that the country we lived in was unfair, that it catered to relationships like theirs, who could say things like we need to dismantle the system of privilege that benefits men, enter a relationship without pause? If they stayed together, got married, it would make their lives new-asphalt smooth, away from any of the bumps and struggle they always complained about and fought against. Why didn't they ever look guilty when they were walking around hand in hand?

At their wedding last year, they held hands in front of seemingly everyone they had ever met and everyone their parents had ever met. We were all asked to wear white. Snowflake, marshmallow, moonglow, milk, dad-bar-of-soap white. They held hands and said traditional vows. Luis promised to protect her body, soul, and mind from evil. To see her for who she really is, to be her anchor to the world we live in, to keep her soul in God's protection. His voice was firm and confident, like he had practiced saying these words by watching action movies where a hero gives a fantastic third act speech. Around me, people were crying as the minister spoke. I watched the garlands of pink fake flowers and fairy lights blow in the wind. A woman had to use one of her hands to keep her elaborate feather-covered hat from leaving her for the distant fields and clouds.

Being there, listening to those vows, made me feel as if I had never truly known either of them. I wondered whether my parents had said the same things at their wedding. I couldn't imagine my mother ever agreeing to let my dad vow to protect her soul from evil.

Once, Gwen had said to me, "Did you know that in half the states, women have to prove they're not witches before filing for divorce? It doesn't even matter in cases of domestic abuse. You still have to prove 'evil' isn't breaking your family apart." She had paused and said, "How do we keep living this way?"

In college, Luis had written a letter that had gone viral about how hard it is for women of color to have any rights in this country. Because on average they were less likely to get married by thirty, because on average they were less likely to have family members who had the resources to support them when they were forced to leave the workforce, because some states could make active claims and take any children they had outside of wedlock. He wrote about his older sister, whose death he blamed on all these systems and the mental health strains they caused. "How," Luis had written, "can any person who is a woman, who is not cis, be expected to do more than survive in this country under these circumstances? We should want better."

At the wedding, they stood together barefoot in a field: Luis in a white suit, his dark hair near his white collar; Gwen's dress fitted on top, an anemic, curtainlike mess on the bottom. Beautiful only because of the way the wind was fussing with its edges. The minister with his high collar, the only person not dressed in white.

My father told me once it wasn't true that people get more conservative over time; he said they just get tired and it's easy when you're tired to be agreeable. I tried to remind myself that was the case and then was sad thinking that at age twenty-six, Gwen and Luis would already be tired enough to get married.

Gwen's voice broke as she vowed to be a good wife, a good mother, to allow herself to be embraced in the warm hands of God and her husband if she were ever tempted to stray into darkness. "I can't wait to be married to you," she said, as if it were years away, not three lines away in the ceremony's script. But I could tell in that moment, the way her wet eyes gleamed, she truly couldn't wait. She loved him.

In my room, I reread the survey again, looked at the reminder letter. Thought in some ways, it would be an intense relief to find myself suddenly turning into a vapor—my body a mist rising and pushing against the ceiling. I would be menthol-cool and finally, at last, no longer a person. I texted Preston. I said I just wanted him to know I was thinking about him. I hadn't been, but writing it down put me in the right direction.

8.

It was the first time we had met for dinner, and Preston had chosen a trendy basement restaurant. The bar area had a custom neon sign that read, "We're all friends while drinking." It made me want to turn around and leave. A twenty-first birthday party—at least fifteen people—spread around a big table. Everyone was wearing crowns custom printed with "Maddyison's My Queen" in holographic letters. A young woman who had to be Maddyison was sitting in front of rows of drinks. Martinis of all colors, cocktails, shots making a fort around the birthday girl. She took a sip and a selfie with each drink while her friends chatted with one another. The hostess led me to a quieter area where couples were seated at small tables tented with mosquito netting. A bottle of red wine and water were already at the table. Preston stood up when I approached, bumped the netting, winced, and sat back down.

I pulled my way through it, sat down. "I know this is supposed to be romantic, but."

"It's scaring the shit out of you?"

I nodded.

"We can go if you want."

"No, no. At least not yet. I feel better seeing that these are LED candles."

He poured me a glass of wine. We talked about how it tasted. Earthy, but that meant it was expensive. We were so pleased with ourselves, we talked about going to a wine tasting together in the future. Or one of those coffee tastings. We agreed we liked the idea of saying the sentence "It tastes like minerals." What did that even mean?

"I think it's a sophisticated version of saying, this tastes like the vitamins my parents made me take as a child," I said.

Preston wiped his face with his napkin. "When I say it, I mean it's like licking a clean rock."

We talked about the weirdest things we remembered putting in our mouths as kids. I remembered taking a branch from my mother's study and gnawing on it even though I thought the branch was disgusting. He talked about how when he did math homework, it somehow helped him do a better job if he had a red Lego in his mouth.

He shared food the way I liked to share food, by gingerly cutting off a piece for the other person and putting it on an appetizer plate. He asked me questions. We held hands under the table. I realized we had never done that before. His fingers were callused in a way I hadn't been aware of. He was taking guitar lessons on the weekends. I said approving things, but I wondered if I would have to listen to him play "Ring of Fire" and big-smile like I used to for the guitar boys in high school.

"Sometimes, I wonder how anyone can know a relationship is real," I said. I cut a piece of steak. Slowly chewed it and tried not to watch his face for a reaction.

"I'm just going to be direct here. Is this something where you want to talk about us, or are we talking generally?"

"Right now, I think I'm talking generally." An older couple was seated near us, both were drinking a martini and scrolling. "Like, can anyone be truly happily married with the way things are? There's always going to be this element of." I searched for the right word, paused. "Coercion, I guess?"

"One of my aunts didn't get married until she was thirty-five,"

Preston said. "And she said you had to go to a center twice a week, you had an assigned monitor. Like a parole officer. She would go in and speak to him. He would write some notes. It sounded mostly annoying. She could only make money by working under the table for my dad."

I took a sip of wine. I couldn't tell where he was going with this.

"She eventually ended up marrying her monitor."

"And do you think they're happy?"

He let go of my hand. "They laugh a lot. She says he knows everything about her. A lot of people think it's a sweet story."

"You know, I didn't understand this, not fully, until I turned fourteen. That's the year when all the girls, you know, went to a separate classroom from the boys, and our teachers reminded us that we were now at an age where we could be credibly accused of practicing witchcraft. But the focus was more, you know, don't accuse each other of being witches. False reports can be prosecuted. They showed us pamphlets about how to know if you're a witch. What to do if you think you've been cursed."

"We were told the same thing about accusations but given one of those speeches about being good role models, looking out for our female friends, telling a male authority figure if something seems wrong."

"Almost everyone talks around what happens to women. So many euphemisms." I picked at a roll, turned it into shreds of dough on my plate. "Why should it make people so uncomfortable if it's the right thing to do?"

He put his glass of wine down. "I'm not arguing that it's right."

I realized I was starting to raise my voice a little. I let go of his hand, poured myself some more wine, offered him more, which he waved away.

"Go back to what you were saying about coercion." His voice

was gentle. I could tell he was truly interested in what I was thinking.

"Is it possible for it to ever truly, really be love—the kind where you agree to stay together forever—if someone has to do it to maintain the life they know?"

Preston looked up at the mesh above us. Someone said loudly, "This is a lemon drop." I put my hand on the table. A small red wine stain was setting into the cloth.

"Jo, what are your absolute ideal circumstances for falling in love? If you were queen of the world, no one could ever tell you what to do, how would it happen?"

I thought immediately, None. Those circumstances didn't exist for me. I opened my mouth, closed it.

"What does your life look like in five years?"

"I don't really think like that. I can think maybe in six months. I'll still be at the museum, I'll be here, I'll be making videos, maybe I'll finally start learning how to knit."

"Do you want kids?"

"Sometimes. Let me go back to your first question. Maybe the ideal circumstance is, quietly, unconsidered. I'm walking with someone, they say something, I laugh, and suddenly I think, oh, I love you, and then I can't stop thinking it. There's no consideration of being thirty, of having kids. I mean, it's connected, I guess it would be impossible for it not to be connected. But I keep thinking, I love you, and rarely think about the pressures on it."

"Do you really think that's possible for you?" His eyes were kind. I could see he wasn't trying to start an argument.

"What do you mean?"

"I mean, I've known you for almost a year. And what's between us is. Well, it's not ordinary. There are some very basic things about you I don't know. Until last week, I didn't know anything about your mom. I don't even know your middle name. I've met your friends, twice?"

"Are you saying it's impossible for me to fall in love?"

"I'm just saying, it's impossible for you to not overthink things."

He pushed his hair off his forehead. Huffed a little sigh.

In his apartment, we already would've been having sex. I would probably be fifteen minutes away from putting on my shoes and going home. His apartment building's stairs creaking under my tennis shoes, music and video game sounds sliding under doors, the lobby stinking of the rose-scented air freshener plugged in beneath the mailboxes. I put my fork down.

"I'm leaving tomorrow for a short trip," I said. I told him about my mom's final wishes. He took my hand again. Together, we looked at a picture of the apples I was supposed to gather. Online they were wondrously purple; Preston made me promise to bring one back for him if it looked as intense in person as it did online. He asked me if I wanted to talk about my mother. I said not yet. We sent Maddyison a glass of Scotch we were sure she would hate. Split a piece of chocolate cake and made plans to see each other when I got back.

When we walked outside, Preston put an arm around my shoulders. He smelled good, like a perfumist's idea of what tobacco should smell like. The air was crisp. We decided maybe it was better to keep getting to know one another before having sex again. It was clear to me he did really like me. I couldn't understand why, though. All I had seen throughout the night was how annoying I must be.

"Tell me two important things about you," he said.

I told him I hated going to the dentist and there was an episode of *Unsolved Mysteries* about my mother's disappearance. I'd never finished watching it, but I wouldn't mind if he watched it by himself.

Preston squeezed my shoulder. "I'll watch it, but we don't have to talk about it."

"Tell me two things about you," I said.

He said he loved cooking, it was one of his favorite things to do in the world. And that he was on medication for anxiety but his parents didn't know because they would be weird about it and it would just add to the cycle of anxiety.

We walked through the night together. Preston started talking about how he didn't trust anyone who could say things like "my parents are my best friends." He knew the term was gross, but he said the best way to describe his relationship to them was, "They're my frenemies." Maybe this could work, I thought, and squeezed his hand. I could tell he had moisturized it for our date. Thinking about him taking the time to put lotion on his hands, considering how they would feel to me, made me smile. Then, I paused, and wondered if my standards were too low.

9.

The last time I saw my mother, it was a Monday. September 28. A few silver balloons were still bobbing against my bedroom ceiling. It was the year I loved that color. For my birthday, five days before that, she had given me three delicate silver rings, and I wore them all on my right hand. My dad had given me a gray sweatshirt with metallic silver sleeves and a necklace with a small robot on it. I felt lucky every time I thought about those gifts because it was clear my parents were paying attention to who I was. For Angie's birthday, her mom had given her a large stuffed rabbit as big as her fourteen-year-old torso. Angie had wanted knee-high combat boots, a long cardigan, and/or a biography of Valentina Tereshkova. Or to be allowed to change her name to Valentina. "Your parents, they just get you, man," she'd said. "My mom wants me to stay nine forever."

And I nodded, but I also remembered how much I'd wished when we were younger that my parents would be better at parent-stuff. They always forgot to pick me up on time from field trips and after-school things. They rarely looked at my homework. When I cried and wanted to go home from sleepovers, my mom would refuse to come get me. She would sigh and remind me life was tough and there were worse things than being at a nice friend's nice house for one night. Angie's mom was always there on time, would drive out even in the middle of a snowstorm to pick her up from somewhere, was front row and paying rapt attention at our basketball games. My mom would read a book, marking the pages lightly with a yellow pencil.

That last morning, my mom had made what she called her harvest hash: reheated leftover roasted vegetables from dinner the night before, an egg over easy with crushed red pepper on the yolk resting precariously on top. She talked to me about a book. It was about a cavern system in Kentucky where runes were on every surface, even the ceilings. People swore—and this got my attention, this is how I think I remember everything—that they had seen silver bats in these caves.

She drove me to school. It was very bright out, but unusually cold. Felt more like a November day than fresh-out-of-the-package autumn. The day was a middle school blur: orange lockers, terrible people who smelled terrible, me a terrible person who smelled terrible, *Romeo and Juliet*, French-fry scent. In almost all of my memories from middle and high school, someone is eating French fries or their grease is the air's humidity, wheezed out from the drab cafeteria with its permanently stained linoleum.

When my mom picked me up from school, it was snowing. "Fucking climate change," she muttered while glaring at the glittering flakes. That was at 2:45. I can't remember what she did for the next three hours, but it was general Mom-at-home stuff. She made me unload the dishwasher, threw together dinner, complained about the weather but not in a way that made me think, Oh, she's going somewhere. At 6:30 p.m.—and I remember because I had to tell this story so many times—Mom made us all cocoas. She seemed preoccupied and said very little. "This is this week's dessert," she said as she handed me the cup. "Happy cheat day." I went to the kitchen with it, added cinnamon, whipped cream, and marshmallows. When I went back out into the living room, she raised an eyebrow at my mug.

We were on strict diets—she called it our staying-alive-in-case-of-an-apocalypse diet, but the "fun" name didn't make me feel better about it. Angie's mom told her all the time it was better to love her body as it was, to not overthink what she ate. I thought how my mother would never say anything like that to me. She always wanted me to be the best possible version of myself. Even at fourteen, I wondered how she could know what that was. In the grand scheme of being a person, I had barely started.

We watched the snow in silence. I hated it, worried it would stay until the following March. Then I read a book for school, watched TV. I assumed at the time my mom was simmering over my cocoa additions, that she wanted to say something but my dad had asked her to cool it with the diet talk. He so rarely asked her for anything that when he did, she took it seriously.

She was also bidding on something private on eBay. I assumed it was either a late gift for me or one for my dad's birthday in November. She kept looking at her laptop screen and muttering to herself. It sounded like she was saying, "I am watching myself get robbed."

We would find out later she had been bidding on a set of decorative cushions. They were hideous: mustard and pea-green paisley front, the back a scarlet and cream spiral pattern. When we opened the package, after her disappearance, my dad was sure they had sent the wrong thing. I was disappointed. When the package first arrived, I thought it might be her head, like in a movie. Then, for months, those awful cushions sat in my bedroom. At one point, I tore one apart; maybe a letter was inside. Nothing. In my notebook, I wrote to myself: cushions = ??? Now, we say things like, "Those cushions were a cry for help," or "Maybe the bigger mystery is how she could've thought these were worth buying." The remaining two cushions are still in my dad's basement.

My mom went to bed early, hugged me good night. She smelled like almond oil and grass and something else. I thought maybe she was getting sick and that was why she smelled a little sour. In the morning, she and the snow were gone. The car was still there. Her hiking boots and coat had left with her. It was September 29, and everything was different.

The last thing she said to me, standing in the doorway of my room as I bent over my desk, barely turning to look at her, was, "Don't stay up too late, okay?"

10.

Angie helped me pack up my car. She was wearing a long robe, her slippers shaped like pugs, and I could tell she was seriously thinking about asking to come. Her mouth kept opening and shutting, she was tugging on her pink sleeves, kept saying, "We should at least have some breakfast." The pug slippers with their black button eyes looked up at me coldly.

"I want to stop in The Loon before I make my way up," I said.

We hugged. Her hair smelled like weed and lavender. There were a few months when I thought I was in love with Angie. This was right around the time when I was ready to understand that I was bi, but I was also tired of feeling like the most complicated person anyone had ever known. I was already the only Black person in my grade at school, I was already the girl whose mother might have been murdered. Teachers and the guidance counselor were always looking at my face as if they were checking for tear stains or red eyelids.

Sometimes, though, we would be watching a movie in my bedroom, sitting together on the gray loveseat, and I would be so aware of the space between our hands on the couch, her juicy apple shampoo, the way our thighs would touch against each other, her toenails painted almost always hot pink, her long fingers, the nails cut short, the gleam in the blue television light of the clear manicures she preferred. I felt sure saying something to her would only put distance between us; and more than having a crush on Angie, more than thinking it could be fun to be her girlfriend, I needed someone other than my dad to feel like family.

The crush was 99.9 percent gone now. There was an awkward pause after the hug, a moment when I had an impulse to lean forward, to see if she too would lean in. I got into the car, waved goodbye. In the city, the roads were mostly clear. People were waking up, each yellow light flicking on felt like a benediction. A few college students were on the sidewalks getting enormous cups of coffee, looking dazed and tired as they waited for caffeine to cleanse their hangovers and return their souls back into their bodies. The streetlamps took a bow from bright white to clear globes. Behind me, the sky was still orange.

A woman walked out in front of my car. Another almost-Mom. I hit the brakes in time. She screamed as if I had smashed into her; the sound became a chorus of fuck you, you dumb bitch. She slammed a hand on my car, made eye contact with me. Then, she walked back to the sidewalk. A car honked behind me, another one. I took a deep breath, kept driving toward the freeway. A cop car was behind me. Had it been following me for miles? Had I been that distracted?

Panic brewed and fermented, gassed into my lungs and throat. I tried exhaling a deep breath.

"Peanut butter toast, walking alone in the rain, Obama Kush, Holy Ghost, Gorilla Breath, YA novels with dragons in them, Ludacris songs," I said. It helped me when I was alone and anxious to list the things I liked.

My breath kept catching in my throat. The fact I knew I was overreacting to the situation but couldn't stop it made everything worse.

My skeleton felt like it was melting inside me.

I tried listing more things—black leather Chelsea boots, candles that smelled like candy, black cats, the sound of the old dishwasher in the house I was renting—but it didn't help. Turning on the radio, a song about having only superstars at a funeral was playing. I shut it off. Turned into the closest gas station. Covered my eyes. If I saw the wrong thing, thought the wrong thing, it would turn into a full-blown panic attack.

My phone buzzed. Once, twice. I grabbed the water bottle from my cup holder, took a slow sip. Water dribbled down my chin. I wiped it off with the top of my sweatshirt. Angie was texting me. I ignored the link to an article that she thought was funny and asked her if she would come with me, meet me in Clair de Lune.

Yes, of course, she texted back within seconds. Probably won't be there till noon at the earliest. Have to pack, eat, maybe get new waterproof boots.

I read her response three times as slowly as I could. Each time made me calm down a little more. Thank you, I finally responded.

* * *

When I got to Clair de Lune, instead of driving home, I went first to the woods my mother loved. I put on my purple coat because I couldn't remember whether it was hunting season and it was the only unnaturally bright-colored thing I had with me. These woods were one of the other places where I had been sure, briefly, that magic was real.

A huge tree was in the middle of the woods—it was hundreds of years old. One of her desk drawers had a small layer of dried leaves in it she had collected from it. When we decided to move the desk to her storage unit, I found they had become brown fibrous dust. I decided I would gather some fallen leaves, keep them to leave at the place where my dad would put up a headstone.

Once upon a time, when I was ten, my mother had brought me here on a spring Saturday morning. She was hunting for herbs and

I didn't want to stay home because I knew my dad would make me help him clean house if I stayed. It was damp and chilly, the ground soft near the tree roots. The green and yellow herbs my mother was looking for were supposedly sprouting. My breath was visible, and seeing it curl out of my mouth reminded me of a snail scooching on a lettuce leaf.

I wandered away from my mother. I ran my hands along the base of a tall tree. I picked up a stick, wrote "Josie, Josey, Jo, Joey, Josephine" in cursive on a soft patch of dirt. When I think about these moments, I remember myself feeling at home there among the trees. No thoughts about homework, school, or the books I was reading. I was the dirt, I was the stick, I was each and every still branch waiting for all the birds' spring return.

Then, I turned and looked at my mother. She was crouched over a plant, flipping through a small yellow book in her hand. Her identification book. Behind her was someone who was watching the back of her head. The person was dressed in light brown clothes: leggings, a scratchy-looking coat, gloves. Talking, gesturing emphatically, so close to her high ponytail. With hair that was male cardinal red. A shock against the ugly spring.

The person could feel me staring. They turned. Their face made me drop the stick I was holding. Their eyes were like a great gray owl's—a third of their face, black with a yellow ring around the outside. Skin pink from the cold air. A small nose. Their mouth open, as dark as their eyes. I could see no teeth. Without realizing it, I took a step back, another. Tripped on a root, fell back on my butt.

When I picked myself up, the person was gone. My mom was still crouched over her plants, lips pursed, thick eyebrows close together. She hadn't noticed someone had been so close. I told myself maybe I had imagined them. This was around the time when my mom had started asking me things like, Is it magic or are you just scared? A creak in the night wasn't a monster—I was too old to be thinking like that.

My dad had been talking to me around this time about his own anxiety. It felt like when I turned nine, something inside me snapped on. School was harder. Sleep felt an arm's length out of reach almost every night. It didn't matter if I ran or played basketball or hadn't slept the night before. My dad worried. My mom said the same thing happened to her sister and it would go away once I got my period. Sometimes on Sundays, my dad and I would meditate together. We would listen to classical music, close our eyes, and lie on yoga mats. "Try, Jo, to get your brain as empty as possible. And if that's not possible, visualize good things happening to you." Getting 100 percent on my spelling test. Singing my solo for the school play with the lights on my face, my hand making the right gestures, my expression showing none of the effort. A pizza party. He told me my life would be easier if I started finding ways to make my brain have soft, comfortable places I could come back to. I know this is weird, but sometimes when you're older, the worst place in the world might be your own brain.

His face looked so sad when he saw I already understood.

In the woods, I turned away from my mother. The bird-faced person was in the distance now, their eyes yellow bright against all the brown trunks. I did what my father always did when he wanted to feel calmer—yes, I listed a few things I liked: "fruit roll-ups, fuzzy socks, pizza parties." It helped until I noticed a small door, only about two feet tall, a foot wide, at the base of a tree near me.

It had no discernable knob, but I could see in the bright, almost-afternoon light a dark edge as if the entire night sky slept the day away in that particular tree trunk. A smell of rot in the air. Each strand of hair on my forearms stood up, my mouth felt full. The door opened slowly, pulling into the tree, until there was only a dark hole.

I turned back to look at my mom. She had moved farther on. From behind a tree, I could see only a hint of the neon pink windbreaker she was wearing. Something—an animal? a thing?—slipped out of the door. I saw it from the corner of my eye. It moved like a ferret. It looked like a garden gnome except it was made from moss, clay, sticks, and what looked like maitake mushrooms, slick as if they were starting to die. Dirt brown eyes. It turned toward me. A mouth filled with gray pointed teeth. My eyes were dry. It picked up a pinecone from the ground, pushed it all into its mouth. Chewed, then spat out a brown-black paste, let it dribble on its gray face. The thing ignored me but kept coming closer and closer. Birds argued. There was no reason for me to be scared, I told myself. My mom had told me to say that whenever I felt frightened or anxious; she said it would help me feel in control.

I'm still scared of so many things. Mice, men walking behind me at night, being in a vehicle that I'm not driving. Anytime someone leaves me a voicemail. Sometimes, when I'm alone in the grocery store, I think about someone shooting me in the back of the head and I have only the half-second before my brain dies from the bullet to realize my time on Earth is done. To realize: I've been fucking murdered. Fear is part of my life now; I accept it.

"Mom," I whispered, although I knew she couldn't hear me. The thing was so close, if I stretched out my foot, we would touch. It darted forward and brushed against my jeans. I seized up for a moment. It left a slime I could feel through the thick fabric, a stink so pungent it made my eyes water, made me sneeze. It ran under an upraised root, was rummaging through dead leaves.

I ran to my mother. "We need to go home."

"You smell awful." She spoke to me as if I were a much younger, very stupid child. "Did you run into a skunk?"

"Please, can we go home?"

"I've told you so many times you're not supposed to scare skunks."

"Mom. Please."

We were back at the root of most of our disagreements at that time; neither of us could tell what she wanted from me, who she wanted me to be. Now looking back on these fights, I can see her reaction to me being nine was a confusing mixture of rage that I was getting older—there were things about me she no longer knew, things I kept closed in the palm of myself—and frustration that I was not yet old enough so she could be completely herself when she was with me.

The stench came back when I took a deep breath to ask her again, in a more polite voice, to take us home.

Still standing in front of the tree, my mother ignored me, marked a line in her book. I waited to get used to the smell, but it persisted. I leaned over and vomited. A small screech in my head told me to take all my clothes off, but it was too cold. I still feel like I can't adequately explain the depths of sudden misery and disgust I was plunged into. It was like playing one of those life simulator video games and you're in the mood to just fuck with your characters. So, you put them into a very small, empty room with no doors. The person hates the ugly space, and their happiness meter lowers quickly from deeply happy verdancy to pee-yellow to emergency-siren-red. The character shouts at heaven, it doubles over. It is hungry, it has to pee. Thought bubbles of all the things it needs to feel better speed over its head. But you don't let it out of the room. It's so unhappy, its soul leaves its body. The digital avatar you spent hours creating, making it look like you or a friend, is gone; a tomb-stone is all that remains in its house. The process on fast mode takes two minutes at most.

My mom made me wait fifteen minutes more. I smelled so bad, she joked about making me ride home in the trunk. We had to burn my jeans.

In the car, I told her what had happened. Described in as close detail as I could about what the person and the thing looked like, acted like, smelled like. I tried to keep my voice calm, but I got more and more excited. My mom kept her eyes on the windshield.

"You're too old to be telling stories like this."

"It happened."

"Try thinking about it this way." Her voice was gentle. "You are the only person in the entire world that saw these things? To have experienced this situation?"

"This could've happened to other people. I don't have proof it didn't. I just know it happened to me."

She sighed. "Your imagination is too big."

In the woods now, I looked at each leaf. The petiole, the veins, focused on the venation patterns. On each part, I wished for a safe journey. I tried to visualize myself picking the purple apples, and above else, feeling filled and settled with acceptance of the situation. You will feel peace, I told myself.

The tree's scent was light, and I leaned closer to try to inhale it as much as possible. The leaves were red and brown in my hand. The veins so deep, they made me think of engraved rings: a secret message pressed against my finger. I felt a breath on the nape of my neck. A hand close by, reaching for me. Fingers longing for mine. I turned. Two people I didn't know were walking together, pausing only to take photos of some mushrooms growing on the trees.

When my mother had first vanished, I had come to these woods.

I walked among the trees calling for her. Mom. Tiana. Ti. I looked for signs of foraging, pretended once a small scrap of fabric was a sign. The woods were a shadow box filled with all the memories of the times we had been there before, decorated with me, pacing, filled to the brim with missing her. I looked for the small door I had seen in the tree when I was ten, but it wasn't there. A bird called and it sounded like "Not here, not here." Another joined in. Another added a downbeat of "No, nah, no, nah." Then it seemed like every bird who had made a home, was visiting their fellow passerines, joined in. I listened. As I walked out of the woods, trailing a finger across every trunk I encountered, I said "I understand" over and over again. It didn't matter. I knew my mother wasn't here. But the birds didn't stop until I was back in the adjoining meadow.

11.

Another story my mother used to tell me was called "The Witch of the Seven Chickens." There once was a witch who was the caretaker of a small town near Lake Michigan. Her mother and mother's mother loved the shore, the meadows, the small cluster of homes, the bushes covered in purple and lake-at-night-colored berries. And that love was a part of her, as visible as the long black hair on her head or her large ears that were always announcing themselves when the wind blew loud and pushed her thick hair back.

This witch had seven black cats—the largest was the size of a small pony, the smallest no bigger than a mouse. The largest kept the town safe from the men from other towns who might come thieving and murdering. The smallest crept in the shadows and listened to gossip. It would return home at night and tell its mistress of everything; no detail was insignificant.

In addition to the seven cats, she had seven chickens. The eggs they produced were so large that one of them could feed an entire family of four at breakfast. The chickens' feathers were always snow-white, their beaks yellow, and they smelled like hay and warm springtime. The second-largest cat guarded these chickens from predators.

When people were threatened, the cats were sent to protect them. When people were on the verge of growing hungry, they would open their doors to find a basket of berries, eggs wrapped in red cloths, and wild asparagus bound in twine. The witch said blessings over babies, held the hands of the old and dying, and kept away the harshest snows.

Over time, the other towns simmered in their jealousy. Their people died younger, their people grew hungry, men from other towns came and went—stealing or slaughtering their livestock, uprooting or burning their crops, carrying their daughters away in the night. How was this fair? Some towns didn't try to rebuild. They lived in the ruins and broken-down bits. It was impossible to get ahead without a witch's blessings. Why bother even trying for a harvest?

When the witch heard of the growing anger against her town, she sent her cats to the various town elders, inviting all those people to join her. There was room for everyone, she said, as long as everybody respected the land and the water.

The first time my mother told me this story, she paused here and asked me, "What do you think happens next?" I was, I think, eight years old. Wrapped in a floral quilt, a glass of lukewarm just-like-I-wanted water on my nightstand. My hair smelled like fresh bath. My father was in the kitchen, making warm cider, and I could smell the cinnamon, orange peel, and cloves. "They all lived together," I said. "And it was great." My mother shook her head seriously. If my father had heard this, he would have told me to stay this sweet forever.

My mom continued the story. The old town residents were jealous of the witch's divided attentions. They said this was no longer their home—with all the new people, it was a farrago where they always felt unsafe. It had been arrogant of her to invite them here.

She asked them for patience. "Give it time," she said. "You will know them, you will build a life together in the fields, on the waters. Your families will become one, and as you knot and loop yourselves together, you and your descendants will flourish."

The witch went to the outskirts of town to take care of an old dying woman she had known since the woman was a child. She made her soups and tinctures to help her go easy, held her hand, and listened to her speak and breathe, until she was still. The witch made her old friend a garland of rosemary, covered her hands in tiger lilies, and knelt for hours singing and speaking poetry for her friend's soul.

When the rites were done, the witch returned home to find her hut on fire. All her chickens were slaughtered. The soil refused to accept their blood, so it sat upon grass and dirt, bright and foul in the afternoon sun. Her cats had scattered, but there were signs of struggle—a man's pale arm on the grass, its thick fingers bruised violet.

The witch knew what was expected of her: confront the townspeople, order the new members of the town to leave, restore the peace. The witch would have to bring suffering to the newcomers, would have to burn the edges of her soul in an attempt to return the town to life as it had been before. She couldn't see how she could trust any of the townspeople again. Even if the new people had been the ones to do this, all she could see was the want inside all men for more, more, more.

When my mother said this line to me, I said, "But those were just some people. Why not just go somewhere else where the people are good?"

She said it was more complicated than that. It's possible for someone a lot of people might say is wonderful—kind to his wife, donates to charity—to be something bad, like a racist. And it's just as possible for someone who is a murderer, someone people say is absolutely terrible, to show sudden kindness, to find something beautiful to believe in and work toward good, but there will always be some people who will think of him only as evil because of the one bad thing he did.

I leaned my head on her shoulder. She smelled like rosemary.

"But most people overall are taught to think only of themselves," she said, "and maybe their family first. As long as you think only about how you can get more things, you might never be able to be good."

I yawned and asked her to finish the story. I didn't want to think about what she was saying. It was all too big and hurt my head.

The witch gathered what could be salvaged. She walked the fields and meadows. And when she was ready, she walked into the lake. Let the water cover her head. Went down to the bottom and began to build herself a new home made of driftwood and seaweed and stones. The whitefish and yellow perch would be her neighbors now. They would all have to work together, the seaweed, the fish, the stones, the very water, to survive. They would give and take from each other, and there would be no acrimony.

The second time my mother told me this story, she asked me what I thought the story meant. I was eleven and trying to impress her when I answered, "The only safe place for a woman is 100 percent alone."

"Yes," she said. "Remember that."

12.

I went to my dad's house. It smelled like bacon and toast. In the kitchen he was chopping a bright yellow tomato.

"It's a Brandywine." Then he dropped the knife, hugged me close. "Jo Jo."

A thing that has surprised me about growing older is I've learned to love so many of the things I once hated. Tomatoes, the smell of incense, being called Jo Jo, winters, doing mental math, shrimp. I had expected a tightening as I grew older; I would like what I liked and that was the essence of who I was. But my personality gets easily seeped now with new details. I read something new, I watch something new, I eat something new and the world feels again like a place where I want to stay.

My dad is moderately tall, his hair is the color of wet sand, although near his temples it was lightening, blond and snow. He is very white, but we have the same dark eyes and chin. We talk in the same slow way as if we want to be very precise with what we're about to say, even when we're just shooting the shit with a friend. We both have the same birthmark on our forearm near the elbow, a dark brown paint splotch, although his looks much more dramatic than mine.

He met my mother at one of the memorial days for witches. Two of my relatives on his side were murdered for witchcraft in Sault Ste. Marie. It was a time when all women were in danger because "no regulations were in place." That's how it was described in school, in a passive way where no one was to blame because that was how life was back then. If you were a woman who got in an argument with a friend, and she fell ill hours later, it was within her parents' rights to have you taken to an ice-covered lake and made to stand in its center for an hour. If you didn't fall in, you were a witch. If you fell in, they tried to save you. A man could claim you had given him a dazzling look and he was not in his right mind when he took you. He had been bedeviled. There was no punishment for raping an accused witch. A woman could even be burned at the stake for defying him.

To be considered a true witch in the state of Michigan, you have to have at least three acts of magic on the official record. They don't have to be large magical events. They can be something as simple as a dream written down that predicts an event with 70 percent accuracy. I once looked it up, and there are four registered witches in the state. Guidelines are vague about what happens, state stewardship, insurance policies, registrations; there is a precise clause that no witch is allowed on the Mackinac or Ambassador Bridges because of "infrastructure concerns"; but each plan is subject to approval by the state committee for witch regulations. Sometimes, people say, Isn't it lucky to be a woman now?

The memorial days for witches. People—descendants, historians, witch rights advocates—gather in areas where known trials and burnings and executions had happened. They carry white and pink candles or large amounts of rosemary and fern. They say the names of the remembered dead. Someone plays a flute. They say, "Let it not happen again." Someone rings a bell. They say, "Let their souls have peace." The bell rings again. "Let it not happen again. Women need equal protection and security in the face of the law. Let it not happen again."

I hate the passive voice of "Let it not happen again." I went to memorial days a few times with my dad as a teenager, and once I asked him, "Why don't we say something like, 'We will beat the asses of anyone who tries to start this shit again'?"

He laughed and said, "This is about understanding the past always informs the present. It's never about revenge."

When my parents met, they were standing next to each other and started whispering together, which led to their leaving early and going to a bar. Two beers, finding out they had the same favorite song—Nina Simone singing "I Wish I Knew How It Would Feel to Be Free"—became dinner. (Younger me gobbled this detail up. Older me suspected my dad lied. The only albums he listened to were by the Rolling Stones and Wilco and men who liked the word "yeah" a lot.) Then a walk along the river. My dad knew it was corny, but as they talked, his eyes moving from her face to the stars so bright they felt just out of arm's reach, he thought this could be his whole life. They went to another bar. He walked her to her hotel. He went back to his hotel. He thought that even though it was very late and he was buzzed, he should call his mom and thank her for guilting him into attending that memorial day ceremony. Instead, on the hotel stationery, he wrote my mom a letter, walked back out into the night, and left it at her hotel's front desk. They had breakfast together the next morning. Within a year, they were married.

My father hugged me again. He seemed thinner but not tired. I let him look at my face. He could see the slight bags under my eyes, probably some tear stains or puffiness from earlier. I was aware as he studied me of all the strain and tension that I was holding in my shoulders, and I tried to relax, be less rigid. I hoped he could also see I had been going to the gym, that I ran. I wondered if he could see that sometimes I made myself green smoothies for breakfast. I hoped he could see the deeper things, too.

I wanted to go up north and do what Mom asked not for the

money but because I felt ready to be a different person—someone who accepted she would never know what had happened to her mother. It felt too stupid to say aloud, but I wanted to say something like, "I'm done being angry." He pulled a leaf out of my hair, patted my back.

I got out the plates, the glasses. He put black grapes, chips, BLTs on the table.

We were quiet for a few minutes as we ate. He used goat cheese instead of mayo and I told him it made the sandwiches seem like we were at an expensive restaurant. "These are twelve-dollar-lunch sandwiches, Dad." He laughed but was obviously pleased.

"Your grandmother is on another one of her gambling cruises."

"Big surprise."

All of my grandmother's active income since she retired came from going on gambling cruises, traveling to do poker tournaments. All my friends who know about it say she's addicted to gambling. But it's hard to tell because it seems like she never bets too much, she treats it like a job, and will sometimes take months off to do other things. She says things like, 99 percent of what people call lucky is patience. She alternates between telling very long stories and saying things that would make her a hit on social media. Her name is Honoria but she goes by her middle name, Jane. She says both names are musty, but her parents were musty people who expected their children to be just as musty. I love her very much.

"She said she won five thousand dollars on slots," my dad said, "so she's just relaxing now."

"Grandma doesn't play slots."

"They're for dingdongs and suckers. I know."

"Do you ever feel weird about her traveling alone?"

"She's not that old, Jo Jo."

I picked all the grapes off their stems. Clouds were traveling slow and large across the sun and the light in the dining room dimmed. The house cleared its throat with a loud wooden creak.

"Whenever I read one of those news articles about people getting pushed off cruise ships." I said.

He took a bite of his sandwich, smiled; we'd had this conversation before and he finished my thought for me. "Those articles are always, like, the perfect crime, death in international waters."

"I hate that."

My dad put his sandwich down. He looked at me with his head tilted. I was a teenager again. It was like we were in the car and he was taking the opportunity to ask me questions because we didn't have to look at one another. Should we move? Do you like your therapist? Are you okay? Is there something you want to tell me?

"I love you." His voice caught a little between the words "love" and "you."

My eyes watered. They always did when someone told me they loved me. My sandwich crust, the picked-free grapes, the light gray plate with the chipped edge were easier to look at.

It's strange, but being around my father has always made me feel the most weighted and the freest from grief. Wanting my mother to open the door, to kick off her shoes, to sing to herself as she starts the coffeemaker—that desire tied us together more than most fathers and daughters. I sometimes thought I had an advantage over so many of my friends: Every birthday, my father told me he loved me. A big chunk of my friends had never heard their dads say it. But my friends, some of them, anyway, talked about how remote their fathers seemed. How it was their mothers who were the glue that kept them having any relationship at all with their dads—"Oh your dad is right here, let me put him on the phone," "Your father is feeling ___." And an awkward text here and there. My father is a person who needs comforting. I'm the only person who has always, forever, been on his side about my mother's disappearance. But it's the only deep thing between us. He couldn't tell you about my life beyond the fact I work at a museum, couldn't tell you my interests beyond art, and anything he could tell someone about me would be from when I was seventeen at the latest. I am frozen in his brain as his teenage daughter; he does not like to get glimpses of the person I've become in the years since.

That doesn't mean there's nothing between us. So many people find grief tiresome or indulgent or contagious. I don't tell people about my mother anymore because I feel like most of them are thinking, Shut up about your dead mom. It's something about how scrunched-up and tight their shoulders get. When their mouths get smaller and smaller while I'm talking about how my mother is probably, definitely dead, they are thinking about how everyone they love will die, they will die, their dogs will die, the Arby's we're walking past will die, the Earth will die, and so will the universe, spreading out into a nothing state we cannot comprehend, and I have infected them with death. Or they're thinking about how they're such a benevolent listener: "It must feel like a relief to have a space to talk about her." It did, Asshole, until you said that wild sentence. Meanwhile, my dad wants to always talk about it; the hole he feels is in the center of everything.

When we're together—eating meals, celebrating holidays, sitting in a movie theater, an empty seat on either side of us—he makes it so I can sometimes feel like she's stepped away for a moment, will be back in two minutes. And then the minutes pass, she doesn't sit down and ask what she's missed, and every emotion I've had about her rushes in feeling brand new and unmanageable. We don't move forward.

"I know, Dad."

He asked me how Angie was doing. I told him about how she

was trying to talk me into taking a glass-blowing class with her. "So, you're going to learn how to make bongs." He said "bong" in a way that made me laugh, as if it were a foreign word he had just learned how to pronounce correctly and relished saying. Baw-ong.

"She thought it would be cool if we learned how to make ornaments."

"Yeah, ornaments you can smoke weed with."

My dad was making himself laugh so hard he almost knocked over his glass of water. "Instead of a Christmas angel, the two of you are going to have a bong slipped over the tree's top. You can send out a Christmas card together wishing everyone a dank new year."

"Oh, my god." I was laughing and also wondering when and how he had learned the word "dank."

My dad stopped laughing, cleared his throat, started laughing again. "I feel like your mom would be so happy weed is legal here."

I echoed her words: "The great gift from the Earth, criminalized by the white man, the Christian, to keep us all under the steel toe boot of capitalism."

"Sometimes, she said 'riding boot.'"

"You know for a while, I was finally not thinking about her every single day, but now this."

I rubbed the edge of the plate. It was dull and scratchy, but it was more pleasurable to touch than the treated and smooth intact line of the rest of it.

"Do you really think she's gone?" I asked.

He coughed. Bent over. "Wrong pipe," he said. Kept coughing. His face blossomed deep red.

"Can I do something?"

He waved me away. The cough was horrible, he was bent over. I stood up, hovered, wondering whether I should do the Heimlich.

"I'm okay." Coughed. Gasped. Coughed. Sat up. A large vein in his forehead was now prominent and looming.

I saw my mother holding a spindly green herb up toward the light. "Can't tell if this is poison."

My mother pointing at my face. "You have your father's chin and eyebrows."

My dad continued coughing. I continued hovering. I shut my eyes for a second. She was gone.

"You probably shouldn't have said that while I was drinking." His voice was still a rasp.

"I probably shouldn't have said that at all."

"Do you think she's still alive?" he asked. "If you do, why did you suggest that we stop looking?"

I was still caught in the surprise of having said anything at all. My arms crossed over my chest.

"You have to tell me why, Jo. An actual logical reason why. We have to." I knew he was going to say what he had been saying to me for months. "We have to move forward."

"She's dead, I know." I could hear a hesitance in my voice.

"You need to move on with your life. I thought this would help. You're twenty-eight."

I couldn't meet his eyes. His hands were on the table, the tips pressed down white, the knuckles pink. His breathing still ragged from the coughing. I pulled out my phone.

"I should get going."

"You need to build a life. I'm getting letters in the mail that say you haven't registered yet. I'm responsible for you, kid."

"I registered two nights ago. I'm sorry for putting it off."

"You need to get serious. You're so smart, so creative, Jo. You need to stop blowing up your life."

"Dad."

"Find a man to love. Please. Try to make things easier for once."

I heard all our past big fights as he spoke. When I came out to him, when I turned twenty-five and he said that was the year to find a man, when we were at my cousin Jennie's wedding and after three whiskies, he said, "Why can't you just pull your shit together?" and I knew he was talking about my girlfriend, my life, my stubbornness. I opened my mouth to start another fight. Shut it.

"I should go. It's going to be a long trip."

We stood up. My dad hugged me. The force of it surprised me. "I'm not trying to be an asshole here. I'm your dad. I just want you to have a good life."

Here's the question I've been trying to figure out how to ask him for years: Did my mom actually like being married? But I couldn't think of a way to ask him. I didn't want to hurt his feelings. I was afraid he might think I was finding a way to blame him.

Out in the car, I pulled my vape pen out of the glove compartment. Clicked it on, took a long hit, and felt indelibly seventeen. A fight with a parent, sulking out, smoking in my car. But I was almost thirty. How wonderful to know time was a deep lie, that for the rest of my life I would be surprising myself by saying something mean and sudden to ruin a nice meal, then retreating somewhere to sulk and consider how terrible I was. I could have gone in and apologized, told him I would try to do what he was asking, it was what I had spent my entire life already trying to do: follow the rules, register, hopefully get married, not be a worry to him. If he had said even once, ever, "I know this isn't fair, it's bullshit you have to follow these rules. It's disgusting how we treat women. I'm sorry I told you once I loved and supported you, but I also hope you end up being with a man because your life will be so much easier, I'm sorry, I should have thought about you first," I would have gone back inside. But he hadn't. So I didn't.

13.

After my mother's disappearance, the usual protocols happened. While the police quietly investigated my dad, I was taken away by the Bureau of Witchcraft to be questioned. A woman who can vanish might not be in danger; instead, she might be a danger to everyone. And if you're the daughter of a witch?

The facility was in Lansing, about forty-five minutes away from home.

I was wearing a pair of black overalls with one of her shirts underneath them. The shirt was too big and flapped around my armpits and moved beneath the black denim around my stomach. The outfit felt important because it was one of my favorites, but afterward, I couldn't wear any of it.

There were two white women who wore bright pink lipstick and told me I could call them Mrs. Andrews and Mrs. Mason. They were wearing gray suits and floral shirts. They reminded me of Angie's mom a little. They had a vibe that made me hyperaware that everything they asked, everything they noticed, was meant to build some weapon against me. Angie's mom was always sure we were up to something, like cool kids on a teen show would do: breaking into a liquor cabinet, sneaking in boys or sneaking out to parties, smoking cigarettes. I gave Mrs. Andrews and Mrs. Mason my biggest talking-to-moms-smile but knew instantly from their weak smiles back that I had done the wrong thing.

"Has your mother been in touch with you?"

I shook my head. It was better when you were behind with an adult to act shy and guarded, but not wary.

"Has anything unusual come to you?"

"I don't know what that means, Mrs. Andrews."

I looked around the room. It was mostly geared toward younger kids. A pastel play mat in the corner, a toy box with yarn-haired down spilling out a crack. The chair I sat in was the purple only found in hulking, mostly silent characters created for children who are still learning how to delineate between cute and creepy. The posters on the walls were about safety and how telling the truth was the right thing.

"Like a bird saying something to you, or words in the sky, or your computer typing by its own volition," Mrs. Andrews said.

"None of those things could happen," I said. My tone was a little bratty, in the way of a young teenager who felt as if her age and intelligence were being underestimated.

I did not entirely understand the danger I was in.

"Did you ever see your mother do something like that, though? Something that seemed impossible." I was looking at my feet and their voices were so similar I couldn't tell who had said it.

My face felt too warm. I wasn't thinking at all about my mother. I thought about the small gross monster that came out of the tree, the person with the bird face, the deer in the attic, other things in my childhood. Toys, dolls, all things now that before this moment I had felt certain were all symptoms of my too-big imagination.

"No," I said. "Never."

I covered my mouth and started crying. I expected them to hand me a tissue and say something vague but aiming toward kind like teachers or guidance counselors at school did. They waited until I was composed. Mrs. Mason bumped her knee up and down, pawed at her hair, and fiddled with her clipboard. Mrs. Andrews buttoned and unbuttoned a button at the wrist of her floral shirt.

"I miss her," I said. "Where is she?"

"You tell us."

"I can't."

"Have you ever done anything impossible? Did your mom say something that upset you before she went away? Did you threaten her? Did you point at her while thinking something awful?"

"No. I promise."

Mrs. Andrews raised her eyebrows. Her eyes were green, and even in that moment, scrutinizing me for magic, they were beautiful.

"Does my dad know I'm here?" I asked.

"Of course," she said. "Your dad is a good man."

Later, I thought this was the first step toward the distance I now felt with him. He had let his fourteen-year-old daughter, a girl who was barely sleeping, who was trying to figure out how to exist without her mother, go to this facility alone and be questioned without any warning. He didn't try to go with me. He never asked me what happened or checked to see whether I was okay. I would read later about these meetings and investigations, about how parents had the right to attend them with their children. Some states don't let any minors be interrogated for witchcraft without a guardian present. My dad had forfeited these rights and let me go on my own. He had decided his own safety, even over mine, was the most important thing. Or at least that's how I understood it. Every time the subject of this meeting came up, he left the room or said, "I did what I had to do."

Mrs. Andrews handed me a set of cards with different shapes on them. Rhombus, star, circle, triangle, and three parallel lines. She told me to study, give them my full focus. Then she took the cards from me and had me guess which ones she was looking at. Mrs. Mason took notes, but mostly searched my face, her eyes dark.

I stayed the night in a small bedroom at the facility. The quilt was Barbie pink. Cameras watched me sleep. It was hard to get comfortable or feel like falling asleep. I looked up at the ceiling and it was tiled, like my dentist's office. The room was pitch black. In the hallway I could hear someone walking around in sneakers that kept squeaking on every third step. My own breath felt too loud to me. I missed my mother desperately. I pulled the covers over my head and cried; I couldn't bear the idea of Mrs. Mason and Mrs. Andrews watching me through the cameras. I wanted to be at home on the couch, watching a movie with my dad, hoping both of us would fall asleep.

Even crying didn't give me enough of a release to fall asleep. My brain spiraled to the English paper that was due; the algebra that a week ago I had understood and now back at school none of it made sense; the girls at school who said they were watching me, my mom was a witch and I had always been weird; a teacher I had overheard saying, "It's always the husband who did it when a woman disappears"; the boy who had stepped on my shoe yesterday and then said, "Don't curse me, bro," and a bunch of people had laughed in a sharp way that made them all sound anxious. I moved to wondering about where my mom could be, what had really happened, and whether I would have to live here the rest of my life. What if I were a witch and didn't know it? My brain scrabbled for ideas about how I could persuade these people to let me leave.

When I had gone to dinner, some other girls were in the cafeteria, but I wasn't allowed to say hello or share a table with them. We ate our sandwiches and chips and looked around the room. All of us were Black and Latinx, except one white girl who was dressed goth. Her skin was cream white and she wore black lipstick. Her hair was dyed blue, and she was wearing large black jeans belted tight and high at her waist. She kept smiling while the rest of us were clearly unhappy. I was almost jealous of her because the only reason she was there—I was sure while I picked at my off-brand barbeque chips—was she wanted to be seen as a witch, that she thought something was to be gained by being affiliated with the dark arts.

After hours of lying still, I finally fell asleep. In the morning, still exhausted, I changed back into my overalls and my mother's shirt. They smelled like fresh laundry and vinegar.

"Josephine Thomas," Mrs. Mason said from the doorway.

I looked up.

She was wearing almost the exact same outfit as the day before. Only today's flowers were red and looked more abstract. "Are you a witch?"

"No," I said. I didn't have the energy to even be annoyed as I said it. I yawned and tried to meet her gaze.

"I know," she said. "But you're going to have to be careful your whole life."

Mrs. Mason gave me a long talk that could be summed up as: get married by age thirty, don't do anything reckless, follow the rules, get good grades, make people like you, don't get pregnant, try to dress respectably, don't join cliques that like danger, be a good girl. Throughout the rest of my teenage years, my dad said the same things. He would look at me sometimes, his eyes suspicious, suddenly cold when he thought I wasn't looking and then when he met my gaze, he would soften.

In the facility, I shook Mrs. Mason's hand. Her grip was tight on my fingers, soft on my palm. "I can do all those things," I promised.

14.

Angie laughed when she saw me waiting outside in my car rather than in the house, but was nice enough not to make me talk about it. We loaded all my things into her car. One of the pleasures of driving through Michigan is the trees. Farther and farther north, they shift, become taller and thinner, go from full Christmas tree to pipe cleaner versions. The sky changes too. The clouds come lower, the blue always feels a little brighter, the towns spread farther apart, and there are more dips, hills to make up the distance. It wakes up something animal in me, makes me want to drive faster, makes me not want to think but to be completely absorbed in traveling.

When I was a child and I couldn't sleep, I would think about what it would be like to be a cloud. I could travel thirty-five miles an hour on a good day, looking at treetops and tiny people. Sometimes, I would think about being a thunderstorm, one hundred miles per hour, filled with lightning and devastation. Sometimes when I was playing I would throw all my dolls around, knock over the houses, flip the cars. "You're dead," I would say, and in my head my voice was filled with lightning and gusts. "You're all dead. Oh god," I would say, pretending to be a mother. "Oh shut up," I would say in a gruff man's voice, "my dog was electrocuted."

"Stop that," my mother would say, "that's a serial killer game."

Angie and I drove through a town where several people had signs and flags that read WE BURN WITCHES HERE. A lone ranch house flew a confederate flag. "Which one makes you more uncomfortable?" Angie asked. Each kind of flag was an I-need-attention-red.

"I can't drive for twenty-five fucking minutes without someone finding some way to tell me how much they hate me," I muttered. "If it's not a flag, it's a bumper sticker. If it's not those, it's some weirdo's road sign."

Two miles later we passed a sign that read GOD SAVE US FROM BORTION, WITCHES, AND LIBERALS. We laughed at the missing A.

Angie pulled the town up on her phone. Just three years ago, an eighteen-year-old girl had gone to a party, ended up being burned to death, and no one said anything except that she had been a witch. The girl's name was Samantha. The high school football captain had been captured in a web of nauseated lust for her. She had insulted a girl and the girl had fallen into a deep, incapacitating fever. Someone said they had seen Samantha walking down the street, a crow alongside her. That was how the Old One worked. There was a podcast about the incident, six episodes, that really dove into the town's politics, its history, Samantha, and who might've done it. The most recent review said, Too many ads for seltzer! and gave it four and a half stars.

"If I die young, don't let anyone make a podcast about me," I told Angie.

Traffic slowed, closer and closer together. We couldn't tell what was happening. A lane closure? An accident? We talked in the half-sentences that annoyed people use when they're trying to sound deeply chill. It would be fine. The boat I was supposed to meet left at 9:30 the next morning, so why did I feel the impulse to grit my teeth, to swear a little bit, as if that would make everything move faster? In the distance we heard sirens. "Could walk faster than this," Angie muttered. "Bet someone hit a deer. Some driving noob panicked."

"Did you say 'noob'?" Angie rolled her eyes at me.

During the wait, we started brainstorming a sketch we called "Midwestern or White?" There would be two teams: one composed only of white players and one of people of color. We would hold up cards and ask players, "White or Midwestern?": "loving good deals over ethics," "hot dish," "being afraid of cities," "church softball league," "honeymoon at Disney," "talking with a nasal A," "calling themselves a moderate," "family cabin up north." The answer would always be "White." The final card would be "always saying 'Midwestern' when you mean white middle class." We were laughing as we wrote it, which was always a good sign. Angie felt a little nervous, sure it would make her mom uncomfortable. But that also felt like we were on the right track—when the joke was there, but we knew enough people would be uncomfortable with the big idea behind the humor. It was wild to me that we could know all these things but still be too scared to let people we didn't know see these videos.

When traffic finally moved, we drove past a semitruck, its front black and crumpled. An explosion had happened. No one could have survived. A fire truck with its lights still on was parked behind it, a cluster of four firefighters having what looked like a solemn discussion. We shriveled with embarrassment about our bad attitudes. I wondered whether the driver had purposefully caused the accident on this ideal September day. There was no animal carcass, no other car or people seemed to be involved. I thought to say it aloud would turn the rest of the car trip into something acrid.

Years ago, when I was very drunk, I had stared up at my bedroom ceiling and asked Angie if she thought my mom had committed suicide. If that was why there was no sign of her. My eyeliner and mascara were crusts in the edges of each eye. I was crying so hard, my lungs were raspy, my throat trembled with the force of it. I wanted her to say no. Instead she said, "Please don't kill yourself." She started crying. "You're my best friend." I was surprised she had heard the question I had really been asking. We sobbed for half an hour, then washed our faces, put on pajamas, and walked to the closest taco truck. I ate an elote. The corn was sweet, the lime was sour, the stars were bright, and I felt briefly sure life was the right thing for me. We never returned to that conversation. I tried never to bring us even near the edge of speaking about it again.

Police officers asked us if we had seen anything. One looked at our hands as Angie rolled the window down.

The other asked us what we were doing up here. We were clearly from out of town.

"Going to nature? Alone? Without men?" They smirked at each other. Their hands were near their holsters. Neither of them had identified himself.

I tensed. Our faces were mirrored in their sunglasses. Angie gave them her widest, most flirtatious smile and then did her best witch cackle. I was envious in that moment. I've never wanted to be white, not once. But I wanted the ease of feeling protected and beautiful enough to try to make a joke, to not have my hands on the dashboard, to not text someone pulled over by cops, please call in 15 minutes if you don't hear from me by then.

The first cop did not smile. He kept his face aimed toward me, his mustache and mouth contorting his face into double frowns.

The second one laughed and said, "Be careful. Drive safe."

Over the Mackinac Bridge, we stopped, ate. The fast food place was gray, white, beige. When I was a child, they were all yellows and reds and blues inside. Now, they're all American interior design show ideas of tasteful. I checked my phone for the first time.

Preston had texted me a video. I realized I had started thinking of him by his first name since dinner. He was on a skateboard, dribbling a basketball. A metal song was playing in the background, like it was coming from a car's speakers. Whoever was filming this was loving it. "Holy shit, man," he kept saying in a very bro voice. Preston shot a basket. It hit the rim, hovered in midair, went in. "My dude," the cameraman yelled. The camera shakily moved back to Preston, where he was still on the board, a fist raised in the air.

I showed it to Angie. We laughed. Watched it again. Again.

"This is the most I've ever liked him," I said.

She stopped laughing, clouded over into furrowed eyebrow seriousness. "Do you think you'll ever fall in love?"

"With him?"

"I mean sure, yeah, but I mean anyone."

"I love you."

"Yeah, I know. But."

"I've been in love." I put my phone down. Reached for a French fry. A person I assumed was a mom was at a table with her two daughters. The mom was listening as the daughters talked about basketball. They kept saying, "I'm the LeBron of our team." Two older men were eating hamburgers and sitting in silence. A teenage girl was staring into her phone while very slowly eating one French fry.

"Who have you been in love with?" she asked me.

"Who have you been in love with?" I know it's not clever to repeat someone's question back at them, but it was better than the instant immediate impulse I had to lie.

"I was in love with you our senior year of high school," she said. "Sloane for all of my sophomore year of college. Keanu Reeves because he is culturally a lesbian. If Concepción texted me, I would get back together with her."

"You're still in love with Connie?" I asked her. I didn't want to talk about the fact that Angie and I could've been together in high school. The mixture of anger that neither of us had said anything and the relief we still had each other made it impossible to linger on the revelation. What would've come from it anyway? Somehow magically finding two men who were also in love with each other and wanted to do us both a huge favor?

Yet, it had sometimes felt like we had been together. The hurt reactions we both had when the other had a new crush or a date. The way every time we disagreed, it felt like we were on the sudden edge of a cliff. How every time something good happened to one of us, we hugged tightly, the side of her face pressed against my chin. A friend in college when I told her about me and Angie in high school called it "a typical closeted experience: a friendship with all the aggravations of a relationship and none of the great sex." Before that, I'd been able to trick myself into thinking we were special.

In some states and countries gay men could still be accused of witchcraft, but in Michigan and most of the East and West Coast states, those laws had been overturned.

"I still wonder what Connie thinks about things. I check her social media. Sometimes, when something good happens, I want her to be there," Angie said.

"Is that love though or just curiosity?"

I stuffed my mouth full of French fries. Wanted to talk about salt, how much I loved it, how I could have gotten the same value and fewer calories if I had just chugged one of the saltshakers instead of eating these. I felt like saying if I wanted to talk about this shit, I would go back to therapy.

"She's marrying a man," Angie said. Her eyes were very wide, they were soft in the space between green and blue. She knew everything about me that I'm capable of letting other people know. She had seen me barf. Had fought with me and we had remained friends. I cleaned her hair out of the bathtub drain, pulled a thick glob of it out with three fingers, but I didn't tell her or bother her about the clog; I just did it. Wasn't that silent cleaning its own way of saying I love you?

Angie often smelled like roses. I could tell her anything. Sometimes, when we were drinking, we held hands and walked down the street together, and her fingers felt like home. But we had never kissed even though there had been so many opportunities. So many times alone, our faces tilted toward a looming moon, a dying sunset, a yellow firework.

"Are you okay?" I asked.

"It is what it is," Angie said.

"Why can't it be special enough to love someone as a friend? Why can't we as a species recognize friend-love? That intimacy is just as important as romantic feelings?" I plowed on, knowing Angie wanted to think about something else. We were allowed to pick at my feelings, but everything for Angie had to be at the right time.

"Isn't love a permanent curiosity for the other person? You've kept them in your life because you want their point of view, you want to fucking laugh and cry and argue with them."

"Isn't that friendship?" I asked. "Aren't you just proving my point?"

"I mean, yes, but, they're not distinct entities for some people."

"What are you going to do when you turn thirty?"

A dad at the next table was giving us a dirty look. He ate his hamburger aggressively. His kids were coloring and ignoring the world around them.

"Do you want to split a strawberry milkshake?"

I shrugged. "Sure."

*　*　*

Back in the car, we listened to a song that sounded like Earth, Wind & Fire but with heavy distortions to remind us it was very now. In the Upper Peninsula, roads had sudden expressive curves and on either side, lakes. The water was so bright, it looked tropical. The sand was ash blond. I wanted to run on every beach we passed. I would be on all fours like a dog, kicking up little clouds, pushing through reeds.

"Are you going to text him back?" Angie tapped her hand on the steering wheel, slightly off rhythm.

"I think so." I rubbed my face. Put my right hand on my forehead. "Do you think there's something wrong with me?"

"There's something wrong with everyone."

"No, I mean, the love stuff. Is that why you're bringing it up?"

"I mean, maybe. But you have all the mom stuff. And you're bi. I don't think that means anything about falling in love, but it's probably more complicated for you because you could love anyone."

I wasn't sure what I thought of that, but my brain was still feeling full from our conversation. My idea of hell at that moment was spending the next two hours and forty-five minutes dissecting the areas where sexual attraction met romantic love inside my brain. A sigh, one I felt in my bones and liver, rushed out of my mouth.

"My mom keeps pressuring me to register with a matchmaker," Angie said. "Some specialize in finding safe relationships for gay women. So."

"I'm sorry."

"I think it's what I want, though." She reached down, pulled out a pair of cheap white sunglasses. Put them on slowly with her free hand. I wanted to help but couldn't figure out how to do it without being annoying. The air was getting colder.

"We could go to a party tonight."

"Whose?"

Angie told me she had texted a girl we'd known in college. One of those people we never hung out with alone but who knew most of our friends so we were at all the same parties. The last time I had seen this girl was three years ago. We were at a Halloween party and she was dressed as a rose. Shiny green leggings, matte pink fabric rigged around her. It was a pretty good costume, but people kept bumping into her and putting creases in the fabric. After an hour, she looked crushed like a fist. We ended up alone together on the porch. She was holding a bottle of gin and looking out along the street. "When I was fourteen," she said, "I thought I would have two kids by now." A couple walked down the street together—the woman walking forward, the man walking backward—kissing. They kept almost tripping and laughing and kissing. "I thought I would be dead by now," I said. She laughed and laughed, told me she had always thought I was funny, and handed me the bottle of gin.

Apparently, the girl was living up here now. She had opened a wine store with her uncle. The hook was no bottle in the store cost more than thirty dollars, that it was entirely possible to drink good wine without paying an embarrassing amount. This from a girl who I remembered yelling, "If it isn't Grey Goose, it's goddamn moonshine." But maybe I had been too wasted at the time to understand she had been doing a bit.

I leaned back in the seat. Being in a hotel, crisp white sheets, cable TV to click through, eating a salad in bed to make myself feel better about my choices sounded like what my soul needed. Doing a skincare routine, washing my face, toner, exfoliating, a face mask, rinsing my face, putting on moisturizer. No liquor, no weed. Putting my silk pillowcase on the hotel pillow. Treating my hair with the respect it deserved.

"We could go for an hour," I said, "I have to get to the boat early."

After we checked in to the hotel, Angie texted, got the address, and we drove straight to the party. It was outside of the city—although it felt strange to call it that, it felt mostly like a small town with a university attached to it. Maybe it was because of the lake. On the right side of everything was Lake Superior. I couldn't stop looking over at its glassy pink, orange, violet already fading into night. Almost everything I knew about it was ominous. The famous song-inspiring shipwreck, how cold it remained in summer, how it was carved from glaciers. At the party, from the second floor of the house, you could look out the bathroom window and see past the trees to the lake. A few people walked along the shore, but they were already fuzzy and hard to distinguish in the ebbing light.

Outside, people were passing around a vape pen and roasting marshmallows at a bonfire. Inside, a long table was covered with bottles of wines and real glasses. There were index cards next to each bottle, and a man was encouraging everyone to write their reactions to what they were drinking, but people were mostly doodling on them or writing things like, it tastes like wine. All the wine bottles were clearly not from a grocery store, no horses or roosters or men's names in sight. Instead, a compass in foil gold, a full moon above a dark lake, an embossed poem in a font meant to look like old-fashioned cursive. I said hello to a few people I recognized, then turned back to the table to choose something to drink.

A woman with beautiful long black hair stood close to me and asked me a question. I pretended not to hear her, she repeated it.

"Are you Black or Mexican?" she tried again.

"Give me twenty dollars," I said, "and I'll tell you."

"Why?"

"Are you white or are you white-white?"

She pulled out her phone and looked at it intently. It took all my willpower not to say I know no one is texting you.

I poured myself a large glass of wine and left the room. In the dining room, there was a smaller table. The wall facing it was covered with framed paintings and photographs. They ranged from children's art—what looked like a child's excited rendition of him holding a PlayStation—to a faded black-and-white photograph of two old white women clutching brooms. People were discussing a recent movie about a terrible family who all wants their slightly less terrible father's family money. It had really made them think and it had a good mystery. I had liked the movie, but mostly because I like any movie where people wear very nice coats, so I didn't feel like I had anything to add to the conversation.

A small cluster of women dressed all in black and wearing big glasses were talking about Mississippi, where a woman was scheduled to be burned for witchcraft. "The laws are so lax there," one said. "Not just there, this country," another woman earnestly said. "I cry sometimes thinking about how we're the only developed country to let this still happen." I blinked and took a step away from them. They talked about how exhausting everything was, how unsafe they felt, while most of them wore large engagement rings. Statistics spilled out of their mouths about where it was only a misdemeanor if a man killed a woman who he thought had ensorcelled him. The law making its way through the Florida legislature that encouraged the state to give out gift cards to people who reported potential witches in their midst. "But we're safe here," one woman kept saying. I drank a large gulp of wine and understood I had made a huge mistake coming to this party.

A woman came up to me and held out her hand. "Rose."

"Jo."

"I'm a psychic."

"Telephone or the kind that works for police officers?"

"Internet."

She pulled out her phone and showed me her website. The main page was a picture of her gazing into what looked like a bright light. For twenty-five dollars, you could send her a question about your personal future or a past event, and she would give you a paragraph's worth of divination. Rates continued. You could even Skype with her. Within the next year, she was going to start the process to be a registered witch with the state of Michigan. I could tell she thought this was the coolest thing. It seemed stupid and reckless to me.

"You're doing what most people do when they meet a psychic— clam up," she said.

I said, "Yeah," and looked again at her website.

When my mother disappeared, our local police station had brought in a psychic who worked on cases with them regularly. When he came into the room, he was wearing pleated khaki pants, with a small grease stain on the thigh, and a button-down white shirt that looked old, a little yellowed on the buttons. His hair was cut short to his scalp, his skin was dry, especially around his nose. He looked thoroughly not prescient.

We perked up a little when the psychic told us he had a long record of being instrumental in disappearance cases. He rattled off situations where the only link between them was everyone had been found alive. As he spoke, his dark brown eyes became shiny and wet. I wanted to hold my dad's hand but felt too old to do that. My mother would've asked this psychic so many questions. I could picture exactly how her eyes would light up, how she would be easy, make him laugh, and then ask him something devastating to show she didn't believe in what he did. The psychic said two different times, I can tell you're going through a hard time.

My dad pulled out one of my mom's notebooks, the long cardigan she used to wear on cold mornings, a small bar of the violet-scented soap she had made only a few weeks before. The psychic told us, even though two police officers had told us the same thing the day before, that he would need these objects for a week. The objects people loved couldn't help but be steeped in their essence. Once he got a feel for Tiana, he would be able to get a sense of where she was. It could be the precise location, or it could come as images.

"Once," he said, "I saw a girl walking in a stream and it was filled with apples bobbing up and down. I saw a spray-painted phrase, FU SOAP." He gave me an embarrassed look. Cleared his throat. "On one of the trees. That was enough for them to find her."

The psychic stopped, looked down at the objects. I understood the girl he was talking about had been dead.

He started gathering my mother's things off the table. As he reached for her cardigan, on impulse, I grabbed it. Home was having it hanging over her chair at the table, her shrugging it on and off throughout the day, it traveling from the couch to the desk back to the chair. It was dove-colored and she let me wear it when I wasn't feeling well.

"Jo," my dad said softly.

"I'm sorry," the psychic said, "but you're contaminating it. If you want to find your mother, you have to let go."

I was crying. Rationally, I understood it was just a sweater. But it was like waking up again and she was gone. I held on.

"It'll be okay," the psychic said. "I'll find her. Please, let me do my job."

I wiped my eyes with the top of my shirt. My dad touched my shoulder.

Rose asked me if people ever remarked on my energy.

"What does that mean?"

"Like what colors do people associate with you?"

"I don't think anyone has ever told me what color my personality is."

"I felt like I could feel you calling to me across the party."

My fingerprints were visible on the wine glass. I took a sip. It made my tongue feel dry, but it tasted great.

After two weeks, the psychic asked us to come back to the police station. We sat in a small room; he handed us a paper bag from the local grocery store. I looked in it to make sure everything was there, didn't care about being discreet. A woman had called the tip line and said she had seen my mother in Detroit. She had been sitting on a bench, drinking a Vernors. The police were looking into it but were sure it had just been some other Black woman. It was hard to believe they were following up on tips. None of the newspapers or news TV shows were talking about her at all. A white college student had gone to a tropical island and disappeared; she was on the news everywhere. Last seen drinking a mai tai with a man no one could identify and waving at a cruise ship. Every day another breathless update. The same picture of her laughing and wearing a bikini, her blond hair saturated with sunlight, her skin in the zone between burned and bronzed.

"What did you find?" my dad asked.

The psychic got up and closed the door. He ran his hands over his scalp. I wondered if it felt like touching a dog after it had been groomed. It had to feel good, he wouldn't stop doing it. The psychic kept his eyes on the round white table between us.

"I didn't see her. She never came to me."

"What does that mean?" I could tell my dad was angry. His mouth was tense. He had the tone I recognized as the one he used when he had just been on the phone with his dad or someone "is driving like an effing maniac."

"I never even got a hint of her. This has never happened to me." His voice broke a little. Softened.

"It sounds like you're blaming her." I crossed my arms.

"They come to me in dreams or visions. I'll see a memory of theirs, something to do with each object. And then the memories lead me to where they are or the last place they were."

"Just try again," I said.

"It won't work. It's like your mother walked completely off this planet. Or like she was erased."

I slapped my hand on the table. "You're being a fucking baby."

My dad said nothing. I looked up at his face. He seemed torn between wanting to tell me how to behave and wanting to see me bully this man who had gotten our hopes slightly up.

"Do your job." I slapped the table again.

He put his hands over his eyes.

"Please don't tell them about this," he said. "I don't want to get fired. Just one incident like this could make them think I was just lucky before. But I wasn't."

I stood up, took my mother's things, and stormed out. The door slammed behind me; I didn't care. A police officer in the lobby gave me a look. His hand seemed too near his gun. I slowed down, walked normal, tried to make myself just a girl again.

Rose told me my aura was significant. She put her free hand on mine, squeezed.

"It's this gorgeous sunset pink with a big gray gash in the middle."

"So, a wound."

"No," she said. "It's like when you're watching one of those space movies and they go into a wormhole. And it could shoot you out anywhere. A whole new galaxy and a planet full of people who somehow have the same language as you but better fruit. There's gravity to you."

I laughed. She moved closer.

"I can tell you're very creative."

"I'm writing a screenplay in my free time. It's a Black, feminist adaptation of the movie *Commando*."

She laughed in a way that showed she had no idea what I was talking about but wanted me to understand that she thought I was deeply interesting. It was one of my favorite kinds of flirting—where someone laughs a lot, touches my wrist, touches my shoulder, doesn't say anything that could make me pause and think, Do I really want this person's tongue anywhere inside me?

"Did you know they have an alien flagger here?" Rose asked.

"I have no idea what that is."

"It's a sort of sculpture set up to attract aliens."

"How do people know what kind of art aliens like?"

She shrugged and the gesture made me think about what it would be like to have my hands on her shoulders. Rose's hair was dyed mustard yellow, the edges were plastic-unicorn-toy-pink. She was wearing lip gloss that made her lips shine, but bits of red wine were stuck in the creases.

We went outside, walked past the bonfire. Angie was talking to the girl from college; they seemed to be having a deep conversation about life and the paths it takes us. It sounded like Angie was consoling her as we walked by them. "Your life probably wouldn't have been better if you had gone to France." The path was gravel. I almost slipped. Rose's perfume was more noticeable out here—leather, orange peel, and something else—though I couldn't figure out what it smelled like other than sharp. I wanted to kiss her but couldn't tell if it would make me feel good or bad. It was a skill I wanted to learn: How could I properly evaluate, before I did things, what would help me and what would harm me? How could I be almost thirty years old and not even have an approximation of this skill? I wanted to feel her tongue on my nipples, her hands in my jeans. It would be good, no, great, to do this. Wake up in the morning, kiss one more time, and then send each other awkward texts for the next three months whenever we were drunk. Think long term, Jo, I told myself. Plant larger happinesses, not three-hour bursts. You are taking steps toward having a boyfriend. Hooking up with someone at a party would be a big step backward.

Surrounding the flagger was a small circle of motion sensor lights. They shone yellow. The sculpture was shaped like three trees. They were painted neon: lime, aqua, watermelon. A placard next to it read: We are peaceful, and we welcome you. We call this planet Earth, this place Michigan. We are excited to know you.

"What do you think?" Rose said.

"It's shockingly sweet."

"They paid fifteen thousand dollars for it."

"Well, that's wild, but I still like it."

Rose moved close, kissed me. I dropped my wine glass. Somehow, it didn't break. Her mouth was soft. She put her hand on my face. She tasted like nothing. The rest of me felt very cold. She held on to her wine glass as we kissed. Her other hand stroked my waist, went beneath my sweater, stroked the curve of my back. Warm mouth, warm fingers. I shivered once, but she didn't seem to notice. It felt as if someone were watching us. I opened my eyes, hers remained shut. A flash of red like a cardinal for a moment. A pair of shining owl eyes. I blinked, and they were gone. I kissed her harder, wanted to be absorbed only in the feel of her mouth, her tongue, her hands. It didn't work.

She sighed, stopped kissing me, and turned toward the lake. She finished her wine in a long dramatic pull.

"You don't want to sleep with me." She said it as if no one in the entire world before this had been satisfied to just kiss her.

Kissing someone new and having it be melt-into-each-other good is one of the best things about living. I couldn't believe how little she valued it.

"I mean, I might someday, if we knew each other better. Or maybe if I drank more. But." I took a breath.

"Sleeping with me is an incredible decision," Rose said.

Out by the lake, a blue light was shining. It reminded me of a haunted house. A light meant to lure me to the next room where a person in a clown mask was waiting to make me flinch, scream. It drifted along the edge of the shore.

"What's that?" I pointed. The light undulated like a jellyfish. It expanded. It was hard to breathe whenever I looked at it.

"Aliens?"

"Witches?"

We paused. I wanted to go down to the shore. See it close. The light swirled. It was beautiful. My mouth opened.

"Whatever it is," Rose said, "it's not our friend."

"Nature doesn't love people. It doesn't think about friends. It exists."

I walked away toward the light. She let me go. I knew as I went alone that even if she didn't live hours and hours away from me, we would never be in love. Love, or at least the kind I thought I wanted, would mean she would at least try to stop me or take my hand and go toward the adventure together. Say something. Not stand alone by a sculpture, looking at my wine glass on the gravel.

The lake sang to itself. When I got as close as I dared to the blue thing, the air was bonfire warm. Two arm's lengths away, it was so bright; I saw dots in the corner of my vision. The air stank of lilacs and rot. The thing undulated; drips and spots of color flecked off into the air, lingered, vanished. My feet sank a little into the sand. I kept trying to think of a way to describe it. Like a jellyfish's ghost, like the aurora but too close. I shut my eyes. The heat increased. I took a step backward, stepped on an old Rock and Rye plastic bottle, and slipped. The tall grass and sand were soft so the fall was mostly startling, not painful. The thing didn't react.

I sat close. My forehead dripped with sweat. I pulled off my sweater when I got too hot. The light hurt my eyes the longer I looked, but I couldn't stop. It was beautiful. I felt sure this would be the easiest way to die. Walk gently into the heat, allow it to consume me, and then, disintegration. No mess for someone to clean up. Some people would miss me, sure. But here it was. I stepped forward. Sweat slicked down my cheeks, dripped off my nose. My eyes closed against how bright the light was. I let myself count to ten, to thirty. The impulse dissipated. My skin and hair would burn. My heart and liver and intestines would cook and it would be the last thing I would ever smell. I took a step back. I pulled my sweater back on. I said to it, "Be at peace." I repeated myself three times, each time a little louder.

The thing undulated, then collapsed and began shrinking. It went from the size of a floating small child to a baseball in seconds. It stayed hard-to-look-at bright and then faded until it was only slightly brighter than the night sky.

I walked back to the party, pulling leaves and grass and plastic from my hair. I told myself I should have been afraid. "What the fuck is wrong with me?" I whispered. Inside, someone was yelling, "I hate Canada." I went to the table, poured myself a large glass of wine, drank it in one long gulp. It made me feel queasy. My forehead was still sweating, my hair needed a deep conditioning, my mouth puckered.

I poured myself another glass.

Angie came over, touched my arm. "Are you okay?"

She was drunk, maybe high. I got away with nodding.

"I saw a will-o'-wisp down by the lake," I said. A white man with a long ponytail took a step closer to us. He said will-o'-wisps were the souls of women who had died violently and their bodies have never been found. He was smiling in an inappropriate way, as if we were all having the best fucking time. Their souls were bright and hot because they were stuck on this Earth, rotting, rather than being cherished. And how did we do it? he wondered. Weren't we scared every day being women? He quoted a joke from a former deeply popular stand-up comedian who had turned out to be a notable piece of sex trash. I could tell he thought he was being smart, kind, attractive. He oozed with look at me being such a great guy who can relate to women. I wanted to take his hand softly, put his fingers in my mouth, and bite the tips and knuckles while he screamed.

"Okay, thanks," Angie said and turned her back on him. She led me into the dining room. Pizzas were on the table.

"Eat."

"It might make me barf."

"Everything you're feeling will feel a little less, I promise, if you eat something."

"Pizza is not emotional penicillin."

"Eat."

I took a slice, leaned against the wall, took a bite. At least the bacon was good.

Every party has a point when things become threadbare. The downstairs bathroom was locked, a couple was ostentatiously hooking up in there. A few people joined in the spectacle, knocking on the door, trying the knob, and yelling things that ranged from their own exaggerated sex noises to "just go home, ya pervs." I wanted to leave, but somehow I had lost Angie again. She had gone to get me water, crackers, and the kitchen had become an ocean to cross. I texted her a few times, no answer.

Rose was flirting with another girl, this one short and blond and holding a light beer. Rose was holding on to her palm and tracing the lines. This means that you're good at math, this means that one day you'll adopt a Great Pyrenees that will break your heart, this crease means you'll kiss a beautiful woman tonight. I was annoyed only because this strategy would've worked so well on me. I wanted someone to hold my hand and tell me I had a own-a-big-dog-have-lots-of-hot-sex future.

I texted Preston, I am the worst party.

Want me to come get you?

I wish. I'm in Marquette.

I realized I had left off the "at" in my first text.

The worst party would be a good band name, I texted and put my phone away.

In the kitchen, four people were playing euchre. It looked pretty wholesome, except at the edge of their game was a ceramic plate with small lines of cocaine.

"Want a toot?"

I laughed. I couldn't help it. Nothing took away the possible fun of coke faster than calling it "a toot."

Out by the fire, a few people were eating, and Angie was there again with the girl from college. They were looking at each other, holding hands. The firelight made them look like a couple on a movie poster. I didn't even know they had liked each other. Maybe they had been chatting on and off. Maybe the only reason Angie had really wanted to come to the party was to see her again. I would have to learn her name, find a way to make her feel welcome and not at all intimidated by me.

I went upstairs. On the wall next to the staircase was a family picture where every member, from grandparents to a little baby clutched close, was wearing a white button-down and blue jeans. Why did every "wholesome" family think that was such a good look? One of the doors was open and a woman was sitting on a bed watching TV.

"The party too trash for you?"

"Yeah," I said.

"Me too."

"I'm Roberta. You probably know my sister, this is her party."

"Yeah, from college."

I came inside and sat on the floor. The carpet was soft but a deeply ugly purple—like McDonaldland's Grimace had been mur-dered and was a splayed-out hunting trophy. She was watching an episode of *True Witches of Salem.*

"Is this the Indiana, Oregon, or Massachusetts show?"

"Indiana," she said.

"I haven't watched this one."

"The main character is Rachel. She grew up in one of those churches that is deeply proud of their role in burning witches. The types who say things like the only way to get magic is to fuck the Devil. That sort of wild shit. But she keeps levitating in her sleep."

"How does she know she's levitating in her sleep?"

"She falls onto her bed or the floor every time she wakes up. She falls asleep in her car and her husband sees her floating."

"You know all of this is fake, right? There are, like, wires and CGI."

"No shit." Roberta rolled her eyes at me.

"I find these shows super-offensive. They always take place where some of the worst mass slaughters of witches were." I was excited and still not sober, stumbling over my words. "The killings are really glossed over in most places. The language around it is so passive. They were killed. By who? They can't even really do anything harmful. Flying? Cool. Making some potions if they study for a long time? That's just chemistry. Talking to animals. Prophecies."

"We can change the channel if you want," Roberta said. She had the tone of someone who regretted being kind to me.

On the screen, a white woman was crying and gesturing at her Indian friend. The white woman threw a glass of wine on the ground. "You ruined the ritual," the other woman said. Her friend crossed her arms. "I've told you about using that tone with me."

"They were trying to get supernatural Botox," Roberta explained. "Let magic heal their faces instead of poison."

The women began the ritual again.

"Most of their spells are them trying to figure out either how to get more wine or how to give themselves round-firm-butts-that-are-the-right-amount-of-big."

"I would love being able to fly," I said. "Or to talk to an animal. I'm always wondering what dogs are really thinking. If witchcraft was all about flying and gossiping with birds, I would be super into it."

"Even if it was just that, it still doesn't seem worth all the drama. When I was in fourth grade, we started accusing each other of witchcraft. A girl said I was getting straight A's because I could read the teacher's mind. A bunch of kids threw the apples and bananas from their lunches at me one day while yelling, 'Witch! Witch! Witch!' We had to have a school assembly to talk about it."

"What happened?"

"We were reminded you can't just accuse someone lightly, how we were all committing a crime every time we called anyone a witch. They told us about the penalties and jail time. Some adults came in and did a presentation about the history of witch burnings, even showed us brief footage of one. It was terrible. One of those things where you don't really learn anything because you're too busy being embarrassed."

"Why do schools always talk around it? It's part of our history."

"Do you go around telling people the worst thing you've ever done?" Roberta reached over, pulled a vape pen out of the nightstand. She took a hit. It smelled like a candy that was supposed to be mango flavored.

The know-it-all part of my brain wanted to talk about how on average if you were a Black or Latinx student at a Predominantly White high school, you were 66 percent more likely to have been accused of being a witch by the second semester of your high school career. I had never been accused; instead, people talked about how my mom had left her family to fuck the Devil. How it was clear she had always been tainted by great evil. How lucky it was my mother had left my family before she had tempted me down the dark path.

Roberta's eyes were glassy. She looked like she was exhausted and just wanted to let her brain slide closer and closer toward sleep.

The women onscreen were crouched around a collie. It was majestic and proud, with a long snout.

"This (bleeped) is so rude," one said.

"Spaghetti, you are a snitch," the other one said.

The dog panted, its tongue was out and it whined a little. I thought it might be trying to say something like, "I hate being on TV," but I can't speak to animals.

"Sorry. I know I'm being way too intense," I said. "I drank way too much tonight. And things in my life have been so wild." I ended on a yawn.

Roberta made a thinking sound. "Where are you staying?"

I told her the name of the hotel. She laughed and handed me her extra pillow and a blanket. I made myself as cozy as I could on the floor. On the TV show, one of the women went to her library. They had grimoires on the shelves rather than locked away to avoid tempting women into a dark fate. She opened one, went to the index, the camera zoomed in, so it felt like the viewers were looking over her shoulder. Spells for anti-aging. One began: Kill a rooster with a silver dagger. The woman closed the book.

15.

I was having a dream I wanted to stay in. I was at a funeral and in charge of making sure everyone got a slice of cake. Whipped cream frosting and a salted caramel surprise layer. People kept saying things like death doesn't matter when the cake is this good. I was so proud every time someone said that.

Angie's voice pierced the dream: "Jo, we only have an hour to get you to the boat!"

A boat would be waiting for me at a marina. I had to trust my mother's lawyer had somehow arranged everything perfectly. I pulled the blanket over my head and considered why my father and I hadn't questioned this. It suddenly seemed likely that my mother had written all these things down in her will and hadn't had a chance to follow through and prepare the adventure she'd planned.

"Jo, you're going to be so pissed if you have to wait another seven years."

"I know." I sounded thirteen and bratty.

"Shut up." Roberta's voice was muffled.

I sat up, rubbed my eyes, felt my hair. I was sure I could feel every germ, the beginning of each tooth's rot in my mouth from one night of not brushing. I tried to fold the blanket I had used, then gave up and rolled it into a somewhat neat ball. My back felt great.

In the hallway, Angie leaned against the wall, her head pushed forward from the force of her hangover. Bloodshot eyes, hair a little greasy, her skin dull.

"Maybe you should stay here," I told her.

She waved melodramatically. "No, no, I just need coffee."

I went to the bathroom, washed my hands, opened the medicine cabinet. I pulled out toothpaste and put some on my pointer finger. I tried to scrub my teeth but only felt the urge to gag. My finger felt unnaturally large and terrible against my molars, my tongue. Dentist office flashbacks. I washed the toothpaste off my finger, put my mouth by the running faucet, and drank.

My pupils were large, but my eyes were mostly clear. I forced my hair into a ponytail while thinking how white people usually didn't truly know when a Black person's hair looked bad. Everything else was fine. I reminded myself that I was, despite how I felt, still young. There would be a day ten years from now when I would wake up and no matter what I had done the night before, something would hurt.

"Jo, come on!"

I yawned. "You're not my dad."

An empty wine bottle on the stairs, someone's tan clog. In the kitchen, a small amount of cocaine that made me admire the user's restraint. Empty wine bottles that were now a deep pleasant green as sunlight streamed through the windows. Index cards scattered on the linoleum; someone had written "lol this wine tastes like overpriced butt" on two of them. A greasy pizza box I was tempted to open to see whether there was anything inside I could scrounge for breakfast. Out by the fire pit, birds were pulling apart the left-out-overnight bags of marshmallows. A small bird flew past me, a marshmallow clenched in its beak. It felt like a good omen and I fell suddenly into feeling like everything was possible, like I could whistle for the birds and they would drop gifts at my feet.

In the car, we drove quickly to the hotel and grabbed our things.

I rummaged through my bag, double-checked twice that the doll was still there, and checked out, only pausing to snatch some bananas and coffee from the breakfast buffet. I drove even faster to the address the lawyer had given me. The lake was dark blue, so beautiful it made me feel like I could burst into song.

Angie leaned her head against the window. "I am trying really hard not to barf."

"I can pull over."

She sipped from a water bottle; I had no idea where or when she'd gotten it. "No. Not yet anyway."

At the marina, a boat much larger than I expected was docked. White, a blue cabin. In my mind, I had thought I'd see a rowboat with a lantern attached to the front. A surly man rowing while I sat shivering in the back.

"I think this is it."

We parked Angie's car. I grabbed the backpack, which included a parka because I assumed it would be cold out on the water. A person was sitting in the boat but didn't come out to us.

The air smelled like the lake. Gulls were perched on the dock. The boat gently rocked in the waves.

Angie gestured with her water bottle. "It's a little ostentatious."

"Yeah, like you're not going to take a million selfies on it."

"I can come?"

"If you want."

"The idea of being on a boat right now makes me want to die, but I'll come on board for a minute."

"Remember that movie. The one where there's a haunted house. And the main man in the movie is a complete dingdong."

"Be more specific."

"It's black-and-white. A brother and sister buy the haunted house. And the brother somehow starts dating the very young woman by taking her on a surprise boat ride even though he's miserable while on the water."

"Jo, I don't remember this at all."

"I'm sure we watched it together."

The boat's steps were out. A tiny sign was taped on the cabin window: "Welcome, Jo."

I grasped the railing as I climbed the four steps. The person in the boat was a woman. She was wearing a white captain's hat and told me it would take only about twenty minutes to get to the island.

"Can my friend come?"

She shook her head. Apologized.

"I have to have a picture of me taken on the island, it's part of my mom's will."

"I know and I'm happy to do that for you."

I turned to Angie. We hugged. "I'll be back in a couple hours."

"Do you have the doll?" the captain asked. I paused, surprised she knew about it. I handed it over to her. She smoothed down the white collar, stroked the braids, and picked at a stray thread near the eyes, then handed it back to me. I put it back in my bag and sat down.

The boat did a foxtrot with the lake. Everything was close—the water, the clouds, the gulls' conspiracies traded back and forth—but I felt like I was looking at them through a pair of discount binoculars. This was the last thing I would ever do for my mom. I was crying softly. The boat's engine was loud, but I still didn't want the captain to notice.

Squeak of the leather and vinyl steering wheel. I was clenching my jaw. The inside of my right palm furiously itched. My dad had always told me it meant good luck. A sudden memory: My dad saying that to me and my mom shaking her head and saying No, that's wrong. It's the left hand because that means you're going to be receiving money. Right hand means you're going to have to give something away. They started bickering over it. It was an argument I could tell they'd had before, would have again. They were smiling while they disagreed, each holding a cup of coffee, their forearms touching. I was eleven, maybe. I realized long before I'd even existed as a concept, they'd had each other. And they thought they would always have each other.

The sky and lake were mirrored. There was a succulence to the clouds on both. I thought if I opened my mouth wide enough, they could float in, dissolve sweet on my tongue. But the sky changed as we moved farther and farther away from the shore—from September-day brightness to crepuscular. The air turned colder. We slowed. The water's texture transformed into something closer to a velouté, the sky total-eclipse dark.

The boat groaned with the effort but went faster. The push and pull between boat and lake made my stomach churn. The captain urged the vessel forward. I felt an impulse to laugh, giddy, as if I were on a rollercoaster. That's always my reaction after the initial hands-clasped-tight-on-knees, the lurch, the crank and crack and climb up to the edge. The free fall, the velocity, and the turns always make me laugh hard and wild.

Now the air smelled of nothing. Before, there had been the dissonance of lake water, the rot and the clean. My rose-scented deodorant. Gasoline. In the distance, someone burning leaves. We moved on so quickly I let go of my knees and fell forward, almost falling to the bottom of the cabin floor. I clung to the vinyl seating though it didn't want to give.

"You wouldn't have believed me if I told you weather like this was coming," the captain yelled. I kept trying to compare the experience to mundane things—it's like being in a snowstorm, it's like watching an astronaut movie in IMAX, it's like being on a plane with momentous turbulence—but it didn't soothe me because they all felt like obvious grasping. In the darkness I could feel every movement of the boat as if it were going to be torn apart.

"Besides, it's better—magic—first time—oh shit." The motor and engine and burst of rain blanked out most of what the captain was yelling at me.

By gradients, the light moved from cave to charcoal. From charcoal to pigeon wing. Mixed into the rain were soft hits and spatters that sounded close to hail, but wrong, somehow too soft.

Then it hit the windows. It was gold. By far the brightest thing I could see. Even in the inexplicable gloaming, it caught light. It shimmered. I took a deep breath. The gold fell down in blobs, the rain in streaks. Mist rose off the water from the meeting of warm and cold.

In the distance, peeking through the storm and gold and gray, was an island.

We approached the shore. White sand like the postcard ideal of a beach. Shorter trees with violet fruit, brighter than they had looked online. A crow was working at tearing one off the branch, not fazed by the bad weather. There was a statue of a woman wearing a cloak, moose antlers coming out of her head. Candles and baskets of apples at her feet.

A woman wearing a blue sweatshirt was smiling and waving at us. It was my mother.

16.

Since I never finished watching the episode of *Unsolved Mysteries* about my mother, Angie told me how it ended. A reenactor steps out into the night. It is lightly snowing. The woman playing my mother opens her mouth, lets snow melt on her tongue, she turns back once toward the house. Her expression is unreadable, half her face in shadow. The actress walks into the night. There are headlights in the distance. They, and then she, fade into a moonlit night. The screen stays navy for another second, then the white tip hotline text shows, reminding people that this woman is still missing. Her family still loves her.

Golden droplets were falling from the sky, harder than rain but surprisingly soft. The statue my mother stood in front of was well-maintained except for its head. The chin and eyes and mouth were covered in furry green moss, only a cracked large white nose poking out. Half of its hair was broken off. The apples in the basket at its feet were slicked with gold. I was purposefully looking everywhere but at my mother's face. The basket's dark brown braid, the black boots she was wearing even though it was still warm—swamp boot, stank boot, my brain was trying desperately to find a joke and I was annoyed that if my brain had to do that, why couldn't it find a good one? My mother's hands were still young. She was saying, "Jo, Jo."

The air was different here. It smelled like rain and metal and incense meant to soothe unruly brains. Everything looked saturated, bright, and important. I felt too alert. My mouth was open as if I were desperate for more air. The gold continued to drip down from the sky. There were huts around us and the gold droplets were tapping on their tin roofs with a rhythm that would make some people leap from their couches and twist and turn around in their houses.

Magic was everywhere. It felt like when you're young and with your best friend in the world and you look at each other and feel as if you're the most attractive, interesting, fun people in the entire room. There's nothing embarrassing about this confidence because it's the truest thing and it lets you be your best selves for hours.

I hugged my mother, let my chin bump on her cheek and held on to her and sobbed things like, "how," "why," "Mom," "I'm here."

My feet were wet from getting off the boat. In the distance, other women were talking with one another. They were wearing black cloaks that blew in the wind, puffing them up like scared cats. On the tree branches, the purple fruit was beautiful, closer in texture to peaches. Despite the light furring, they were the most vivid purple I'd ever seen in nature. My mother was talking to me, saying something banal like you got so tall; her hands were on my shoulders. She was crying and our faces were so similar I tried to take a step back. She pulled me close again. It stopped raining. Her breath smelled like cigarettes.

I had spent years wondering where she could be, why she had left, how she had died.

I was crying. I hugged her, pulled her close. My mother smelled like summer body. And beneath the ick of that, like when I was a kid and was feeling shy and would bury my face in her side or stomach or shoulder, I would breathe in that mom smell and feel better. Now, I was three inches taller than her, so I had to stoop, but my nose was buried in her shoulder. I had never felt more grateful in my entire life. Or more angry.

My mother sobbed. Above us, the sky was turning pink as if time had moved impossibly fast. A sudden sunset. The colors blurred together, pink and crimson and gray, and I was still trying not to feel too much, so I kept thinking, Oh, look at that sfumato. I remembered how I embarrassed myself the first time I said that word aloud for the first time, how it was not the mispronunciation but how clear it was to everyone how much I wanted to show that I was so intelligent. Why couldn't I just say I thought the painting was beautiful, like everyone else had? Here I was again, trying too hard to be cool, smart, collected. Look, Mother, I am a fully contained, rational adult. I don't do things like get overwhelmed in emotional situations.

Then a deluge. Blood and feathers and bird parts fell from the sky. I screamed, and a small terrible amount fell into my mouth. I spat and spat while my mother said in a voice like she was watching the news, "I didn't know it was going to storm today." She took my hand and we ran toward a hut. Beaks, bones, blood. Feathers like soft fresh snow fluttering down. My brain was running through possible explanations: a flock of birds was struck by lightning in midair, they all were sucked in and vomited out of a plane's engine flying overhead. Everywhere was gore and beige and white and red, and it was the hardest thing not to scream or get sick.

Blood doesn't taste like copper or pennies like people are always saying in books. It tastes like iron and having a big cavity that makes a dentist say "oh wow" while he brushes a gloved finger against your gums.

We ran and ran. I tripped in the sand, nosedive, a face of sand and eviscerated passerine wings. It was hard to see, the blood fell so thick. My mother pulled me back up. Sharp little beaks felt like hailstones; a few left small cuts on my arm. My mom looked almost on the verge of laughter as we finally made it to a hut. Inside, I leaned against the door, panting. She grabbed a dark towel from a hook and tenderly wiped my face and hair. Another visceral nostalgic feeling hit me even though she looked like a demon from a painting we used to display in the lobby at the museum. Her eyes were dark and wide, face splattered with blood, a clot of tissue near the base of her neck, dirt and blood beneath her fingernails, and her teeth were still so white against it all. Mom wiped her face, then she sighed and laughed a little.

"This happens only a few times a year. I can't believe I'm saying this now, but you'll get used to it."

I couldn't think of anything to say other than, "Okay."

She said her friend Aster called it "the great menstruation," proof nature was truly our mother. Mom took my hand and led me to a small bathroom. On her wrist was what looked like a perfectly intact miniature intestine, black and coiled. I reached out to flick it off. Paused, thinking about how gross the impulse was, how I would spend the rest of my life having to know what it felt like, and put my hand back at my side.

"Where are we?"

"Clean up first."

The bathroom was lit by candlelight. There was a small sink that worked, although all the water was cold; a pile of dark washcloths; a bar of soap that smelled like herbs. Mom handed me a robe, then left. I took my clothes off, tried to rinse them in the sink. Scrubbed at the blood until each stain looked like a wound, the foam and water combining to look like ichor. It was briefly easier to think of that small, insurmountable thing, getting my clothes clean, than to realize for the first time in fourteen years, I was with my mother. The sky had rained gold, then blood and dead birds.

My mother is alive, I thought, while scrubbing my clothes. The first time I decided to let go of her, I was fifteen. It was Mother's

Day. The weeks leading up to the day, I couldn't help myself. I constructed a fantasy she would walk through the door, I would post a picture on social media of the two of us reunited. We would be eating pancakes or laughing with our arms around each other. I wanted to rub it in the face of every person who had ever said to me, "Oh, this time of year must be so hard for you." Fuck you, I always wanted to say, every day is hard for me. Where had she been? It didn't matter because she was home. We would hug. We would be a family again, we would be boring, and we would fade away from being weird or extraordinary over time. When she didn't come home that night, I waited until I was sure my dad was asleep. I drank a large glass filled to the brim with vodka, then got into the bath. I wondered if it was possible to drown myself. Instead, I threw up into the warm water, emptied the bath, and had to take a shower instead. I fell asleep miserable on the bathmat. The next morning, my skin was dry and my cheeks were imprinted with the pattern of the rug.

I scrubbed at myself with cold water, stooping over to rinse my hair, finding another beak. I was old enough now; enough time had passed that I wanted it to not matter where she had been. To instantly forgive her for not coming home, for not finding a way to get in touch with me. Why couldn't I just say, I missed you, or Welcome back? My fingers were puckered from the cold and too much water. I dropped my clothes into a metal tub. A howl in the air, her footsteps on the creaky floorboards, and I was shivering in the thin black robe. "Well, this is my life now," I said to myself. It made me calmer to hear my own voice.

I opened my bag. Inside it, the doll had fallen apart. It was fluff and strings and fabric and a small cut braid that must have been made from my mother's hair. I forgot what I had been looking for and closed the bag.

Outside the bathroom, the air smelled of campfire and onions cooking in butter.

"Let me see you," my mother said.

I stepped closer to the fire. She paused, looked at me everywhere but in the eyes. She was surprisingly clean, all remnants of blood and tissue gone except for some small flecks on her neck.

"I thought when you got older, you might look like him more. But you're still all Marshall. Maybe starting to look a little more like Alyssa though than me?"

"Aunt Ali is doing good."

"She married?"

I nodded.

My mother pursed her lips. "Does she love him?"

"We don't really get into stuff like that."

"Is he Black?"

"Nope. He's Indian. They met at work. Aunt Ali says it's impossible to find a Black man her age who wants to marry a Black woman. Only young men are interested in that game." I resisted the outrageous urge to mention her own husband was white.

She rolled her eyes.

"Have you always been here?" I asked.

"What about your aunt Carol?" she said.

"She had cancer. Kept it from everyone until she knew she was fine."

My mother sucked her teeth. She was the spitting image of my grandmother. The grudge part of me was already doing the math: How long will it take for her to apologize? How long for her to explain? How long until she wants to know about Dad, about me? Her eyes were back on the pot. She sprinkled a little bit of what looked like salt, but in the firelight it was a deep, sensuous orange. My mother was complaining about Aunt Carol like they had been having regular phone calls, not as if Aunt Carol had been spending years of her life begging people for any information about her sister's whereabouts, letting herself cry in front of TV cameras, on true crime podcasts, at the thought someone out there held the key to helping my mother come home alive and safe.

The second time I had decided, enough, my mother is dead, was the day after my twenty-first birthday. Angie and some of our friends from college had planned to celebrate my birthday in a haunted hotel. I stayed in a room decorated to look like a forest. Pine tree wallpaper, a brown comforter, dark green carpet. In its desk drawer was a pamphlet that explained how the owner before the current one had been burned as a witch, this hotel had been seized by the state, and it had taken years for it to be returned to her family. It was still legal in thirty-five states to burn a witch at the stake for practicing malicious magic. We could donate to a lobbying group—the safety of witches and all women went hand in hand. I agreed with all the pamphlet's points, but it depressed me to be reading about that, alone in a dim room on my birthday, so I took out my vape pen, took a hit. Supposedly, the room I was staying in had been the owner's room. I heard what sounded like a woman's voice coming from the closet. Without thinking, I said, "Mom?" And then I thought, Oh, she's dead, I think she's dead, and it was such a sudden relief. I was moving on.

I ate cake, I laughed, I danced until we got shushed by the hotel staff, I kissed the wrong person because my boyfriend at the time hadn't been able to get off work and join us. I stayed up all night kissing her, until my mouth was dry, her mouth was dry, and I thought, This is the best day of my life. In the morning, I drank a glass of champagne, and then I couldn't help myself. I went back on Reddit and looked at one of the forums for a podcast that had done an episode about my mother's disappearance. Someone the night before had sworn they had seen her in New Mexico. A blurry picture snapped from a distance that made me think, Oh, maybe.

"Where have you been?" I tried again.

"Here."

"Why did you come here?"

My mother sighed. It was petty, but it was annoying that the stew smelled so good. I could tell it was rich and filling, and knowing how much I would probably enjoy it made me want to kick the pot over, watch the luxurious brown slop glop all over the floor.

"We thought you were dead." My voice shook. "There was a theory I thought about a lot. People were sure a serial killer had found you in the woods. That you were murdered, and then your body was dismembered, burned, your ashes scattered around Michigan."

"I'm fine, Jo. I was here. I'm safe. You're safe." She gestured with the wooden spoon she was using; some stew fell off it and she winced as it burned her forearm.

"What are you talking about?"

"You can stay here, too. With me if you want. Or we can build you your own hut."

I was shaking, but I refused to let emotions take over.

"I know. The journey, the storm, the magic in the air—it's a lot to take in," she said. "You should eat, have some water, rest. A lot of people feel overwhelmed their first time on the island. I was sick and exhausted the first week."

"Tiana."

"Mom," she said automatically, like I was a child pushing boundaries again.

I sat down, tried to force myself into relaxing. When you lose someone—even when you think about them every day, even when you read their journals, running your finger over every stain and scribble thinking it could tell you something deep, even when you watch some old videos of them when you're in the thrall of a deep missing—you reduce them down, over and over. For years, my mother had been a wound I could never fully stitch, one that when I was being honest with myself, I didn't ever want to scab over, fade, disappear. She went to bed early one night and the next morning was gone.

My mother had become the stories I could only half-remember, the gaps filled in by my father. The time she had caught a fish with her bare hands, the party she had thrown for one of her friends where everyone wore sunglasses and anytime someone yelled a pose, everyone stopped mid-conversation to try it. The mushrooms and herbs she gathered that were always delicious. How she made nature feel so big and luscious and worth falling in love with. She was sweaters in the back of my closet with holes in the elbows, rips at the collar, a wedding dress with short sleeves and a full skirt in a shiny blue bag. Books with her inscrutable notes in the margins. For so long, my mother's absence had been—I was sure—the source of some of the biggest, ugliest parts of me. And because of all that empty space around her, because of time, because of sadness, I had idealized her, too. Here Mom was, being annoying in a kitchen again, not wanting to be forced into saying something. Here she was, being like most people when they mess up—trying to get past the moments when they accept blame or guilt and instead push forward to the place where everything is forgiven, everything is normal. And wasn't that what I had wanted for fourteen years?

"I missed you," I said.

My mother pointed at the cuts on my arm. "Let's take care of those."

She left the room, came back with a small bag. As she dabbed at my arm, she said, "When you were a child, I told you stories when

I did things like this so you wouldn't cry. This one is called 'The Witches and the Island in the Middle of the Lake.'"

* * *

"Once there was a lake," my mother told me while wrapping a clean cloth tight around my arm, "and the lake was the daughter of two glaciers. These glaciers were told to stay apart, to stay in the ocean, to let penguins and bears and seals come and go off them; they never lingered, only either died or made death there. The glaciers wanted to bob with one another, stay close, to be in the water and the sky and only think about life. They loved each other enough to flee. They created mountains and ridges in Canada. They carved and dug and kissed until they melted and became Lake Superior. The storms that rage across this place are the tantrums and sorrow of a daughter who is desperate to know her parents, yet knows she exists because of their destruction."

I am too old for this shit, I thought, but my mouth wanted to hang slightly open, my eyes wanted to be half-focused in the distance as I imagined these glaciers moving across the world. What is it about love? Why does it make everything seem so important when most people give their love so carelessly to people, to pets, to objects that will never love them back?

My mother checked the cloth one last time. "We'll clean it again in the morning."

She went back to the pot. Cleared her throat and continued.

"Their love was so strong that the lake became a perfect place for magic to safely enter our world. It seeped in from the northern lights, was launched here by meteorites, bubbled up from the Earth's core. The light and stone and rock became this island.

"Stories have been told about it since people could tell stories,

Jo." My mother's eyes were shiny with excitement. "The native peoples who lived in this area, they came here only when they truly needed something. They understood the risks of being in a place like this. Some people called this island the home of the fountain of youth. Not Florida—it's here among the tall pines and the black bears. A pond near a cave where, if you bathe on the solstice, you can become twenty again and again. All those smooth-face years that are so hard to get right. There are so many ways to lose yourself when you're young, Jo, but you know that now. Other people said a rich man had hid his treasure here. That what was once a million dollars in gems and gold in the 1800s was now worth a billion dollars.

"A billion dollars, Jo. You can be anything or do anything, be a witch, be a single woman, buy anyone off, live whatever life you could ever want, with that kind of money. I've been telling you about this island for your entire life before bed. Don't you remember? An island with a heartbeat of rubies and diamond necklaces. People have been trying to come here forever. To get the coordinates for the heart of this place, steal its treasure, and build the life they want. You would say, Let's go there if it's so great. Let's take a trip."

I ate my stew. It was delicious. I remembered this vaguely, but I also remembered saying similar things after watching a VHS tape I owned that was essentially a well-produced forty-five-minute advertisement for an amusement park. Music played while a happy white family went to all five sections of the park, encountered ghosts, rode up into space, watched some fireworks, and said things like, We've made memories we'll have the rest of our lives.

"That was why I came here, too," Mom said. "I wanted treasure and adventure too. And freedom."

She said the money was to free both of us. It wasn't that she didn't love my father. He had been as good as a husband could be. Really, truly. But was it possible to ever love someone under duress? How could you ever be certain what you loved was having the most amount of freedom you could have as a woman? As she said these things, I couldn't meet her eyes. My gaze drifted from her mouth to her hands. The way she was gesturing to make her points. She kept saying things like, How could you keep loving someone who was supposed to monitor and report on you if you ever showed a sign of being something different? You must have thought about these things, Jo. You always cared about how things truly were. You like and actually care about fairness. You could be anything, Jo, have any life, if you have enough money.

"Tell me, Jo." She drank a glass of water. "Have things suddenly changed out there? Are they still monitoring women? Have they outlawed burnings? Do you get to keep your job if you're unmarried at thirty?"

I shook my head. I raised a hand, stop, she didn't have to keep going. I heard the echo of everything I had said at dinner with Preston.

"When I came here," she continued, "the sky was gray. I thought it was snowing, but it was ashes and dust slowly falling. The fruit on the trees was like when you see crocuses stretching their way out of the snow. A woman was flying in a long black cape low over the trees. She could have been a large crow. There were no men here at that time. I knew suddenly how much I had been holding in my entire life. Here, I was me. I could be anything. I ate one of the fruits; it was delicious. The insides of it are violet with a brown pit. It stains your palms for hours, even after multiple hand washings. I didn't fly but transformed into an animal, like a badger or a raccoon, but new, entirely me. I scratched at the ground for hours, and the memory of my claws, my fur, it feels as meaningful to me as anything else in my life."

I said something stupid like, "Did it hurt?" And she ignored me.

"The witches have been here for hundreds of years. They can leave the island freely if they're strong enough, stubborn enough, want children enough. But most prefer to stay with one another rather than explore the rest of the world. Why leave? Why risk everything? Everything they need for their rituals and spells is in the woods, on the beach, in the hills and caves at the center. Their statues and art are safe here. Their fruit can't be exploited."

Our bowls were empty. She offered me more stew, but I was full and tired.

I told her I felt as if I had been here before. That the instant I stepped on the sand, I'd felt something in my bones, I'd come home. It was inexplicable, but I felt welcome here. She bit her lips. I asked her what was wrong.

"I love you."

It was what I had wanted to hear, but it wasn't an answer. She had been talking around me for what felt like hours. I understood it was better to wait. I tried to put myself in her place, realizing she probably felt scared and anxious and excited and guilty. Over the years, I had forgotten something crucial and uncomfortably normal: I had never heard my mom apologize to me. She had changed the subject again, talking about the woods, how there were set paths most people should take, but all the best things were found by slipping away.

"Even in normal woods, I follow the trails, Mom."

"Well, that's disappointing."

My mother put another log on the fire. In the firelight, she looked so much like me it was as if I were talking to a more knowledgeable version of myself. Her posture was straight and relaxed, she was talking and gesturing. We wore matching robes. My hair was pulled into a ponytail I kept tugging, a nervous tic I thought I had left behind. I was slouching and my back hurt from it. The wind was making a scene outside the window, but we refused to acknowledge it.

She told me later tonight, under the full moon, if I wanted, I could go to a ceremony and eat the fruit. It might just be some-thing delicious, a first taste I would think about forever, like honey that has the tang of pine needles. Or it could be the bite I needed to take to find my truest self. You eat the fruit, you shut your eyes, and something wakes up inside you. Witchcraft.

I laughed; I couldn't help it. Yesterday, I had been at a party considering what it would be like to be nothing, and here I was only hours later with my mother, who was suggesting that maybe I try to find out if I was a witch. Underneath everything else, I was happy again to be alive, to be surprised at the way a Friday and a Saturday can be so completely different.

"All I have to do is eat the fruit? I don't have to praise the Old One or sell my soul or give a gift?"

My mother laughed even though I hadn't been entirely joking. "No. No. Under the moonlight, by the fire, with witches present, in the heart of the woods. It's not dangerous, not at all." She added "They might sing," as if that could be a huge deal breaker, and it made me wonder if for years my mother had listened to a cappella singing and thought, Jo would *hate* this.

Who had I become to her over all these years?

The third time I thought I had successfully let her go, I had been driving home from Preston's apartment. It was 2:17 a.m. and I called my dad.

"Hello?"

The moment I heard his voice raspy and ancient with sleep, I knew calling him in the middle of the night was a bad idea.

"This was a bad idea. I'll call you in the morning."

"What's wrong? Where are you? I can come get you."

"I'm sorry. I didn't mean to wake you." I was sitting in a Meijer parking lot. I had stopped to buy a large bottle of water, some chips, and now I was watching two teenagers who were leaning against a minivan each holding a vape pen and looking at one another. They were in love, I could tell, and it made me feel like a slammed-shut window with the blinds drawn. I wanted to be someone who could feel that, even when I was talking about something as dumb as what some girl they clearly mutually hated had said in homeroom. What a fucking dumbass she was, and the love they were feeling was in every disdainful syllable.

"What's going on, Jo? It's two in the morning."

"I think it's time that we officially declare Mom dead," I said in a big rush. He couldn't understand me. I had to repeat myself slowly.

"Did something happen?"

"No."

"Why now?"

"I want." I fumbled at the chip bag but couldn't get it open with one hand. "I need to move on."

He was silent. The teenagers laughed. One even wiped at his eyes as if he were hearing an incredible comedian just killing it.

"Let's wait three days," he said. "And if you still feel that way when it's not night, when you're not emotional, then we'll move forward."

I covered my mouth and yawned, then agreed to wait. I felt nothing and decided that was a good sign.

* * *

My mother gestured as if urging me to get into a car, Hurry up, we've got places to be. "It'll be fun. It'll be like nothing you've ever done in your whole life."

"You have no idea what my life's been like," I said.

Her face was blank for only half a second, and then she laughed as if I had told a joke. Outside, it began to rain again. Ordinary water, like home.

17.

We walked along the island's west side. It was the golden hour, the time the beasts who lived in the waters liked best. My mother said we were more likely to see them on evenings like this after two different storms than at any other time. Near the shore, I saw two, a parent and child, their bodies akin to dolphins. Silvery and plastic-looking from their permanent wet. Their heads like those of birds. Black beaks, gills in a bold black-and-white pattern and yellow eyes that I felt were watching me. There was a shine of gold and blood on their beaks, and I felt sure they had surfaced to open their mouths wide and to eat both feasts the sky had given them.

"So, it's not safe to swim here?" I asked.

"They only like this side of the island. We don't know why. And most of the time, they just avoid us."

The baby cried and it sounded like a human child at the playground. The sound startled me. It cried again.

"They're beautiful," I said.

"They're so ugly," my mother said.

"Both."

We walked to a small shed that had a *T* painted on its door. We stepped inside and were overwhelmed with odor. Herbs were drying from a long birch rod. The strings of herbs were so long, they almost made a curtain. A box was filled with candles, different colors, dipped in dried herbs and with long white wicks. Each one, my mother explained, could help with something. A candle that could cure a cold, one that had taken her two weeks to make that could summon an owl spirit. My mother lit it and the spirit appeared. The owl with its golden eyes said, "I have nothing to tell you because your daughter is here."

"This is Josephine," my mother said. I held out a hand. It nodded and disappeared. The candle melted and slid to the floor, only a mess to clean now.

"That's the only spirit who'll talk to me," she said, and I didn't know what to say.

I wanted to learn everything. There were ways to set fires using only a gesture, there were ways to relearn the languages of animals. Here a woman could fly herself home at night. You could turn yourself into silver or glass to protect yourself. You could heal plants with your hands if you studied for long enough. My mother pulled out each book that explained each spell and showed them to me. The world I had lived in felt small and childish; after a few hours, I felt like I was a haughty twelve-year-old cleaning out her room and mercilessly throwing all the dolls and toys and soft stuffed animals in a box marked "Donate." I no longer needed those things because I was an adult who saw the path of her life.

"Think of magic like music," my mother said. "Everyone is capable of something. A hum, a stomp, a clap. Even their heartbeats and the rhythm of it is music. But some people." She paused for a moment to find the word, and I couldn't help myself.

"An entire song or a full opera." I sounded like I had in college when I was eager to impress a professor.

"Exactly."

We visited beehives. Women who felt too drawn into their work to attend another bonfire, another feast, and instead were in small sheds writing runes, stirring cauldrons, sculpting wood, weaving dolls, or talking to spirits. Two women had a shed filled with sand. They kissed, and from each embrace something new formed in the sand: a vase, marbles, a bowl erupting, sizzling hot. Their shed smelled of lightning strikes and sex, and I felt a tingly discomfort being there with my mother. And that felt good because I'd never had to feel it before, because she had disappeared before I had become interested in sex.

Each part of the tour made me feel as if I could see a new path for myself—even when I saw the women who had been damaged by their spell work: a sudden cat's tail poking from their robes and knocking over trays, an eye that was a golden mirror, and a mind that could string together only two sentences before being pulled toward other conversations, other images, other times. None of this scared me. I only wanted to know more.

A long workspace where five women sat in a row and used hammers to smash plates in a two-four rhythm. Each break and splinter became pink and yellow peonies that burst forth into the air and flung themselves around the room. One woman with an ordinary video camera was filming it. I felt as if she looked familiar, I could visualize the presentation on her video art. If I was remembering right, we would be bringing in an installation of her work next summer at the museum. The video that had made the chief curator desperate for this witch's work showed a woman sprawled across a couch wearing jean shorts and a white T-shirt. She was drinking something fizzy, and each burp that came from her mouth was accompanied by a cloud—tiny and dark and carbonated with electricity. The clouds dumped small rains and electric zaps around her head. "Excuse me," the woman kept saying. "Excuse me."

"I'm a fan of your work," I told the woman when the group had taken a break. My mom hovered near me, pleased I was the kind of person who was comfortable praising another person.

The video witch smiled. She stepped down and handed me a peony. I took it. She instructed me to shake it. In my hands the petals fell loose and glamorous and became small china plates with little peonies printed on them that looked like their old selves. I gasped. We watched as the plates broke onto the ground and became ant-sized flowers.

"Forever and ever," she said to me.

I clutched the stem. She showed me a book and told me to come back and borrow it when my mother said I was ready to learn the more complicated stuff.

Already, I was daydreaming of my own shed where I could think and learn and make things. Beyond everything else—society, anxiety, money—maybe it was hard for me to find a path out in the world because the only thing I loved was creating. There was no specificity to this love, and that was why it was hard for me to feel ambitious in the way I needed to be. But here, all these women were dabbling. The emphasis was on learning and making, not being famous or rich or special. Seeing that, it was easy to feel infatuated. I understood what it meant to feel at home.

I was swept away by a premonition. I could see my mother and me here in the mornings: She would leave for her hut after an early breakfast. I would come to my own an hour later. In midmorning, we would meet for tea and talk about the things we were learning or doing. She would show me how to read the leaves, how to nourish the only variety of tea that could accurately tell you things. I would talk through a spell that I was struggling with understanding. In our work, we were family. I let out a breath. I felt sure this wasn't just a wish, but a promise of things to come.

"We'll go to the other side of the island in the morning," my mother said.

I realized this might be the only time in my entire life when it felt like we were on vacation. There was no pressure behind her words, there was no other meaning behind her words. We both loved seeing how things were made, learning the practice and ideas behind them. We were talking to each other like we had just seen an exciting movie. Can you believe that happened? I wanted to laugh so hard when her tail knocked over that glass! I was like holy fuck when that woman showed us how to turn things small. She gave herself baby hands. I hated it and I loved it. I could never do that. Imagine having one eensy hand your entire life. Our voices were blurring together, we sounded so similar. Tones, excitement, and even pronunciation. I wanted to say something earnest about missing her, in some way that wouldn't make her slink away from me, that this was what I had hoped life would be like with her. But we were laughing and I was scared to be the reason why the fun ended.

18.

It was an impossible fire. I kept wiping my forehead with the top of my shirt, my hands on my face. Around me, the women were alive. Kissing, bickering, poem-talking about the last full moon and how it felt inside their veins. My mom was clustered with some friends at the edge of the circle, behaving how I always thought she might at parties. She had called this a ceremony when we arrived, but that was clearly wrong. My mother was slowly sipping her glass of wine, looking dubiously at a book a friend was showing her. The light reflecting on the cover made it seem as if it were also on fire. A woman near me was saying in a voice of nasally complaint that this morning she had woken up and it was like her taste buds had fallen out and grown again while she slept. Even the air tasted new and weird. It was a curse. I have to be aware of the air. The fucking air, she kept saying.

Almost every person was dressed in black, mostly cloaks, but a few younger women were dressed like they were going to a cool bar. Black tank tops, tight jeans, pointed black boots, and ostentatious earrings—hoops, starbursts, obscene glaring tigers I kept making eye contact with—that made me simultaneously want to know them and feel already as if there were a large crawl space between who I was now, becloaked on a beach, and the woman I had wanted to be seen as before.

I had assumed everyone on the island had to be a woman, but there were some people who looked clearly like they might be men, others who were androgynous like my friends from the protests, the ones who reminded us all that gender was a cultural construction. Maybe it was because there was no cell phone service on the island, but I felt safe and relaxed. Some people were singing closer to the water, facing the lake. I couldn't understand any of the words, but the melody was a lullaby. It was easier to people-watch by myself than fixate on the fact my mother hadn't seen me for more than a decade, but when we got to the party, she had left me to go chat with her friends. She hadn't even introduced me to them. Just told me to go have fun and strode away, easily shaking off the laughter and moments we had shared just twenty minutes before.

Women were flying overhead. Not a broom in sight, and I wondered how that idea had persisted for so long. Some floated so close to the fire it seemed like the soles of their feet were in danger of being toasted to a perfect marshmallow-brown. Most of the women were shadows, black on black, hair loose and making tiny clouds in the wind as they soared away from the gathering. I wondered what my mother had thought when she came here—all those years of believing magic was a lie and then being confronted by women flying, dead-bird derechos, and people arguing about the best herbs and environment to begin brewing tinctures to ease arthritis. I hadn't thought to ask her earlier.

A woman whose hair was a glorious tangle of iridescent feathers. A person with talons instead of fingers. A woman sitting on the edge of the party crying icicles. She kept pulling them off her face and letting them melt in her hands. Women with gills. Women with raccoon ears and markings around their eyes. It used to be one of my favorite facts: nature gives predators masks to help them blend in. I had to keep my face neutral whenever one of them came close; I kept reacting as if I were the rabbit or trash can they might use for a buffet table. Women were having conversations with people I couldn't see.

My cup was empty. As I was getting another drink, a woman took my wrist gently, by the tips of her fingers, and made eye contact with me.

"Do you want to try?"

"What?"

She leaned closer, tried to clarify, but all I could hear was the sound of her voice, the swamp of her mouth. She smelled good. Like tomato plants caught under a warm rain. I could feel my heart inside my chest the way I always did when an attractive person was in my personal space.

I nodded anyway. Her hair was buzzed down, her lips were painted red, her brown skin shone with sweat. She looked radiant, like someone who had danced for hours, not caring about anything but the relationship between the beats and her hips. When my own skin shone like that, all I looked like was someone who needed to refresh her deodorant. I felt a carbonated mix of wanting to be her and wanting her attention, wanting her to lead me away from the party and kiss me at the edge of the woods.

The woman guided me through the circle. I told her my name was Jo, but she didn't seem to hear me. A few people greeted her, but I couldn't tell what her name was. Liv? Soft fingertips. Her nails weren't painted. She led me to a table close to the forest. Piled in a woven basket were the purple fruit I had been instructed to gather in my mother's will. I picked one up. It was the size of a satsuma. Firm in my hand. An almost-sickly sweet smell, closer to the smell of a lilac bush clumped with rain and blooms than fruit. Holding one, it was impossible to think of it any longer as an apple.

My eyes watered. Someone in the woods was smoking a joint.

Even here, every party had a space where someone could try to get farther and farther away from everyone, including herself. I had the sudden desire I'd had at every party I'd ever been to—to walk away from all these people, to hear myself breathe, to go find the stars and sit silently until I was filled with the night. Why was it so much easier to think about people than be with them?

The woman took the fruit from me. She stood over the table, squeezing the fruit until it became mush and liquid and a few large seeds in a small bowl. Her palms and fingertips were stained purple with the effort.

"I'm Linden. Most people call me Lin," she said. "You're Tiana's daughter, right? Jo?"

She didn't look at me but continued to squeeze and mash and smile at the mess her long fingers and short palms were making. I said yes and she continued her work. It was like watching a demented child take all their rage out on a container of slime. When Linden was satisfied and her hands were glistening with mess, she reached into her left jeans pocket and fished out a small plastic bag. She sprinkled the dark powder into the bowl and then smashed it all together with her fist. A dumb little whoa escaped from my mouth.

"Don't eat this, okay?" She lifted her fist covered in glop. The orange lighting made it, her face, the woods behind her, suddenly ominous. "You apply it to your skin. If you want, I can help you with your feet."

"What is it?"

Linden said it was a way to open the path. Other things could also help: meditation, chanting, mugwort, wormwood, snorting crushed bat bones, intense emotional shit, drugs—so many cultures out there with different methods. Her eyes met mine. "It lets you know your potential," she said. "Some people fly, some transform, some hear voices, premonitions." Linden's voice was excited. She was explaining that for a lot of people, it was like smoking really good weed. You got relaxed and chill and nothing big happened, but that could also be nice.

I sat down. I took off my shoes and socks and offered her my left foot. My hands touched something hard in the sand. A bird's beak and skull. Linden's hands were strong. She focused mostly on the arches and my heels. It looked like she was humming, but it was too loud to know for sure.

Everything was blurring out—the people around us, the singing, the fire. I looked at her hands, her fingers, her dark nails. My eyes shut. My mouth felt dry enough that my tongue was cumbersome. I envisioned it falling out of my mouth, and the idea felt effervescent.

Once, when I was a girl, I'd had a stuffed bear named Lia. I spent hours talking to her: nights when I couldn't sleep, when I wanted someone to tell secrets, when I wanted to play with someone, or when I was angry and needed someone to lash out at. Lia was my sibling replacement. Maybe a replacement for my mom, too. It was a year when she had gone back to school and owned a bakery with one of her good friends. Almost every time I saw her, she was either exhausted, distracted, or doing multiple things at once. My dad learned how to take care of my hair that year. And he got really good at making me tiny pizzas.

My fingers weren't touching anything. I opened my eyes. The air was cooler. Stars revealed themselves. There was a layer of mist in the air from being higher and higher. I laughed with surprise, kicked my legs out like I was swimming, and pushed through the air. My hands were tinged purple and the surprise of that made me feel more connected to the air, the mist, the night than my arms or legs.

One night, I'd woken up because something was touching my face. It was Lia. Her eyes were sewn-on buttons, her nose was rough against my cheek. She opened her mouth over and over. I yelled, "Dad, Dad, Dad!" Lia told me to shut up. Told me that he would take her away from me. I would be alone. I'm your sister, the stuffed bear said to me. I'm your sister.

The trees looked like bottlebrushes, the fire an extravagant streetlamp, and Lake Superior was spreading farther out, getting larger and thinner before my eyes like spilled-out paint. Never before had I truly felt capable. Now, I controlled everything. My arms close to my body made me race through the air. My legs pulled into a squat made me into a bullet arcing toward a target; straight, I lost altitude. I saw a door made of pink light lingering above me. It had an ornate gray knob. I pushed closer to it, the sky giving little resistance.

My dad opened my bedroom door. He saw the bear speaking. He shut the door. Opened it again. Lia said to me, "It's your fault." I covered my eyes. My dad scooped us both up and took us quickly to the backyard. He said nothing, but as he held me, his hands were shaking. Lia was saying any awful thing that we had heard adults say on TV and I had whispered into one of her half-moon ears. You bitch. I'll kill your whole family. When I had said those words, I had felt the thrill of saying them and knowing I could do something bad and there was nothing my parents could do to stop me. And here was my stuffed animal, saying all the putrescence back to me.

The door in the sky swung open. Inside, only matte gray, no shapes, no people, but still I felt a gaze coming from the depths. A scream slashed out. So loud that it seemed tangible, painful, and I willed myself to fall, to get closer and closer to the shore. I was hugging myself as if I were trying to cannonball into a pool. Women were still singing. Another scream. All the hair on my arms stood up. It felt like an electric shock; I knew I needed to be anywhere but there.

"Be nice," I told Lia. The bear kept swearing. Her voice sounded like she was talking through a large brownie. My dad stacked firewood in the pit. He took a lighter out of his pocket, started speaking to me, telling me that I could never tell anyone, not my mom, not a teacher, not Grammy, not anyone about this. That if they heard, they would take me away from everything I knew. My father had never spoken to me like this. He told me I should tell Mom that I had lost Lia. He promised me that he would buy me a new toy, but I could not ever talk as much to it as I had with Lia. This next one would have to stay a toy. He reached a hand to me. I handed him Lia. He tossed her into the fire. I loved you, the bear said. It was an accusation. We watched her burn until the heat made our eyes water. I loved you.

19.

At the shore, the song echoed. Lyrics about a ship, the men on it who drowned, the lake's harsh chill. The women were singing like they were in a church, giving praise. I let the spray hit my cheeks. What will I do, I thought, with the rest of my life? My legs felt cramped and asleep. I bent over and rubbed my calves, shiatsued them when the rubbing didn't make the pain go away. My mother ran to me, held me in her arms. She touched my shoulders, my arms, the top of my head. Still stoned from the fruit, still adrenaline rushing from flying—I had flown!—I was adrift in myself, unable to comprehend her reaction.

My mother was asking me questions about whether Linden had explained what could happen. Did I know all the risks of transformational magic? Was I intact? Did I feel like something was missing inside of me? She was speaking quickly, holding my face like she had when I was a child and I had tried to touch something hot, or the time I had walked out into traffic and almost been pancaked by an SUV.

"I'm twenty-eight, Tiana," I said.

She winced. Let go of my face, took my arm. "Let's go home. You need water, some bread, or you'll be miserable in the morning."

I understand now she was trying hard to figure out what I needed from her. That she was tied up in knots between never wanting to be a mother, wanting to still find a way to do right by me, and resenting the whole process. Time lets us see the things that in the moment emotions and inebriation cloud away.

"I would like to fly in a sunset," I said, my voice a little slurred. "When everything is orange and pink. Like a sherbet. I would like to also have one of those in a waffle cone. That sounds really fucking good right now."

She led me back to her hut. The path to the woods was different to me on the way back. I thought I saw a man in a long duster and dramatic black hat watching me. His face shone like the moon. His eyes were silver. People outlined in Las Vegas neon were having their own party, holding goblets. They were all laughing, but the sound made the hairs on my arm stand up. What could only be a monster—a mastodon body, bat wings, an oversized head with ridged teeth—cast a shadow on the path. Come sing with us, the people urged. My mother gripped my arm; I couldn't tell if she heard them encouraging us toward the close-knit trees and roots or just wanted to get home.

"You didn't apologize," I said.

We kept walking. I was disappointed that she didn't say anything at all. In her hut, she handed me a cup and I drank water that tasted like acorn squash. I fought the urge to bite into the cup to see if it was made from hardened gourd skin. The bread she gave me was flavored with black pepper, and I couldn't stop talking about how good it was.

My mother was watching me, her chin tilted up, eyes narrowed.

"If you have something to say, you could just say it." My arms were wrapped around me so that my hands rested on the tops of my shoulders. When I was fifteen, a therapist had told me to do that to reassure myself. I'd called the idea stupid, but here I was doing it.

My mother stood up, took the cup from me, refilled it from the pitcher of water she'd set on her small table.

"I thought this would be different," she finally said.

I wanted to ask her what she thought would be different. Did she expect I would see her side? Did she think I would be so grateful to see her again and everything would be forgiven? It would've been easier if she had said that because I would've agreed with her. When I'd imagined ever seeing my mom again, I thought I was the kind of person, the good type, who could forgive easily if I could just have her back. And now I was simmering at the fact that she had been gone for half my life. Safe from the world. She had made me question whether magic even existed, made me consider it was all a lie, made me proud of my ability to think that way, and here she was, probably flying all over the fucking place, studying her herbs, never missing me and Dad at all. I was sure there was magic, a spell, a potion that would've allowed her to tell us goodbye, to tell us she was still alive, that we could stop worrying. She just didn't want us, okay? All the crying, all the years of people asking me whether my dad had killed my mom, all the suspicion I had been under, too. If a woman disappears, it means one of two things: she was murdered or she was a witch. And if your mother is a witch, well, what else can you be?

With a big shivery gulp, all the loud and quiet hate that people said to me in high school slithered down from being firmly locked in my brain and into my throat. The way I felt like I couldn't tell anyone—friends, my dad, my aunts—about the slurs, the chewed gum put in the hoods of my sweatshirts. How sometimes, I would lie awake at night and lie to myself that if she were here, at least then, I would have someone who would make me feel like I truly belonged. All the years of anxiety wriggling inside my veins that came from suddenly waking in a world where my mother was just gone, probably buried in a shallow grave, maybe a witch. The emails from people wanting me to talk about it, to sign away my life rights or agree to be interviewed; the tests I went through; the meetings with police officers, going over the tips that made my father get stupidly hopeful; the stomped-on sticks and slippery gravel that formed inside of me instead of the big heart I'd had before. And all she could say was, "I thought this would be different."

Before I could open my mouth, she said, "Goodnight," and walked into her bedroom.

In the morning, my mother served oatmeal with ginger and seaweed and white pepper. While we ate, she told me the story of "The Woman Who Could Never Stop Flying."

"Once there was a young woman who went to an island dedicated to the element of wood. The people who lived worshipped the firs, the deciduous trees and their ripening, to the birch bark, the spindly branches forever reaching for birds and light. You celebrated the moments of your life—a substantial love, a child, new knowledge—by planting a new tree. You mourned when the trees succumbed to natural deaths. You prayed and gave offerings when you had to take from them to survive.

Because the women on this island treated them so well, the trees gave a gift: a purple fruit that when ripe and mashed and applied to their skin would help them walk the path.

Other islands had similar rituals and gifts. The women who worshipped volcanoes had to run on stones heated by their mothers' lava. The women of the sea had to drink a broth laced with phosphorescent algae and eggs given willingly by fish or turtles. On the island of sand, people had to meditate and allow themselves to be buried within pink sand. They had to consider not their fear but every grain of sand—how it had been made, who had stepped on it.

It's a truth all people should know but they spend most of their lives working actively to forget: there is no power without the potential for harm.

One of the first women on that island began to fly. She said dumb gorgeous things like, I am the wind, I am the clouds. She couldn't stop lifting and lifting. A small bird collided with the flying woman's face and smashed down into the earth. The woman's nose streamed blood.

But still she couldn't come down. The people on the shore watched as first her skin faded, going from tan to clear, then her long brown robe faded until she was only an outline. The flying woman could be seen only if you held a hand over your eyes for shade, squinted. There she was, more of a kite than a person.

Her friends on the shore tried to find ways to bring her back. Brave women flew up and tried to grasp the shimmer of her, but only came away with dew-covered hands and a clogged-up feeling in their throats. They concocted spells that they threw at the flying woman. Some would stain her for a while, making her more visible. Others flew through her and you could hear the zephyr of her moan."

I heard the gravity in my mom's voice, understood some of the story's lesson, but I was irritable and viciously hung over. "There's a TV show," I told her, "that is always trying to position older Midwesterners as being able to speak to one another only through stories and stumbling half-sentences that end with feeble arm pats." I demonstrated one on myself, drank more water. The sound of my voice hurt my eyes, but I persisted. "White men talking to white men across cheap kitchen tables or in dimly lit cars. And it was violent and rude to women but in the way most people call prestigious rather than think about it."

My mom did not understand why I was talking to her about this TV show. I didn't understand either at the moment. Looking back, I understand now that I was trying to find different ways to tell her I was angry. I tried explaining social media to her, how important it had become in her absence, but soon that was another tangent. It didn't even matter.

I told her how we had thought social media were going to be these great places where everyone could connect, where we could learn things and share all our little comments about TV shows without annoying the people watching with us, where there were no limits to the possibilities of language. Then, it became mostly like almost everything else that people touched. White, thin, conventionally attractive people amassed power, white men continued to assert their dominance because they were afraid of change, and sometimes between white people talking over them and being racist, Black people got to be funny. I realized, while talking, my mother would have had no interest in social media if she had stayed with me. Nothing emotionally or professionally about her would have made reading people's attempts to feel important at all enticing.

"Are you and Angie still friends?" she asked.

The question was pointed; I was meant to hear the implication that she knew, had always known, about the crush I'd had on Angie. Here was another thing I had forgotten about being around my mother. Maybe it's a universal thing about mothers in general: their questions have fangs that can pull up and tear out the truth.

"Of course." Before she could keep going, I said, "Last night, I saw a door in the sky. Sometimes, when I shut my eyes, I can still see it. Bright neon pink, Las Vegas style."

"Do you feel well enough to walk?"

I nodded.

* * *

The sunlight was so bright I kept putting my hand over my eyes like a visor. My mother noticed and pulled out a pair of sunglasses from her pack. They were crooked and scratched, but still helped. We walked on the lakeshore, and she pointed out each of the nine statues. They had been built simultaneously and were meant to give another blessing to the island. That, my mother said, was how most safe magic worked: through the efforts of many working in unison.

"We're going to follow the trail," she said.

From the beach, we walked to the woods. In the daylight, the trees were ordinary. Spindly birches, evergreens, growing out of dead leaves and ragged soil. I heard voices but couldn't make out what they were saying. There were deep scratch marks in some of the trunks. A humid smell like going into a reptile house at a zoo. I pushed the sunglasses to the top of my head. The next stop was a circle of trees. In the center was a bench surrounded by tall grass gone to seed. On each tree was a large round mirror painted black.

"Go and sit for a moment," my mother said.

On the bench, I felt the sunlight warm on my hair. I had the summer inclination to shave down to my scalp and let all the heat go free. I closed my eyes. The longer my eyes were shut, the louder the voices became, as if a hand were slowly adjusting a dial. I thought I heard Preston saying, "Work was boring today. Another day at the email mines, knocking out some all-bests and respect-fullys." Some of the voices sounded familiar but others I couldn't place. What sounded like applause. The sound of a match being struck. The scream from last night.

"They're scrying mirrors," my mom said. "The past and present blur."

"I didn't see anything, but I heard things."

"It's usually a one-sense-only thing for people here. You know, touch, taste, smell. It's rare for people to hear, but especially rare for people to see. On full moons, we gather together those who can do the senses all at once."

She was looking at the mirrors. Her eyes were wide, and they made me sure, suddenly, that she was seeing things that I didn't want to know.

The next stop was in a meadow with grass of different colors—blues, greens, pinks, scarlet. I wanted to take a picture of it but had left my phone at the hut. Several women were working together to assemble a large figure made from wire and mud and the grasses. I could not tell what it was supposed to be, but its feet looked like messy hawk talons. The closer we walked toward the women, the hotter the air felt.

"It's magic," I said. "Whatever it is."

My mom nodded even though what I said had been obvious and stupid. She told me it was an icon of prosperity. That it was meant for the holiday. She pointed toward the legs, and I could see a vine snaking out of one that looked like it had small pumpkins growing on it. The other, a vine with velvet bags—like Crown Royal bags dyed black.

"Can we sit for a minute?" I didn't wait for my mother's answer but sat back in the grass, let the blades push against me. I took a deep breath, still tired from the night before.

"If you all can do this," I said, "why hide here?"

She stretched out her arms, pushed her face to the sun. In the light, I could see the new lines around her mouth, near her eyes. For the first time, I could see the years that had passed. It was reassuring to see that time, to not have to look at her and see exactly who she had been fourteen years ago. We were both different people. It was possible to start over.

"Everyone can do magic," she said. "It's not special."

My brain split toward two thoughts: How had she felt when she'd found this out? And how was it possible?

"The lie is that only women can do it."

"Wait, what?"

"Magic, when done safely, takes time and patience and community. You need to work together, to learn together, to create something beautiful. And most people, they don't want to hear that."

"But—"

"Let me tell you."

My mother wiped at her eyes. Already they were rimmed red from the grasses. "This story is called 'The Witch King and the Cursed Caves.'

"In the past, people recognized their need for other people. Hunters needed gatherers. Fighters needed doctors. Farmers needed merchants. You couldn't exploit one another because it led to alienation. And to be alone in the world meant too much risk.

Depending on where you lived, there were different kinds of magic. Most were influenced by nature. People in towns near oceans and rivers built," she paused, "maybe the best word is totems, to those water sources to help their lives flourish. They're not places meant for ordinary lives; they were meant to be places where people could devote their lives to magic and to protect the nature that made it possible. Some followed the ideas of animals. Lava Magic. Yakisugi Magic. Rain Magic. We didn't think of magic as evil or even anything special. It was natural when done in unison. There are records all over the world, some preserved here on this island, about different rituals done throughout the years to give back to the world. It's true everyone was different then, but in almost all cultures, there was one foundational truth: you respected and gave back to any thing that gave you life.

Some overpowered witches throughout history could transform without risk, do curses, hear prophecies alone, but for most of us, magic was about community. You need to be in community with others to make the world a better place for us all.

There have always been greedy people. It's not unnatural to be greedy. If you spend enough time being afraid, thinking of only survival, it leads to hoarding. Cruel isolation can set in. The poison that makes people want to be kings, to do things and not consider the harm their actions bring, to value things and power over life, can saturate a person's brain. Even in the past, people were always making a crucial choice: Is life the most valuable thing of all, or is the most valuable thing of all your personal pleasure?

Once upon a time, hundreds, even thousands of people would celebrate bees, seeds, the snow. If we hurt the Earth, we would give back twofold.

Once there was a woman, a witch with too much power, who decided she would be king. She used her magic to curse her enemies. She would write their names into dough, bake the dough into bread, stab the loaves with a knife, and hang the loaves in caves to molder. So many wasting diseases were born from her magic. The witch who would be king didn't attempt to hide what she was doing. She took credit for her actions, offered life to any who agreed to be ruled by her.

And for a while, most of the world was ruled by the witch king. She trained others in the art of curse work. A person's hair, the ashes from their fireplaces, something they had put a great deal of love into could be used as the foundation for these spells. Some say her appearance was rotted by these spells. That she looked soggy and covered with mold. That only through magic did she not fall apart after taking a step. Others say that she looked normal, even beautiful, but when she opened her mouth, death's scent leaked out.

Her actions took on more and more momentum. People began fighting, went to war, and finally, guns were invented. Why memorize a spell and sit together for hours to chant when you could point and shoot? Why spend your time cultivating plants and bees and knowledge when you could get things done faster by hurting other people? Why work together when people wanted kings?"

My mother paused, pulled out a handkerchief and blew her nose. A wet honk.

"We can go home," I offered.

Her voice was hoarse.

"That's the story of how the first burnings started. People, especially men, started gathering women up. It didn't matter if the women were their wives, their sisters or mothers. Anyone who wouldn't give up the old ways, they burned. There were no consequences."

I looked back at the group of women building the figure. They had gathered around it, holding hands, and each was taking a turn saying something out loud. The wind was blowing. Words came at us in bits and pieces—"healing," "apples," and "mild winter." Clouds were floating in, soft-serve globs melting along the horizon.

"Do you understand now why you need to stay here?"

I shook my head.

My mom took my hand. Our hands were the same size. Our pointer fingers had the same inward curve.

The people went back to work again. Two were standing on ladders, the others passing buckets filled with grass. I still couldn't tell what the figure would end up being. It could be a chicken, an unshapely angel, or a monster.

20.

My mother couldn't stop sneezing. Over and over. I had forgotten that about her. It was never just one with her. Always three or seven. Watching her sneeze and refuse to do anything about it other than use an increasingly useful handkerchief made me feel like a teenager again. Her sneezing meant less and less and to me—only an increased annoyance at having to think about her and her body and remember she was a person. The difference was I was now old enough to be embarrassed that I could react that way toward anyone. I kept asking her if she was sure she didn't need anything. She rolled her eyes as we walked away from the meadow.

"You don't think you should go home?" I said.

"Excuse me?" She paused on the dirt path. Sneezed three times. I could see the clouds of it and felt thankful that my mother had turned, that it was all heading back toward the meadow. "It's allergies. I'm fine."

"You clearly feel miserable." I tried not to let any annoyance seep into my voice.

"You're doing exactly what you would do at fourteen."

"Excuse me?" I said and crossed my arms. It didn't escape me that I had said this in the exact same tone and style as she had.

"I used to worry that you were going to be one of those high school mean girls. You say the most judgmental shit in that nice-girl way. You can't say whatever you want and pretend it's helping."

"I'm just telling you to take care of yourself."

"It's your tone, Josephine. Who would want to listen to anyone who's speaking to them like that?" She wiped at her nose again.

"And you always started fights when you didn't feel well," I said. "If you had a cold, everyone had to be miserable."

The wind blew harder, pushing up dirt from the path. I forgot where she said we were going.

In my head, a long rant formed. It was about the Christmas I turned twelve and how she had ruined it by picking a fight with my dad that went on for hours. I had sat upstairs in my room, eating my way through a fruit and nut basket someone had sent us and watching the *Home Alone* movies, while my mom complained about my dad's family and how she was tired of spending Christmas with them. Her words were punctuated with hacking coughs and silence where I could tell she was worrying down cough drops. My dad kept saying rude things and then ending them with things like why don't you rest, let's talk about this tomorrow, and each attempt seemed to make my mother's rage stronger. I couldn't understand how he could be so stupid to try to fight with her. I couldn't understand how she could be an adult and think she could act that way.

Before I could speak, my mother said, "How are you nothing like him?"

I knew she meant my father and I shut down. My feet started farther down the path. There were no longer any thoughts left in my brain other than get out of this situation before you say something you'll regret. A clamorous insect chattered, emptying out what felt like big concerns. My mother sneezed again, loud, but I could tell she was following me. If I got to the library and anyone was around, I knew the fight would be at least paused until we were alone again. You ruined his life. The heat of the words lingered in my mouth.

You ruined Dad's life.

You ruined my life by making him my only parent.

A white house, so regular, it seemed incongruous, came into view. It was surrounded by apple trees, still studded with unpicked fruit. Something shiny was hanging from all the branches, silver-bright between the leaves. I had to close my eyes because of how the sun was hitting them.

"Wait," my mother called.

I quickened my pace. Behind and far taller than the house was a lighthouse. It was painted in a checkerboard black-and-white pattern. There were four windows, one for each story. Above each of the windows, a large eye was painted—blue, green, brown, and yellow like a cat's. Even from the distance, it made me stop walking and tilt my head up. At the very top was a lightning rod. Somehow when I was flying, I had missed seeing it. What would it be like to fly around the lighthouse, treating it like an art museum, pause, close, but not too close, and look at each eye?

My mother grabbed my arm.

"That hurts." It didn't. I just wanted her to stop.

"It couldn't possibly."

"Mom, can we?"

She moved her hand down to my wrist. She held on. I couldn't finish my thought and instead focused on her hand. There was dirt beneath her fingernails, her fingertips were even rougher than they used to be. "The only way we're going to be able to live together is if we stop being so polite."

"What?" I shrugged her off me, took a step backward, stood up straight. Not slouching, I was taller than she was. "What do you mean 'live together'?"

"I mean, don't you want to stay here?"

"I have no idea what I want to do; I've been here a day. I need time to think."

I was still processing the idea of staying here forever, living in a small hut and slowly merging back into what she remembered of our life when I was a child. It was so complicated. I had clung to the idea of her for more than a decade, and now, it seemed like she was offering me an impossible choice: her, or the life I knew and everyone else I loved.

My mother shook her head, coughed. "You're free. Why would you go back?"

"Tiana, is that you?" someone called.

We turned toward the voice. A person whose face was covered in brown feathers stood only about ten feet away. We had been so absorbed in our fight that we hadn't noticed.

I don't know why, but suddenly, I felt sure the door I had seen in the sky the night before was directly above us. I felt its presence again. The pink light of it, the gray knob, the nothingness behind it. A tense silence. I looked up. Blue sky, white clouds, a single unidentifiable bird.

My mother started walking toward the person. I followed. As I got closer to the trees, it was clear that chimes were hanging from the branches. The leaves moved and rustled in the wind. The chimes moved, too, but were silent.

"They're for spirits," my mother said. "They only make sounds based on ghost movements."

"All books are haunted," the other person said. Her hair was pulled back, but it was a mixture of black curly hair and the feathers on her face. "I'm Lex," she said.

Lex told me the trees looked like chandeliers every spring and in the winter, the chimes never froze. On August 8, October 31, and some other days, it depended on the year—she said that as if, of course, yeah, I would understand—the chimes were so loud they could be heard on the beach. Most of the time, a spirit would appear on a full moon here or there, but one or two made the chimes sing for a minute at most.

"What is a spirit? What does it look like?"

"Depends on the spirit," my mom said, and it took a lot of willpower for me not to roll my eyes.

"What about the lighthouse?"

"It's also for spirits." Lex sounded genuinely delighted. "We only turn it on during special ceremonies."

"I can't go inside it," my mom said.

"Spirits hate your mom. She's got a love-it-or-hate-it-colored aura."

"Auras aren't real," my mother said, sounding exactly like me when I was being pedantic. I winced.

I was tempted to tell them about the woman I had met at the party who tried to use seeing auras as a seduction technique. My aura was sunset pink, she had told me. With a wound, I had added. Thinking about it now, I wondered why I hadn't questioned her about shade, tone, or saturation. I felt sure my soul was supersaturated, no matter what color it was.

Neither my mom nor Lex seemed like a person who would find that digression at all interesting. "We don't know if anything is real or not real," Lex said. "That's the curse of existence."

I looked back and forth at them and wondered if they were together.

My mom coughed and Lex said, "Come on, let me get you some tea."

They walked into the library and I followed. The first room had a long kitchen table, smelled like Earl Grey tea; handwritten posters reminded people they could have tea only while reading from the people library collection. The phrase "people library" made me laugh. Lex opened a cupboard, pulled out a packet of tea, and put it in a large white mug. She gestured for me to come over.

"Put your hands on the cup and say 'feel better' three times."

I nodded and did it. Then Lex did too. My mother took the cup. As she drank the tea, her eyes cleared and unpuffed, her nose was no longer red at the edges, and she sat up straighter. She drank more, and each sip made her look more relaxed, her skin glowing, the cough dissipating. As she and Lex started talking about the efficacy of a spell like that, I went exploring.

The next small room was filled with paperbacks I could've gotten at home. A lot of romance novels with bright red spines. Popular books about thin white people who thought sex could solve their problems, but surprise, surprise, sex just made everything more complicated. I couldn't judge though; I realized I couldn't name the last book I had read that wasn't for work or I had skimmed to help me seem interesting on a dating website.

The rooms adjacent to the people library were what I had been hoping for: thick old books in languages I couldn't even guess at along the back wall, letters in display cases under lock and key. The handwriting was small and spindly and hard to read, but they seemed to be love letters. A long table covered in rolled-up long pieces of paper I thought would be maps but were intricately designed mixtures of art and spells.

I sat down and started going through them. A ritualized burying that must be performed by four people that could save someone from wasting diseases. But what even was a wasting disease? I had never known. A staircase assembled with specific flowers—aster, red sunflower, lilac—attached with a honey-based glue to make a home safe from spirits and hungry men. The flowers had to be alive for their magic to fully work. Quilts that could contain the memories of the maker. A person who fell asleep under them would experience the sewn-in memories instead of usual dreams. A stew made by ten women in tandem to heal spell damage. The drawing on that page showed a woman with a face full of feathers and the feathers wilting off as she ate more and more stew. Schematics for a garden that could bloom no matter the season. I was sure my mother had studied this one and taken extensive notes.

The designs and recipes were so appealing. Hand-drawn figures, steps written out in large, clear cursive in English, printed words in Spanish. They looked like the kind of things that people with velvet-sofa money would have framed and hanging on the walls of their curated homes. Looking at them, I had the feeling I had when I was scrolling through science articles. What I was reading made sense. As long as I took my time, I could explain what I had read to someone else, but I also knew I was missing the deep understanding needed to create or make these things. I wanted that deep understanding—to study, to make things, to have many willing teachers.

The only spell I saw for an individual was one called Extinguish. The drawing showed a woman being tied to a stake over a bonfire. The next panel showed her whispering to herself: I will repay any help given to me threefold. The next was an image of a woman enveloped by fire, but a thought bubble showed rain falling from a cloud, a glacier bobbing in ice, what I thought could only be sand, and waves. A meditation. The penultimate panel was a split screen. Fire around the woman. Rain falling inside her. The final panel: the same woman flying next to a cloud and saying, "Thank you, thank you." Written next to it: All witches who don't show gratitude will face consequences. I looked at it again and again, wondering how this was safe, why the witches still felt even here that this spell was worth learning.

There was one last drawing to unroll. It was the only one not in black or white. I gasped: it showed the bright pink door with its ornate doorknob. In the drawing, there was the design of an eye on the knob. Around it, a navy sky, clouds obviously saturated by moonlight in the foreground. Around the edges of the drawing, many people had written notes: the great omen, the monster's den, the alluring shriek, turn and turn and turn. A pen was on the table; I picked it up, wrote automatically "the abiding mystery" and was immediately embarrassed that I had done so. I fought the urge to cross it out, knew it would only make things worse.

It was a relief to know I wasn't the only person who had seen the door.

When I walked back to the first room, my mother and Lex were sipping tea. This time it smelled like what she had used to make for herself to help with allergies when I was a child. Nettles.

"Linden's going to come and show you around the rest of the island," my mom said in her own fake-pleasant tone. "I'm going to go home and rest."

"It's the lighthouse. She can't go in it," Lex told me again.

"Why not?"

My mother looked at me. Her eyes were softer now, but I could see by the way her jaw was clenched, the way her eyebrows lifted, that she was determined not to talk about it. "Some spirits just don't like people." She took another sip of tea. "When you get home, let's talk more about your future plans, okay?"

What I had let myself forget about my mother is she had wanted to be my life's compass. I was, like her, quietly not supposed to believe in magic. I was supposed to be thin like her. Able to look at mushrooms and herbs and know immediately what was death and what was delicious. If I had to play a sport, I would run like her. Team sports led to cliques, which led to stunted adults whose only personality trait was being able to think high school was the best time ever. I would not ever, ever be ashy, especially in public. Everything about me should be neat, from my desk to wearing freshly ironed shirts. I would be a doctor, or maybe a lawyer. She did not like that I liked being funny. On the rare occasions when I could make her laugh, she would cover her mouth with her right hand.

Once, I had gone to a movie alone. It was one of those weeks when I had already seen everything new and A-plus, so I went to a teen drama about two teenagers who fall in love just by looking at each other through a window and sending each other cutesy emails. There was a scene, though, where one of the teens has a sudden medical crisis. Sitting in front of me were a mother and daughter. The daughter was around the age of the characters in the movie, and suddenly, she was crying. As her crying persisted, I knew it wasn't just a response to the tension, the overwhelming soundtrack, the large, young faces emoting into the camera. It had touched something that was going on in their life together. The girl's mother kept patting her back, but it didn't make the crying stop.

"I'm so sorry, I didn't know it was going to be about this," she said to her daughter.

No one else seemed to notice them.

They were all I could notice.

The mother pushed up the armrest. She pulled her daughter into her arms and held her. Cheek to forehead. They stayed like that the rest of the movie. I cried while watching them, wiping away tears with butter-scented fingers.

At the time, I had told myself I had cried because it made me miss my mom.

Sitting across from her, I wondered if the reaction I'd had was because I knew I would never have an intimacy like that with either of my parents. My mom was not a warm person. My dad told me he loved me on my birthdays, written in a card in a chicken scratch I had to work hard to read. What was it like to be loved in a way that felt immutable? To not be told I was loved, but to feel it, to see it most of the time?

21.

As I waited for Linden, I started making a pros and cons list about staying on the island, even though I didn't understand the rush to make a decision. A definite positive for staying was the way I felt here. At any time, I knew I could lift up into the air. Soar above treetops, brush fingertip to wing with the gulls and be again in the night mist. I realized while thinking this that it was now possible for me to dunk a basketball on a regulation hoop. Would that be a waste of flying to take a basketball, glide above the rim, and slam it and myself down to score? It didn't matter. I longed for someone to stroll up to me and challenge me to a game of Horse.

Later, I would learn that the witches have their own version of Horse, but even more elaborate. You not only have to sink the shot but have to do all the intricate aerial moves that your competitors do while doing them—a double spin in the air, a rolled tuck, moving like you were doing a backstroke in the pool—and then score. I would spend hours I thought I should've spent studying, playing, and sweating and becoming more and more confident. So much of being good at magic relies on believing you can do this spell, follow that path, hear that voice. I told myself that in my own way I was developing a necessary skill.

A big pro on my list was here on the island I could freely do magic. It was exciting to think with practice and community I could be a part of something big that less than a year ago would've felt impossible. I could make things. Not to sell or to survive, but because I loved doing it. In a way it was even more exciting to feel like that again. I could make magic that looked like art. I could hold a fire in my hands. Make flowers out of cups. Be inspired and pushed toward creating. Only two things had made me feel that way in my adult life. One was writing with Angie. There was a space between us where we could laugh and fight and say stupid things comfortably on the way to that potential great thing. The second was my job at the museum. Not the day-to-day meetings or emails, but the moments when I was focused on making sure someone else's vision was exactly enabled, building a space where people could think about art. It was corny, but one of the few things that made life worth living was being able to show how beautiful, how strange, how wonderful people could be. Art was one of the few remedies I had for chronic misanthropy.

No monitoring, no pressure to get married, no being in a social situation and having to grit my teeth and be pleasant because I was worried the wrong expression, the wrong words, the wrong tone could ruin or end my life because it would lead to an accusation of witchcraft. No reading the news and having to frantically call, having to find money I barely had to donate to different groups in different states facing another crisis for women's rights, having to go to a protest and worry someone was going to drive their car into it, no having to email my congressmen about wanting the right to health care, wanting to live in a country where a man did not have to "take responsibility for me," and getting a reply encouraging me to "cheer up and trust in the process." I could actually live a life that didn't feel as if I were constantly being squeezed by careless, hairy fingers.

But here there was no Angie, no Dad, no work at the museum, no board game friends with their cute apartments, no drinking friends whom I thought I was immeasurably close to at two in the morning and then never thought to text until it was time to go drinking again, no work friends to complain with about bosses and patrons and the coffee that tasted like it was brewed not with beans but with shredded-up recycled paper that had been colored with a scented marker. No Preston. No walking on sidewalks drinking a cold brew while the sun made everything feel possible. No cars. No apartment with the big porch and loud dishwasher. No grandma and aunts.

The second day my mother was gone, they had poured into our house. Cooking, cleaning, bringing flowers, arguing, crying, laughing. They had made it so my dad and I couldn't forget about living. We couldn't fixate only on my mom, what was missing. They had made us feel. It was a gift I would never be able to repay.

"What are you thinking about?" I looked up. Linden stood in the doorway. She was again dressed all in black, a tunic and long shorts that looked handmade. No one had explained to me the clothes or supplies situation here.

"My mom," I said.

"She's famous around here. For—what's a nice word for it?—her credulousness."

"That's a good SAT word for it."

Linden gave me a blank look.

"You know, the test you have to take to go to college."

"I've always lived here. Always-always. I was born here."

She told me that her parents—neither of whom used the words "Mom" or "Mother," "Dad" or "Father"—had come here individually, fallen in love, and had a whole life here. Fox and Jam and Linden. A lot of people changed their names here to fit their new lives. They had taught her math and spelling and some science from outside books. History both from the library and also from the people of the island, who had written their own book, were still writing it. Linden sounded uncomfortable as she talked about her life. There was a reaction or question she kept anticipating, but I couldn't figure out what it was. I was thinking instead about how it sounded like a good children's book: *Linden, Jam, and Fox on the Island of Witches. Linden, Jam, and Fox Learn About Friendship.* Watercolor illustrations. A hugs-and-picnics life.

"It wasn't perfect," Linden said.

I stood up, pushed away from the table. We walked out the door and started up the slope toward the lighthouse. "I didn't say it was."

"Your eyes did."

But I did think about what an entire life here could be. Not walking home with your fingers wrapped around a can of pepper spray. Living a life where you always knew magic was real, and maybe on your fourteenth birthday you flew above a meadow. I knew that there were awful things here, too. A sky filled with dead birds and blood. A screaming door. What seemed like monsters in the middle of the island. Linden's eyes were on my face.

When she spoke again, it was in a soft I-don't-want-to-offend voice. "We're people, too. Nowhere with people can ever be perfect."

I nodded.

A bird hopped on the sand, leaving perfect small claw prints. When I was a child, I would've stared at this for a long time— invented the history of the bird.

Long dune grass waved on either side of the path. The lake cleared its throat, announcing itself over and over on the nearby beach.

Still speaking in that same voice, Linden said, "My entire life, I was curious about everywhere else. Now, I'm old enough that I could go see what it's like out there, but I'm too scared."

"If I were you, I would feel the same way," I said, and then felt the immediate shame of someone trying to say something helpful but fucking it up.

The lighthouse loomed. Here the eyes above the windows were intimidating. It was maybe an optical illusion, but I could feel their gaze. They were measuring me.

"Weren't we supposed to be talking about your mom?" she asked.

"Were we?"

"You really like questions."

"That and also not talking about myself whenever possible."

I wanted to be someone who didn't flinch when the subject of me came up. There were so many things I could've told her about myself, about why I was the way I am, but I wanted Linden to like me. I chose silence.

"There's a story about your mom," Linden said. "I think you'll like it. When we tell the kids about it, it's called 'The Story of the Witch Who Believed Nothing.'

"Once there was a witch named Tiana who was from what she called 'the real world.' She came to this island seeking treasure. The only stories that are out in the world about this place now are always steeped in money. Gold and gems and dollar bills. A necklace made from pink sea pearls that had been hunted by actresses and billionaires' wives. A cursed ring made of sapphires that had been worn by a famous poet at the time of his death. Supposedly, it had inspired three of his famous poems that had once been beautiful but now were ugly with the weight of people being forced to explain what they meant.

The witch was fascinated by the value of love. How it could take an object from being worth something clear and easy to parse and make it invaluable. It didn't matter if something were one of a kind; it mattered more if someone important had loved it. She liked to talk about how people could add value to things, but that on average, things couldn't add value to people. And people could maybe add value to people, but most weren't interested in doing that.

Some people on the island said that the witch was saying all these things because she was embarrassed about looking greedy. Saying things like this made her look like some grand adventurer from the past.

Some people said it was true: that this was what society looked like where the witch had lived.

Some people hoped that she would stop talking about this treasure all the time. Wealth was pointless here.

And a few who had actually talked to the witch said to leave her alone. She had left her child behind. The witch was still processing that she was a person who could do that.

The witch was unhappy to find several people on the island. They helped clean her wounds, feed her, and explain what this land was, but her bitterness persisted.

She refused to believe in magic. The women flew under the full moon and the witch asked for proof that what she was seeing was real. It was dark, she said, there could be special equipment. What equipment could that be? the witches asked her, and she changed tactics. She had been intoxicated; 'I was so drunk, my imagination ran away with me.' The witch met people who were half-bird or had claws or were small as pebbles. She claimed these were genetic anomalies, indulged herself in the language of half-science to make her lies stronger.

The only times the witch listened and didn't argue was when the stories of herbs and gathering were told and whenever she heard anything that seemed close to being about the treasure. Tiana claimed that money would give her daughter freedom. Nothing else could do it.

The people took her to the lighthouse, hoping that the spirits inside would convince her magic was real. But the spirits wouldn't let the witch in. The doorway curled itself into a mouth—something none of the people of the island had ever seen it do before—and said, No. When the witch tried to force herself in, the door growled and shook. No.

Tiana called the lighthouse and everything she had experienced on the island childish, cruel, prank show bullshit.

At the center of the island was a place no one went unless summoned. A row of white trees with cream leaves marked the area where no one should pass. The witch went where no one was supposed to go, so no one could follow her.

Three days later, the witch returned. Her pack a little fuller than before. She didn't speak. Maybe she couldn't. Across most of her face was a large handprint. Sunburn red with a bright white border. It looked as if the hand had been traced and pressed onto her skin. Every day, someone would ask how she had gotten that mark, but the witch only sighed and shook her head.

The handprint remained on her face for three years. Tiana said two things about it: 'I demanded proof that magic was real, and I got it' and 'The spirit called me Little-Miss-Gets-a-Slap.'"

I laughed. I couldn't help it. Hearing about my mom mouthing off to some mystical being, still refusing to accept that some things could never be explained, and then a spirit, a witch, a monster got fed up and gave her one big magical slap. It was gratifying to know even a fantastical being could get that tired of her.

Linden reached out and took my hand. I didn't pull away.

"I knew that story would make you feel a little better."

We were at the doorway of the lighthouse. A navy door, a gold knob, a sandstone step.

"Don't worry, a lot of people can't come in here," Linden said. "It doesn't mean anything. Some people are just the wrong flavor. It doesn't mean they're bad; it just means they're not for you."

What she said was reassuring, but I still gripped her hand tighter. There were no sounds except our breathing and my anxious heart. No smells either. The nothing feel of being in a space with a strong air purifier running, except we were outside.

I reached out. The knob turned easily in my hand.

22.

Inside the lighthouse were bird cages, muted gold and spindly. Proud birds that looked like parrots and parakeets were inside them. Birds were flying loose in a dense bright cloud. They all looked as if they had been drawn with pastels and then smudged. Their calls and hellos and chirps were all either too high-pitched or too low-pitched. They sounded closer to electronic music than living birds. It took all my willpower to not step quickly out and shut the door. In the center of all this was a woman, smudged like the birds, holding a large, elaborate loaf of bread with a tree design on it. She ripped it furiously and let the debris fall to the concrete floor.

The birds all turned toward me. "Hello, hello," they called in crooked parrot voices.

I raised a hand and waved, immediately embarrassed by how uncomfortable I felt.

Linden stepped around me. A bird flew to her shoulders. "Hello, baby," she said. Linden smiled, lifted her eyebrows, and urged me closer. The face she made was so cute and warm, I felt like I had to be cool. Relaxed. I walked farther in, and on impulse held out an arm like I had once seen a falconer do. Several birds flew to the arm and landed. They had no weight, yet I could feel their talons and feathers. They were trying not to hurt me. More flew over. They perched on my shoulders, my other arm, my head. Their wings were brushing against my cheeks and throat. I sneezed and then yelped with pain as a few startled birds dug in. No weight, but cuts and blood. Up close, they were even more smeared. Parrots with heads at forty-five-degree angles. Parakeets with beaks in their stomach. Cloud birds. Wings that came out of their heads. Their noise made me want to cover my ears, but I knew moving would make even more of them dig in.

I had a sudden idea of what I looked like covered in these ghost birds and felt weak-kneed. A rush of blood to the head, the sea rocking feeling of my body urging me to faint. The birds whispered and chattered at me. "Welcome, welcome, you should eat a small fish every day for your heart, the weather is too humid, you should go home, no you should stay, go, I missed you, you should wear only black jeans, you're a bad man, no that's not true, you should renounce money, you should eat gold, you're an old woman in a bat's body."

"They like you." Linden's eyes were wide with delight.

"I hate this," I muttered, and all the birds laughed.

"What's so funny?" Linden asked them. Her voice was pitched as if she were talking to a toddler, Tell me where your nose is, baby, that's extraordinary that you already know what a nose is.

"Josephine," they said in unison. They hopped and fidgeted on me. I gritted my teeth. Don't offend the birds, I thought. Each of their movements made me more nauseated. I was desperate to move my arms. There were divots and cuts in my skin from their claws. Some on my hands were nosing and looking at the persistent purple dye. "She flew, she flew!" I wanted to be home in my comfortable bed, pull my quilt over my head, pretend that this was all a nightmare.

"Jo—se—phine Jo—se—phine," they chanted.

"Linden." My voice, small and desperate.

A bird on my scalp pressed in. Blood smeared on my forehead. It made a line down my nose.

"What if you all gave her a break?" Linden spoke in a bright, cheerful voice.

"You're hurting me," I said to them.

Most fluttered off in response. One cozied close to my ear. Its harsh beak pressed into my lobe. The bird told me when I returned here, I would have to bake a loaf made out of the finest grains, write thank you into the dough. I would owe them everything if I didn't pay up. Its mouth smelled like cut grass and something rotting in a refrigerator crisper. It told me birds and people were alike because we couldn't tell the difference between glass and air. And Linden couldn't tell the difference between the power of seven and nine and that was why she kept failing. And in the middle of the universe was a great big hole and we all had inherited emptiness. You could either embrace loneliness or try to make something new. That was the way of people.

This was the moment when I upgraded birds in my head from approach warily to do not trust. After this, they were often in my dreams, telling me things in my sleep that sometimes came true. When I saw crows on trees, picking in the grass, they called out hellos, told me gossip, asked for things. I flinched sometimes when robins or sparrows came close, anticipating their claws and weight.

"Okay," I said. "I understand." I hadn't. Everything it had said felt important, and none of it made any sense. The bird flew away and went back to eating bread off the floor. I walked out of the lighthouse, plunked down on the stoop, and tried to calm down. Deep, slow breaths. Could still feel their talons and beaks. Birds ripped at things as they ate. Linden came out and put a hand on my shoulder.

I shrugged away from her. "Why didn't you warn me they might do that? I would've been more cautious. I might not have even gone in there."

"I've never even seen those birds before. Most of the time there's a woman or a rude cat, or sometimes, I don't know, a floating candlestick." Linden tried to touch me again. I shrugged away again.

I opened my eyes. Linden was clearly shook. Her eyes were so dark it was hard to distinguish between her iris and pupils.

"I'm so used to spirits." Linden crossed her arms, took a breath. "I'm sorry. I should've talked you through this first meeting. It's important you have a good relationship with them."

"A bird said you were messing up seven and nine. Does that make sense?"

Linden tilted her head. She offered her hand and I took it. We walked slowly—her being patient, me taking slow steps and still mostly thinking to myself, Calm down, calm down.

The farther away from the lighthouse we got, the more smells and sounds crept back in. The wind in branches, the lake, living birds. There was a distant bonfire smell. My arms and head hurt from the claws. I smelled and felt sure somehow one of the ghost birds had pooped on my back.

"I need some Band-Aids."

"Mhhhmm." Linden was elsewhere again. She led me off the path, more inland. We walked in silence for ten minutes, hand in hand. The quiet was fine, it helped. I thought about how her hand was so cool, even though the day was hot. How it was already starting to be coat weather in the Michigan outside the island; it was the time of year that always made me feel lost. Everyone around me seemed to have so much energy in the fall and I wanted to hibernate.

Nothing good in my life seemed to ever happen in October. Here, maybe, I could start over. Everything would be different. I could get new feelings about the seasons, new ideas about how to live my life. Then I thought about the birds again, my mother, the menstruating sky, no Angie, no work, no Preston, no Dad, no internet, no nice whisky, and wondered if I should just buy a new SAD lamp, an expensive quilt, and whether those things could help me start having a new, better life.

"My entire life I've been obsessed with why it seems like only curses can be put into objects, but not blessings," Linden said. "'Blessings' is such a musty word, I know. I can't think of anything better." She kept her hand on mine. Her palm was short, but her fingers were long.

"It is a really corny word. What about gifts? Surprises? Presents? I feel like those are better than blessings."

"But they're so ordinary."

"You're the one who cares about mustiness." I looked at my arm; some of the cuts were still bleeding.

"Anyway, I've been trying to invent objects that can heal or protect their wearer," she said. "A hat that lets you transform into an animal without spell damage. A bracelet that can protect you from flames. A ring for fertility or infertility. Gates that can help with carbon output. None of them worked," she sighed. "Right now, I'm trying one that's a house that slows down aging."

"That's wild. How would it work?"

"I thought it needed to be a seven-sided small house built by seven women over seven days in seven-hour increments with seven base herbs integrated into all the construction elements. But maybe nine is better. Ugh. I have to read more. Maybe talk it out."

We flopped down into the tall grass. I was interested enough in what she was saying that I forgave her for not warning me about the lighthouse. She told me about all the research and ideas for spells she had. The more I heard, the more I understood that writing spells was like any other human skill: creativity plus research plus a willingness to make mistakes. You had to be less self-conscious, though, because other people had to be a part of it. It wasn't like me and Angie riffing on our couch in the soft cushions of our relationship. To make a spell that had even the smallest possibility of working, there could be no hiding.

It made me admire Linden, how little she cared that other people saw her make mistakes. As she talked and thought through everything with me, I could tell she had never woken up at 2 a.m. thinking about things like misspelling "refrigerator" in front of her third-grade class, or all the bad jokes she had written in her journal and let her ex-girlfriend read, or the time at work she had insisted that she was fixing the printer's jam but somehow in the process of yanking the paper out had broken a small piece off that could not be reattached and had irrevocably destroyed the printer. Linden said things like, "Everything is learning, you know," without any affectation.

Linden wrote down some ideas in a small notebook, pushed it away into her back pocket, and stood up again. "Dinner?"

We walked together to the shore. People were on the beach picking bones out of freshly caught whitefish, tearing lettuce, and wrapping beets and potatoes in foil. The beehives in the distance were loud enough with the colonies' rhythms that they felt close. I was handed green apples, a cutting board, and a knife and told to dice them for punch. Everyone was helping out in some way. My mother was sprinkling herbs and salt on the fish. She tentatively smiled, and I waved at her until her smile was full and wide on her face.

A woman with thick black hair looked at me and guided me away from the cutting board. Next to some chairs surrounding a bonfire, she pulled out a wooden box. Took out three brown jars and some rags and started dabbing at my arms, my head, my cheeks. Each dab burned and I muttered "shit" over and over until it had no meaning. "Give me your shirt," she said. I took it off and sat as she went down to the water, dunked it in, wrung out the water, and came back.

"How did this happen to you?"

"Birds really like me," I said.

"A blessing," she replied.

The people were brainstorming ways to magically connect to the internet. Even on an island where you could learn and practice magic, there were still arrivals who longed to scroll and upvote. We could talk to family was a common argument. It would make things less emotionally hard. Others said that the internet was humanity's great hubris. It was rotting brains, making people less creative and more cruel. And others argued that it would be impossible to feel safe here if it was, even via the internet, easily accessed by the outside world. Some people were excited by the idea that they could find a way to make magic technology. Others were angry at even the suggestion, given the amount of energy and effort it would take to continually renew, monitor, and make vessels that would house the magic. But it would be cool, some said. Other witches from other islands might be impressed when they visited. It was clear that this was a regular disagreement.

In the morning, I would get my own shed. Linden offered to help teach me spell work. You'll learn from all of us, the witches said. That night, I would practice flying again. The wind and clouds would be waiting for me.

23.

Suddenly, days passed. Walks and talks with Linden. Each walk a mixture of her asking me questions about the world away from the island and her talking to me about spells. On our first walk together, she took me to her hut and walked me through a spell. I rubbed a small stone in my hands over and over and focused until it became a small cloud that drifted around the room. It rained and wisped around my head and I clapped for it as it moved. "That's talent," Linden said and handed me another spell to try.

Some days, we walked hand in hand in silence and I would look at her face and couldn't tell what she meant by the physical contact. I was scared again, like with Angie, of doing the wrong thing, of losing my only close friend.

Fish and potatoes cooked over flames. Sprouts and tubers roasted in ancient clay ovens. Cooking over fire was its own magic. The sweat streaming down my face, learning how to move and shift dishes based on the flames. Learning the language of fires, when to give them more food, when to let them wane.

The sky bled another time. Blood dripped down the windows, bones rattled, and somehow this time, it was beautiful. The way the crimsons and pinks of it slicked on glass made me long for a camera. No one could tell me why it happened. When I asked one woman, she asked me why I wanted to ruin it. The pleasure of life was sometimes learning to enjoy things as they are, rather than asking why.

I joined hands in a circle and floated above the trees, a bug smashing against my forehead, the wind so cold I longed for an overcoat. Most of the wounds from the birds vanished. My mother dressed them in the mornings with a potion she made. It smelled like oregano and took the itching away. "Hold still," she said while dabbing at them, and I watched her face like I had as a child whenever I had a cut or scrape. Her focus, the relaxation on her face as she tended to me, was still reassuring. A few of the cuts became lighter brown scars on my arms.

People liked to hear about the work I did at the museum; they speculated on whether the art we exhibited was done by actual witches and who could have done it. It felt like all the witches knew one another. I kept dreaming of a bird whispering to me, but everything it said ended up being the word "toast." Some of the leaves burst orange.

The evening they threw me a belated twenty-eighth birthday party, I walked out to the beach where my mother was waiting with two cakes, two huge full-sized candles poking out of both. Linden wrapped a necklace made from daisies and sweet grasses and bright flowers I couldn't identify around my neck. She kissed me on the cheek, her lips close to my mouth, and I felt like the heat of her could make me drift off from the ground for a moment. Another witch put a garland on my forehead. They sang to me, and as they sang, the fire shifted colors: orange to pink to peach to blue. Crows flocked and joined in the song, singing in their discordant voices and promising me gifts and safety in the year to come. One climbed on my shoulder and nuzzled me after I fed it a small bit of cake. I drank a shot of moonshine that made me cough. My mother gave me a gift: a golden magnifying glass. It had been my grandmother's. She had enchanted it so that I could look through it and see my memories of my grandmother. "This is a top five birthday," I told my mother. We held hands when we walked home, both a little drunk.

A night when the wind had the nothing-smell of snow. My mother and I circled each other, continually talking around each other. I helped prepare mead. I learned how to make beeswax candles. Goodnight, I love you, my mother said, and the muscle memory of all the love I'd had for her for so long let me say it back.

I read spells. Sewed a doll for a little girl to protect her against animals, spirits, and the eyes of men. Practiced baking bread. My loaves would mean nothing until baking wasn't a task or something I fretted over but something thoughtless, like blinking. People gently reminded me on days when I was very homesick that there were boats back to the outside if I ever needed anything that I missed (a treat, tools, some medicines, even though they warned against most of them and how they affected magic). I could go home, too. It wasn't that I was unwelcome. But they acknowledged it was a lot to say goodbye to, especially without knowing I was saying goodbye to it all. Whenever my mother overhead this, she said, "That isn't an option. It's not safe to go back."

Some came and went, their loved one sewing them dolls filled with hair or nail clippings that would allow them to return. They went out to check on the world, to find other people who might need a safe place, to gather resources. Each time they left, time was out of synch. Sometimes, they returned to the outside world only seconds from the last time they had been there; other times, weeks or months had passed. But for most, the island was everything now. The place was bound by layers of spells. You couldn't come without an explicit invitation in the form of a doll or a bracelet woven from the dune grass. And sometimes, even those failed. A decade ago, they had built an eye made from glass and mud and the blood of everyone living on the island at the time. It was supposed to be able to judge the intentions of everyone attempting to access the island, barring anyone who came to do harm. Instead, it made it impossible for six months for anyone to come and go until the eye was smashed.

"How could it see what people would do?" I asked.

"People are more obvious than you think," a witch said and left it at that.

Everyone but my mom was curious about how I was adjusting. "I miss hot tubs," a woman who had been the newest witch before me liked to say. "And cheap margaritas. I dream sometimes of going to an Applebee's on a Tuesday night. The plasticky cheese, the smell of cheap fajitas."

"I miss Angie," I said. "I miss my boyfriend. Well, it's complicated, well, he's sort of." I was trying to say I missed laughing with Angie. I missed splitting a joint and watching TV and talking about when the writing was especially good and when it was especially bad. I missed lying in bed after sex with Preston. Him handing me a glass of water. The two of us talking in soft voices and the way we felt like the only people in the world for the half-hour or so we stayed in bed afterward. I hadn't been willing to see how much those moments meant to me until I couldn't have them.

I flew in the nights, relishing the way the wind felt against my neck, through my hair, making me aware of even my eyebrows and how necessary they were. There was no bigger joy than being up high in the air and seeing the fire reaching its tongues toward me, and the women gathered in black laughing and singing and kissing around it.

Every day, I tried to understand my mother better. I needed to accept who she was, not who I had made her into when she was gone, not who I wanted her to be now that she was in my life again. Tiana liked helping other people, she was good at remedies, she talked to the pumpkins in the garden in a sweet voice because she said vegetables needed kindness to taste better, she was smart and incisive and let people talk through their issues with her. She liked gossip but not in a malicious way. The pleasure Tiana took in hearing about other people's dramas was more of a delight in how interesting living could be.

But she was self-centered. Tiana was uncomfortable with me anytime I seemed different from her, especially when I did anything that clearly reminded her of my dad. When I tried to talk about my life at home, tried to tell her about my job, my ambitions, Angie, Preston, she was dismissive or changed the subject. I knew even at the time it was because she wanted me to move forward, make a clean break. Her problem with me always was that she thought harshness was best, yet all I ever needed was a little softness to be persuaded.

She did not like it when anyone was more knowledgeable than she was and would later belittle or find a way to cut down that person. She did not have much of a sense of humor, and even when I made other people around us laugh, her lips would stay a straight line, and her gaze would go to the sky or the sand. Tiana liked telling stories. She was good at it; her voice was agile, her hands made big entrancing gestures, and the joy she felt from the actions made it hard not to engage. She was noisy in a way I hadn't remembered. Even reading, she would sometimes think aloud or make a variety of uninterpretable sighs. One day's low sigh of this-is-shit was the next day's this-is-brilliant. I could never tell what she was thinking when she looked at me. She rubbed my feet for me when I couldn't sleep. She walked me through making dough, reminding me to be patient. She sat beside me at dinner in soft silence while everyone else talked.

Each day I was there, I thought in the evening that this could be forever. In the mornings, I opened my eyes and berated myself for beginning another day away. I kept thinking about my dad and what my absence was doing to him. It was cruel and selfish. Sometimes I could see our house again, filled with aunts and cousins and probably Angie, everyone telling my dad I would come back. I was still alive. I wondered how he was taking all this, if the Bureau of Witchcraft had talked to him about what he should do if I suddenly reappeared and if it was the same as when my mother had disappeared: he was to immediately call and quarantine himself, place a line of salt around his bedroom door that supposedly a witch could not cross, wear noise-canceling headphones and avoid eye contact.

Every morning, my mom and I had breakfast together and the thoughts of leaving would seep away as she poured me tea, handed me some bread, gently served me a bowl of oatmeal. We talked about her work and the weather and Linden's spell and sometimes the pink door in the sky. She speculated it might have something to do with time; part of the deepest mysteries of witchcraft was thinking of time as an element. How could you change its speed or walk outside it? It was the hardest of the elements to master. Few did. Sometimes, I told myself maybe the door was something figurative, a way for my brain to process magic after years of thinking it was a big lie. Then I would think of the drawing I had seen of it, and I knew I was being stupid. Every time I said something like that, my mother zoned out and looked into her porridge.

We washed and dried dishes together and sometimes she would warble "The Gambler" and I was small in a good way in those moments. And then, more sewing, seeing something incredible and turning for a moment to an empty space next to me where I expected Angie to be, more growing, more talking, a moment alone and wanting to pick up my phone and text Preston, walking hand in hand with Linden and listening to the birds, wanting more and more, sometimes lying awake at night and wondering Should I have kissed her? or thinking about how her hands and my hands were the exact same size. The smell of her. The way her lips were light pink and brown and full. Her ass in black jeans while she danced on the beach.

My mom's footsteps on the floorboards during the night. Coming out into the front room when I couldn't sleep and she was there drinking tea and reading. How comfortable it was to quietly join her for an hour and then go back to bed. The way her eyes lit up when I told her about a new thing I had learned. A plant I could use to turn my fingernails golden for a week. A small unruly lizard I had sewn into life that had darted up and down her arm and then run away to the shore. "That's wonderful," she said over and over. The lizard was still clearly sewn, but it moved and darted like it was flesh.

It was a rainy morning when everything inside me boiled up. I had made the oatmeal, added chopped apple, and mixed in a dried fruit that also smelled like apple but looked more like tree bark. Put in too much ginger so that each bite bit back. My mom was talking to me about Halloween. It sounded sacred and warm. Gifts and spirits and setting generosity goals for the coming winter. Anointing each other's feet with oil infused with gold flakes and opening ourselves to visions of the days to come. At home, I would've been brainstorming a costume, talking to Preston about what he wanted to do that night.

Last year, we had both dressed up as Zorro, taken MDMA, and fucked with our masks on. Embarrassingly, the matching costumes, calling each other Zorro as he was inside me, really did it for me. In the morning, we had gotten up early and I had watched as he slowly ate chicken and waffles and said, "It's so good I'm tearing up." "Are we still high?" "Probably," he said, and offered me a taste of his breakfast, the syrup dripping down the fork's tines.

"I need to go home," I said to my mom. "At least to say goodbye."

She shut her eyes, took off her bonnet and put it in her lap.

"Look, I'm not saying this all to hurt you," I said. "I just can't do this, not this way."

I waited for her to say something. Her eyes were on my face.

"You know if you go back," she said, "after something like this, you'll be investigated, maybe immediately tried."

"I know that. Mom, they investigated me after you left. I know it won't be easy."

"What makes you think you won't just be burned?"

"There has to be an investigation," I said. "They still do that."

"Why would you trust that? I taught you better."

Everything I wanted to say poured out of me at once. None of the sentences seemed to connect to one another. I talked about how her leaving had broken us. How we'd spent much of our lives trying to find her, thinking about her, dealing with the consequences. I talked about going to therapy. How it had taught me to see the connection between her leaving and how hard it was for me to relate to other people. I couldn't hurt everyone like that. It wasn't who I was. I tried to talk about already having been investigated because of her own escape, but I couldn't get the words out right because I was too emotional.

"So, you're saying I ruined your life?"

"No."

"You value your life so little that you would risk everything to go back there?"

"No."

My mother didn't yell. She kept her arms and hands on the table. Out there I was a woman, out there I was a Black woman, and that was even harder. Wasn't I finally alive here? Wasn't I finally a person here? Wasn't I afraid every day there? She talked about statistics. She talked about how Black women suspected of magic were ten times more likely to be incarcerated or go immediately to trial instead of paying initial fines like their white counterparts. They were far more likely to become wards of the state when they reached thirty and were unmarried. All of this was valid, none of it had changed in the years my mother had been gone, but as she spoke, I became angrier and angrier because it was so distant; she was speaking to me not as if I were her daughter, but like I was a student who she really wanted to see succeed but was a little naive about the systemic issues that would impact me. I could see she had prepared this speech, wasn't responding to any of the things I had said to her. I was gritting my teeth to keep from interrupting her. The only time my mother made the speech personal instead of generally political was when she said, "I don't have to worry about you if you're here."

"You left me alone," I said. "Do you know how hard it was to be the only Black girl with a witch mom in high school? It almost killed me. You were the only person I had who knew what it was like to be in that town, who could tell me how to live, and you left."

The only soft things in the room were two crocheted blankets, brown and blue. Not enough to cut the sharpness of the way we were speaking to each other. Every word was loud and resonant.

"That's not fair. You could at least try to understand me," she said. With her face flushed, I could see where she had been slapped. The fingerprints red and visible on her forehead. Each mark big enough that I thought I could see the ulnar-oriented whorls.

I tried to articulate how necessary going back was for my mental health. How I needed to feel like this decision was truly mine. Each day, I missed home more and more. I tried to get her to understand how I had been suicidal as a teenager. How I had been torn between wanting to be invisible to feel safe and how making myself invisible just made me want to die and get it over with.

She said nothing. Her eyes were on the ground. The red fingerprints brighter and brighter. The silence spread. We were both standing, arms crossed, looking away from each other. I cleared my throat.

"I'm leaving tonight if I can."

"It's not going to fix you. You're not going to learn anything you don't already know. You're only hurting yourself. You'll never have your own life back."

I was crying. Each tear increased my anger. Even my eyes were betraying me. The word of soap opera villains and movie superhero aliens: betrayal. Angie and I, after the smallest annoyance, spill, or slight, would turn to the other and say, "This is a betrayal of the highest order."

"There's nothing noble or special about what you're doing," my mother continued. "You're choosing to be unhappy because you're addicted to it. You could be happy. You just don't want it."

There was no remorse or surprise on my mother's face when she said that. I could tell that she had truly thought this about me, had never put herself into the equation, and refused to give weight to her actions. I would always have the knots of her absence inside me, for better and for worse. There would never be a moment when she would be accountable or would give me anything that I could use as a step toward moving forward with her.

"You don't ever feel bad about leaving?" The question surprised me after I asked it.

"If you let your life be guided by the idea of feeling good or bad." I heard the No in her voice, the way she avoided the direct question.

With distance, away from my emotions, I could see the question maybe wasn't fair. Of course it wasn't easy to leave me. She had engineered a way we could be safely reunited. The way she fought and argued with me to stay was her way of telling me she regretted all the time we had been apart. But she was my mother. I hated seeing any proof that she was fallible. A person.

"I should pack," I said.

"I'll go make the arrangements," she said and quickly left.

At the dock, people gathered to hug me and speak kindness. Safe travels. Take care of yourself. You'll always be welcome here. Linden reassured me that now that I had been here, now that I had flown, it wouldn't be a seven-year wait if I wanted to return. The island would always know me. "I know, cheesy," she said immediately after the words slipped out of her mouth. She wrapped a bracelet around my wrist. It was made from dune grass and seaweed. "For protection," she said. Linden put her hand on my cheek and kissed me soft and sweet. We laughed, I whispered in her ear, "Thank you." And we laughed again but in a way that it was clear we were both annoyed at how timid we had been. The sun was getting low. I looked out at the crowd, waiting for my mother to emerge. I knew it was too much to expect an apology or understanding, even for her to hug me and pretend the fight had never happened, but still I waited for her to finally say goodbye.

She didn't come.

24.

When I was younger, I used to claim I had never been embarrassed. Some of it was because I didn't often care enough about
what other people thought and because embarrassment was so
gendered. Magazines for teen girls had those sections at the beginning where readers shared their humiliations; it was supposed to
feel like a sterile slumber party, one where no one got mad, where
no older brothers acted weird, and where you could go home by
just shutting the magazine and dropping it in the recycle bin. The
humiliations were always a surprise menstruation that someone
noticed, a dropped tampon in front of a crush, an unruly bra strap,
someone seeing boobs through an open window, a whale tail when
bending over while doing a presentation in government class, a vo-
luminous fart when the school sex hunk was lingering. Everything
was meant to reinforce having a typically cis female body was a
mortification that must be endured until you were old enough that
your body was an aged mush helped into baths and rolled over in
beds. And then it was only about the embarrassment of being alive.
None of those magazines pointed toward what I knew of mortification: my brain and how ugly it was, how it was linked directly to
my mouth that let ugly stuff slip from it, and how those ugly things
were then permanently in my brain for me to consider whenever I
was restless at 2:30 a.m.

I was a step away from myself when I returned to the "real world."
On the boat, I'd drunk from a small jar of something awful that
looked like liquefied orange Play-Doh. It will probably help, the

captain had said. She told me I was the first person since, and then got distracted looking out the window. The captain told me the last time someone had left permanently was maybe five years ago. A time that stuck with her was about fifteen years ago: A man had been invited to the island by his wife who couldn't stop thinking about him. But he hadn't shown up looking for her. Clutching the doll she'd sent him, he went looking for treasure. The husband had disappeared into the island's center and when he returned, begged to leave. "He was hilarious," the captain said. "No cell phones! No thanks. Pussy blood sky! A monster! This is my nightmare!" The voice she did while imitating him made her sound like a tween boy on an animated show.

She recommended I make myself look like a woman in trouble when I hit land. I took off my shirt. She didn't have to explain to me. I knew the scrutiny I would be under again. It would be better if I didn't seem threatening, if my absence appeared to be someone else's fault. My mother had vanished and so had I. Even a sympathetic person would assume witchcraft when I returned.

My bra was off-white, with a long coffee stain across the left cup. There were small scars on my arms from places where branches and brambles and birds had nipped at me. A hole was surfacing in the knee of my jeans, and I helped it along. Whatever I had drunk made me intoxicated and tired. I was grateful for it; my head kept turning over my fight with my mom. I was embarrassed I could see her for who she was and still let her crush me like this. The captain reminded me it was dangerous to do magic alone. It was not safe to fly out here. And as much as possible, I should keep my head down and follow the rules.

"If you come back, you should remember that time is different," the captain said. "Sometimes, only five minutes have passed. Sometimes, years."

I nodded. Then paused. "Why do you do this?"

"I love the job."

Her eyes were on the lake. The waves were moving in reverse. Every bird song was backward. They sounded wonderful and wrong. The clouds were lightening from nothing dark to morning pink. Whenever I looked out the cabin's window, it seemed as if everything was moving very quickly, but in the boat everything was still. Fish hung in the sky and then somersaulted into the water in sloppy splashes. Bug smashes on the windows reassembled into flies and dragonflies that darted away. Snow flurries sucked back into clouds. Mist sank back down into Lake Superior. A boat that was the twin of our boat drove past and the captain cheerfully waved at herself. I could only watch in short glances; the dissonance between the cabin's stillness and the frantic broken time outside made me feel rollercoaster sick.

The captain continued, "I prefer a heightened not-knowing. I don't like pretending life is manageable. I like all this because it tells the truth about being alive. People are always trying to make the universe smooth through repetitions and routines."

"The older I get," I said, "the more comforting it is for me to accept anything is possible." It was the kind of thing I said while making small talk that after it slipped out of my mouth, I wondered, Do I really think that? I accepted it more now that I was older. But acceptance didn't stop the days of being so anxious I had to stay home and lie on the couch. And even lying still, my brain would think about a car veering off the road and knocking a Kool-Aid Man—style hole into the front window. The old toaster catching fire and killing me. Carbon monoxide. Someone showing up to burgle my home because statistically most burglaries happen during daylight hours. My dad or Angie disappearing.

"That's because each year, you're a little closer to the void," the captain said.

I left my shoes on the boat and walked back into the world. It was cold and I kept thinking, I am on the beach in my ugliest bra. No one was around. The sky was dark with rain, maybe even slush and snow this time of year. I wished I had said meaner things to my mother; I wished we hadn't fought. Stop crying, I told myself. I wished I had never seen her again; I wished I was still there with her. Goosebumps rose on my arms and breasts. The thick sand took effort to walk in, especially in socks. And still, I was more aware of myself looking around the dock. So many kind faces, so many people wishing me well, telling me I was now family, I would always be welcome, and me peering around all the people who actually were able to be kind to me, hoping that my mother would finally give me something. Embarrassing!

"Ma'am," a white man with long hair and glasses called, "are you okay?"

He ran over. Of course he had a fucking golden retriever wearing a bandana. The dog licked my hand with its sloppy sweet tongue, and I sat down. It kept nudging me and licking the tears off my face. The dog's unyielding kindness made me cry harder. I thought I could hear it saying, "baby, baby, baby," under its breath as it panted at me. I sat up, tried to run away from them, sat down again.

The man called 911. He told me I was safe now. His hair was silvering but his beard was full and brown. If he had teen daughters, I was sure one of their friends had called him hot, old white Jesus. He shrugged off his jacket, asked if it was okay if he touched me, and slung it around my shoulders. It smelled fresh from the dryer. His breath smelled like coffee. You're safe, he said. His eyes were wet. It was clear the man was trying not to cry, to take care of me in these moments. He told me the police and an ambulance were coming. And he was sorry they were coming and not social service people, but he would be with me the whole time, record the whole thing if he needed to. My name is Mitch. I hunched beneath his jean jacket. The wind was picking up. I could tell he wanted to take me somewhere warmer but knew it would make things harder.

A police car and an ambulance rolled up. Mitch spoke to the police officers and kept looking over at me with big, concerned eyes. The female EMT talked to me in a slow, reassuring way. Everyone kept telling me I was safe. It was clear everyone thought they were rescuing me from something ugly or that I was in the throes of a mental health crisis, and their gentleness and kindness were overwhelming. She asked me my name.

"I'm Josephine Thomas."

I had been gone for only a week. On the island, it had been close to six weeks; there, we had been narrowing in on Halloween. The hospital they took me to looked like a blue-on-green Tetris board. The nurses who examined me all seemed to have the same large, concerned brown eyes. They all had brown eyeliner and thick mascara. I got IV fluids. A female police officer asked me where I had been, who I had been with. Had I drunk anything suspicious? Had I been assaulted? Did I have a history of mental illness? Was there anyone nearby they could call?

"I'm sorry," I responded to each question.

I fell asleep. When I woke up, two older white men wearing navy suits were sitting in chairs next to my bed. They told me they were from the Michigan Bureau of Witchcraft. I was going to go with them. One handed me a bag filled with clothes. They turned around but did not leave the room as I changed into black scrubs and black slip-on sneakers. I didn't argue or fight them. There wasn't a point. I knew this was coming. I reminded myself that now that I was an adult, it would not be just a few questions, a test, a one-night stay; a greater danger was coming.

On the website where I registered as an unmarried woman of twenty-eight, all the pictures had been reassuring: women with very white teeth talking to other women, a brick building surrounded by bright yellow tulips, and the smooth web design to reassure you, This isn't the past. We treat you like people. Don't worry.

In a small room, the two white men in navy suits said that their names were Bill and Bill. They asked me:

Have you ever slept with someone for money?
Did you lie when you were a teenager?
Were you with your mother?
Are you a witch?
Have you ever fucked an animal?
Have you ever fucked the Devil?
Do you drink the blood of chickens?
Have you ever cursed someone?
Where were you?
Who else is in your coven?
Do you know that the Devil especially loves Black women?
When was the first time you performed magic?
Do you speak to dogs?
When did your mother initiate you into evil?
Why aren't you married?
Have you ever concealed the birth of a child?
Do you hear voices?
What evils have you done to others?
Have you ever left the state to have an abortion?

Have you ever transformed into a bat?

Is the Devil your true father?

How many other women have you cursed out of jealousy and spite?

Have you seduced a married man?

Do you eat toads?

Have you eaten a baby?

Is this your true form?

How old are you really?

Where were you?

Were you in hell?

Have you ever corrupted or seduced a young woman?

Hours and hours. The questions phrased in different ways. A meandering plea that if I were to just admit I was a witch, if I renounced evil, I could be saved. God's light could be on my face again. Do you know what your name means? God Raises. You could be in his hands again. An exhausted part of me said, "My mom named me for Josephine Baker. Not because of the Bible." It was the first thing that I had said in hours that wasn't a variation of No, Never, I don't understand.

They took me to a smaller room to perform tests. A table with two bowls of water. I submerged my hands in one bowl that was filled with room temperature holy water. They watched with great interest as my hands only became water shriveled. The next bowl was filled with ice water. I longed for the card game they had played with me when I was a girl. It hurt. I kept pulling my hands out, and they kept forcing them back in. They brought out a bowl of ice and made me hold the ice for as long as I could stand it. Their faces were blank and uninterested as I cried and said I couldn't keep doing this.

One Bill wrote notes, and one Bill shook his head in an aggravated slow way as if he were stuck in construction traffic. They both seemed deeply annoyed at me for wasting their time. Occasionally, when I said something that wasn't No, when I tried to just be a person, their eyes would shine with excited dog-sees-a-ball-being-thrown interest. All this time on the job and finally, here was a potential witch to torment.

My hands kept shaking. On the island, everyone had reminded me that now that I had done magic, it would be reflexive. I would have to be especially careful and controlled. If anyone saw me do any magic, danger. If I did any magic alone, also danger. When magic is restless inside you, you feel like a bright red lollipop dropped on the ground and ant after ant is moving on top of you, taking tastes of your slick sugar surface. Most of my thoughts were a refrain of You can do this, you can do this. I wanted to make a flame drift from the palm of my hand and burn this place into ash. I thought nothing would grow where this building had been. The land was suffused with the ugly intentions of the men who had tortured and judged witches.

For another test I held out my hand and they pricked each finger with a long silver needle. "Her blood is red. The skin is penetrable. The skin does not smoke when it encounters silver."

They put a necklace made from silver around my neck. I drank a garlic smoothie that made me burp a lot but clearly did not have the expected result. It was actually kind of good in a way that made me want to ask them for the recipe. I decided they would think I wasn't taking this seriously enough and ramp everything up. One of the Bills lunged at me haunted-house style, and I immediately covered my face and spat out some white smoothie.

"Did not turn into a bird or badger from fear."

When they decided to call it quits for the night, they took me to a large cafeteria where three women were working. All were wearing large headphones and were purposefully not looking at me. The food was a salad with out-of-season watery tomatoes and too-sharp raw red onions. I ate it ravenously, wished I could get seconds. I thought about the last time I had been at a facility like this. The food had been better. I wondered if they had told my dad I was here. And if he knew, was he on his way to get me? Or would it be like last time: no acknowledgment except to tell me to "be good"? After that, they took me to a small room with a Japanese-style futon on the floor, a small silicon water bottle beside it.

I was too tired to be scared or anxious. I slept and woke up in the middle of the night hot and dry-mouthed. In the dream I'd been having, my mother kept telling me I had broken her fax machine. When I went to look at it, the machine was a diorama I'd made in third grade of a scene from Beezus and Ramona. I pushed on the poorly cut out paper figures, the popsicle sticks of their bedroom, and tried to figure out how I could get this broken mess to send a message. It was impossible. In the dream, I had walked out of my mother's house and told everyone I have to live in France now.

In the top left corner of the room was a camera. I looked at it while slowly drinking from the water bottle. How long would I be here? I couldn't remember anything about being assessed for witchcraft under unusual circumstances except it was not considered an infringement of my civil liberties to have no access to a lawyer. I was considered dangerous until I had been thoroughly evaluated. It was for everyone's safety that only trained witchcraft specialists were exposed to me.

The next morning, I was asked to pee in a cup. An older white woman wearing headphones and keeping her eyes lowered accompanied me to the bathroom.

"Is this a drug test?"

She kept her eyes low.

"Do you have to watch?"

She nodded.

"I can't hurt you. I'm just a person."

She pursed her lips. I took that to mean we'll let the judges decide.

"I don't think I can go with you watching."

She shrugged.

I was wrong. It had been a long night. I filled the cup. She took it from me. Her hands were shaking a little and I wondered what she believed a witch's urine could do. I had heard nothing about that.

After the test, a dry granola bar and then back into the room. The Bills returned, still wearing matching navy suits, but today they were both wearing bright red ties. The vibe was very presidential debate. Now that I had slept, the men seemed much younger than they had the day before.

Bill Number Two asked "How are you feeling, Josephine?"

"Miserable."

"Before we get started, let me tell you a story," said Bill Number One.

"When the great creator made women, he made the glue that holds this world together. Women give birth, they care for their children, their husbands, their parents when they age. They create beautiful homes, beautiful meals, and see the world with gentleness and care.

"Women were made smaller and gentler and kinder and obedient because without those qualities the whole world would crumble. Isn't it miraculous? To be made something so wonderful, to always know your path and to never be lost."

Once one of my uncles on my dad's side had gone off on a similar tangent after he had drunk one too many Coors Lights.

My mother had kept saying the word "obedient" in an angrier and angrier tone. My dad sent me up to my room. I walked as slowly as I could, so I saw her slap my uncle's beer off the table. She moved quickly like a petulant cat. The liquid arced into his lap. I walked up the stairs to her laughter and my uncle's complaints.

Bill Number Two said "Amen" like he was in church when Bill Number One paused.

"But there were a few outliers who refused to see the gifts the world had given them. Voices whispered in their ears. Evil loves to break the natural order of things. And most women were so, so good. They turned their backs on this temptation and continued their beautiful lives. But a few couldn't help themselves. They listened.

"These women let themselves be transformed until they were no longer recognizable as anything but witches. Evil and lust and power made them take children and eat them, seduce men, seduce women, talk to spirits, create more and more danger. Can you imagine how amazing it is that people are even alive today? That our ancestors survived the reign of witches and now, here we are today thriving, let alone surviving?"

Both men were watching my face carefully. I was keeping my eyes on their eyes. They wanted me to be small and twitching in their presence, and so I was. I let my fingers press against each other, I let my face always have a plea written across it.

I shook my head slowly. "It's a miracle."

"Finally, our ancestors rose up against these witches holding us back. They brought order and peace and wealth to the world. We built societies where anyone could succeed. And we promised to help keep women safe.

"Good women are the gravity of the world. They keep everything in place, keep us from floating away into oblivion. It's a woman's most sacred duty to make sure she upholds the standards and natural order of things."

"That's all we're doing here, Jo," one of the Bills said. "We're just making sure you're safe, that you're ready to go back to the world and to keep maintaining order. As long as you continue cooperating, I'm sure everything will turn out just fine."

I nodded. No one had spoken to me about women like that since I was a child. My grandmother on my father's side. I rarely thought about her because she and my dad had a terrible relationship. My grandmother hadn't liked that my mother was Black, she hadn't liked my mother's bad attitude, didn't like the church my parents got married in, didn't like the town they settled in, every conversation she had with my dad was about all the ways he had messed up. One of the few conversations I could remember having with her was when she had me come into the kitchen and help her make dinner. While I diced potatoes, she talked at me about the right way to be a woman, how I would never get married if I followed my mother's example, how I had to learn to make a man feel like he was the boss of the family. All families needed a strong, masculine boss.

I knew it was easier to not talk back to her, so I diced and diced, nodded and nodded and zoned out and wondered if anyone had ever nodded until their head wobbled off. I pictured my own head falling on the floor. My grandmother said to obey a man, to let him keep my soul clasped in God's hands was the greatest gift to myself. When the bonding time was over and dinner was served, I looked at all the dishes and realized none had potatoes in them. Later, when I peeked in the trash bin, all my chopped potatoes were on top of the chicken bones and plastic wrap.

The other Bill was on the verge of tears. "Bill, can you believe we're even alive today? It keeps me up at night sometimes." He rubbed his eyes, cleared his throat, and adjusted his tie.

Had I ever had a miscarriage? Did animals obey my will? Had I ever slept with a married man? Was I a witch? Had I sold my soul to the Devil? If I was a witch, it wasn't my fault—it was the culture's. Santeria, Voodou. My ancestors had set me up to fail. Black women are drawn to black magic. Had I ever cursed anyone? Could I see the future? Had I ever told people I was a man? Had I ever killed a chicken for good luck? Did I obey men? Was I a witch?

"Josephine," Bill Number Two said. "We're going to do two more tests today. And if you prove to us you're still a woman, that your soul is still intact, we'll start talking about a way for you to go home."

I couldn't help it. The thought of seeing my dad, of sleeping in my childhood bed even with its back-breaking rigidity, of being able to stop enduring and let my shoulders smooth down to where they were supposed to be, forced tears out of my eyes. As I wiped them away with the back of my hand, the two Bills smiled at each other.

25.

They had me sit in a high-backed wooden chair. It was bearable only if I didn't slouch. A woman wearing headphones tied me to it using bungee cords. Another woman put me in handcuffs. They weren't steel but silver. The women watched me for a full minute, and I assumed the materials they were using were supposed to make witches react in some way. Maybe I would melt or spontaneously combust or reveal that all along I was a talking cat. When I remained a living woman with no reaction, both visibly relaxed. "It's a gorgeous morning," I said. No one looked at me. "Chilly, but look at the sky."

Then two men, also wearing headphones, appeared and lifted me and the chair up. They placed me in the back of a pickup truck.

"I'm going to die," I whispered. They drove the truck slowly; I rocked and bumped around in the bed. Most of the trees had dropped their leaves, but one persisted, bright yellow and orange. I focused on the colorful tree. Tried to keep myself calm. I had known there would be trouble when I came back but assumed it would be like when I was a child—the questions, the isolation. Not this. I had been arrogant.

We pulled up to a lake. The trees were still full with leaves here. The water was still.

"No," I said. "Please. I'll die."

No one heard me. Their headphones were still firmly in place.

I can't remember all the things that came out of my mouth. Begging. Pleading. I tried to move my arms and legs, but there wasn't enough give on the bungee cords. The scream that came out of my mouth was horrible. I would always know what I sounded like when I was begging for my life.

Bill and Bill were watching from a black car that had followed the pickup. They were wearing matching dad-at-the-beach sunglasses. Bright orange and blue and purple lenses with unflattering angles cut near their cheeks. The other two men lifted me out of the truck bed. Again, they didn't look at my face. It was clear from what I could see of their faces they were uncomfortable with what was happening but would still do it. They had probably been told the headphones would make sure they weren't ensorcelled or seduced, but in fact they made sure no one could hear me and empathize.

"Help me."

They carried me to the water's edge, walked into it slowly. Then one of the men tripped and dropped me and the chair. It fell backward and hit against some rocks. My head was submerged, my legs up in the air. I kicked and flailed. Squirmed. Opened my eyes. I could see clear autumn sky through the water. A bubble from my nose rising to the surface. It hurt to hold my breath. The water tasted terrible in my mouth.

Four hands lifted me up.

I spat water. Took the loudest breath of my entire life.

"Are you a witch?" the men yelled.

"No."

They submerged me again.

My heart was so loud. My ears hurt from the rush of water into them. A yellow leaf fell onto the water's surface and stared down at me. I tried again to thrash my way out, I hurt my wrists. My nostrils hurt, somehow my left more than my right.

The hands lifted me again.

"Are you a witch?"

"No, no, no."

A third time. This time I tried to calm down. They'll pull me back up, I said, forming my first thought in minutes. They waited longer this time. I struggled again, desperate for air. My heart so loud I thought my body was transmuting, becoming one unwieldy super heart. Leaves fell onto the water. Yellow after yellow. I wanted to be one of them, placidly drifting on the surface, with no mind.

Hands pulled me back up to air. I was panting now like a dog. My mouth tasted like rot and lake water.

In the past, in some places, the only way people accepted a person was not a witch was if they died during a test like this. I'm going to die here, I thought. I wanted my end to be peaceful. I wanted to be thinking of everyone I loved or to feel comfortable, not die scared, alone, and desperate. I wanted to feel as if I were in control of my death, to welcome it into my arms. That was impossible. I breathed and begged. Breathed and begged.

Finally, Bill and Bill got out of the car. The men who had been putting me under paused, sat me and the chair all the way up, removed their headphones. One of them gestured at how wet another was, then pantomimed wiping out, and all of the men laughed. I was too tired to react. Later that night, I would think about them laughing as I sat there shivering, think every swear word I knew, simmer with a hate I had never felt before. At that moment, I was too cold and overwhelmed. I was using any energy I had left to test the cords, the handcuffs. My right wrist was bleeding. One of the Bills laughed so hard he was holding his stomach.

The Bills strolled over. I couldn't tell which one was speaking, I was so disoriented. "So, we heard you passed the test. We're so proud of you."

"And your other test results came in."

Some of my urine had gone to a lab and some of it had been

baked into pellets and fed to some goats. The animals that had been willing to eat them had lived. They didn't even get sick or act weird, which was apparently a great sign. And nothing unusual from the lab, either. I must have made the strangest face because they started laughing again.

"It's really a great sign." By the earnest way Bill said this, I knew they weren't fucking with me over this. Somewhere, a bunch of goats were being raised with the express purpose of making sure women weren't witches. I coughed.

26.

Angie used to encourage me to try stand-up. She said I was naturally funny even when I wasn't saying things that were funny. I had a tone. I had big eyes with short lashes, the kind of eyes that remind people of cartoon animals. Few things sounded more nightmarish to me than being on a stage in front of a two-drink-minimum crowd and trying to make them laugh. But after she said this, I couldn't stop thinking about what I would do or say in my hypothetical set. My go-to opening would be from my life: Your mom disappears when you're a teen, your dad is suspected of being a killer, and one of your aunts agrees to be on *Unsolved Mysteries* to talk about the whole thing. I know what you're wondering: When did you get boobs?

I sat alone on the futon in the small white-walled cell and thought up different variations of that comedy set. Have you ever found out magic was truly real, flown above an island, been covered by ghost birds, and fought with the mother you thought was dead, and then you come home and have to go to potential witch prison where people torture you? Oh ha ha, you too? Well, okay. Have you ever been to a Meijer on Sunday morning where all the church families are pouring in and all their kids are screaming for doughnuts? No, well, *that's* terror.

Sometimes, I thought my ability to joke about anything, anytime, anywhere was proof something was fundamentally wrong with me. Sometimes, I wondered if it was the only thing keeping me alive.

My feet were still cold; I thought they would be cold forever. My hands and wrists hurt despite the painkillers I'd been given. A cramp on my left side made me feel as if lake water were an inch deep inside my torso, slowly rotting out my intestines and making my gall bladder moldy.

A woman wearing headphones had cleaned and bandaged all my cuts. She had kept saying in a soft-talking-to-baby voice, "Oh, you're okay, you're okay," and each time, it made me feel worse. The peroxide burned and when I winced, she frowned big and clowny like the expression had been suddenly painted on her face. It reminded me of my mom taking care of me on the island—the way she made sure I felt calm and relaxed as she attended to my scratches. How soft her voice was. For a moment, I was no longer angry at Tiana. I wished there were a way for her to walk through the door, take me home, and for neither of us to get into any trouble.

If you can get through this, I told myself throughout the night, you can have your life back. Each time, I knew it was a lie, but I kept doing it. Even if my dad took "responsibility" for me, even if it meant moving back to Clair de Lune and living with him. I tried not to picture it because I wasn't sure he would show up here if I was allowed to leave. He wouldn't like the mess; it seemed most likely he would be immersed in all the feelings, all the accusations of my mother's disappearance again. I wouldn't be able to live alone with Angie. I let my brain poke at the easier math of rebuilding my life: A new job at the Meijer twenty-five minutes from my dad's house. Sleeping in my childhood bedroom. I wanted to tell myself it was worth it because I wasn't making my family go through that pain again.

But a tiny voice in my head that sounded like my mother's asked, "But what about you? Your happiness?" I shrugged it off. Rolled over on my side. Every time I shut my eyes, I felt the tepid water again in my mouth and nose. Heard my own voice begging. Saw the men laughing as if one of them had pushed me into a swimming pool, not tortured me for being a suspected witch.

Eventually I fell asleep. I had a long dream I was made out of ruled notebook paper and simultaneously no one believed me and complained when I did paperlike things. I bent and blew away in the wind, and a man called me dramatic. I wrote on myself, and a woman called me disgusting. How could I do that in a public place? It rained and when I bent over, I tore open my throat. The doctor who stapled me together chided me about my life habits. Kids like you think you're invincible. Do you know what rain can do to your lungs?

In the morning, everyone was still wearing their headphones, and no one would let me shower. I ate tasteless oatmeal and stank. For lunch I ate the bread and lettuce out of a cheap cheese-and-lettuce sandwich they served me and stank. The only sound was the loud spraying of someone washing dishes. I was tempted to wander into the kitchen and scream at the person to rinse me too. In my cell between meals, I was careful not to talk to myself. Sometimes I walked the eight steps of the room. I squatted and dipped against the wall like I used to do in my office at work between meetings, when I felt like I would scream if I had to respond to another email.

In my head I alternated between arguing with myself about if leaving the island had been the right choice and calming myself by thinking over the spells I had read. Linden had shown me one of the few violent ones that were still preserved in the library. Five women who had been wronged by the same man could join hands, recount all the violence he had done, and offer him a chance to repent. If he hesitated or hedged, the man would begin to ash. The spell would kill only the most unrepentant of men, but every one who survived the spell would at least be a little bit shorter and always have the scent of fresh-struck matches.

The door swung open. Two men wearing headphones led me to another conference room, where the Bills were waiting. Today the Bills were Casual Sweater Bills. Ties and formal shirts beneath, but Navy Blue and Camel Bill. I realized their names probably weren't Bill, but they had given me a standard fake name in case I was a witch. So many folktales we were taught in school were reminders that once a witch knew your name, you were toast.

"So," one of the Bills said. They were both smiling. Even their teeth were excessively normal. Straight but with crooked bottoms, not too white, not too yellow. "We found someone who will take custody of you."

The Bills walked me through it. I couldn't live alone with another woman. I couldn't gather with more than two women without a man's supervision for the next six months. The exception to that would be in workplaces where a strong security system was in place. I would have to check in biweekly with a court-appointed monitor. My guardian would also have to go to meetings to be checked for enchantments, as well as to report on my progress. If I violated these terms, I could be fined or subjected to further testing or imprisoned, or all of the above. A minor infraction was a two-thousand-dollar fine, but fines could be as high as a million dollars. If I couldn't afford the fines, it would be an immediate trial. If I did anything suspicious or if there were reports against me, fines or an immediate closed trial. I could be jailed for the rest of my life. I could not leave the country for any reason. I could not possess any cats.

It felt small, but I refused to smile or make my posture non-threatening. I kept my arms crossed. I nodded. I was so tired of diminishing myself. But even in those moments, a small squirrel-like voice inside me encouraged me to stay pleasing, unobtrusive. The whole talk they were giving me was reminding me again that morality and consequences were based on money. There was no such thing as morals or societal norms because it was clear again you could do whatever you wanted if you had enough money.

If I chose, I could register myself as a witch. But if I did, I could have no money in an account in my name, only in a man's; I could be only self-employed to keep companies safe and protected against the liabilities of hiring a witch. No cell phones or social media: I would have to install a landline and hire a court-verified assistant to monitor all my calls. My entire life would be monitored unless a man was willing to pay fees and take responsibility for me. One of the Bills said in a way I could tell he thought was helpful that many witches were employed as artists and performers. They had a man in their life establish an LLC and work as their manager. I would have to get permission from cities to be able to live there or be there without supervision. When I turned sixty-eight, I would have the option of surrendering myself to a state care facility for unmarried elderly women. Another round of talking through the fines and other punishments that could happen to me as a registered nonhostile witch.

"What happens to men who are accused of witchcraft?" I asked.

"Men can't do magic."

"Why not?"

The Bills exchanged a look. One tilted his head, the other spoke. "Why is the sky blue? Why is there gravity? Why does the sun exist? We can attempt to explain, but the root of why our universe is this way is always going to be impossible to articulate."

I knew I had to be careful, that saying the wrong thing would make this all start over again.

"But why are only women capable of being witches?"

In a ramble they talked about genes and parts of the brain and the character of women. They were made to be predisposed toward emotions and overreacting and the forces of everything. There were scientific studies proved women just weren't as strong as men. One of the Bills described magic as an invisible force that was everywhere in the air and water, and women's immune systems couldn't always keep up with the constant bombardment. I nodded and nodded. Each thing that came out of their thin-lipped, spitty mouths was progressively nonsensical. They confirmed what I knew but needed affirmed again: anything can make sense to a person as long as it helps them feel powerful. I could argue with them that gender expression does not equal sex assigned at birth. I could poke at the laws and ask why gay men were still prosecuted in some states for witchcraft if only women could be witches. There were so many flaws in their logic, as they talked and talked. These men could spout off nonsense like this for hours if I continued to listen and nod. Their tones were more and more confident the longer they spoke, and everything was a jumble of imagination and half-understood science.

Were people always this stupid? I wondered, and if so, how did we still exist?

Finally, one of the Bills got bored, cleared his throat, and said we should get back on track. If I chose to be registered as a witch, I would either have an IUD inserted or be sterilized. A judge would rule the best course of action: Did I seem remorseless, irrefutably a witch? Or if I found the right man, could I be coaxed back to a righteous life?

Nothing on any website, nothing in any pamphlet, had said this.

It would have been better if they had looked openly, cartoonishly malicious, their true faces finally revealed. But one Bill was blank and bored, clearly tired of spending time with me and on this case. He did not like paperwork or spouting off legal terms. His eyes were on the form, and I could see that none of this meant anything to him other than some boss above him in the organization would be obnoxious to him if he didn't do all the right steps.

The other Bill was giving me a sympathetic look. His eyes were on my face. His lips were soft. I could tell he thought that finally here was something I could understand. The anger and exhaustion and fear on my face were because I wanted to be a mother. He could see me as a little girl holding a doll or maybe a teenager at a slumber party turning to a friend at night and saying, "I always wanted to have three kids—two boys and a little girl."

I wanted my independence. To let my mind be changed by circumstance, by love, by the ways every person can shift over years and years of living. My hands shook with rage. My signature on the form, acknowledging I understood the laws and what happened next, didn't look like anything I had ever written before—a monstrous scrawl, claws forced to balance a pen.

Later, I would ask myself why I didn't question this more. Why didn't I keep trying to make them answer my questions? Why didn't I refuse to sign? Why didn't I try to run away? My head forced underwater, lungs and nostrils burning, the way the men laughed, the stink of me, the way everything in that place was engineered to remind me because I was a woman who was not obeying, I was nothing. It's easy when you feel like someone to judge another person who feels like nothing.

They handed me a bag with the clothes I had been wearing in the hospital. My wallet had been found on the beach and turned in, but unfortunately, my phone was gone. I signed a form acknowledging I had received everything. I agreed to pay eighty-five dollars so I could keep the clothes I was wearing because I did not have a suitable shirt to leave in. I had to pay another one hundred dollars to cover the costs of my meals. The state comped my medical care and room because it was my first offense. If I racked up additional offenses, at least in Michigan, I could be asked to pay state-assessed fees for the use of those facilities.

The door swung open, and a woman led in Preston. I couldn't believe he was there. I wanted to hug him, I wanted to tell him he was an idiot, I wanted to say this was a bad idea. I couldn't help being flattered he had come all this way to help me. Preston signed the forms agreeing to take custody of me; he made appointments to talk to my caseworkers. They kept talking to him, and I knew it was better to not interrupt. He was wearing a blue button-down shirt rolled to his elbows. His forearms and hands made me close my eyes because just those bits of him made me feel so unattractive in comparison. His hair looked extra shiny, and the few times that he came close to me, he smelled like citrus and cedar. How had they known to call him?

The Bills took the paperwork and left us alone for a moment.

He asked, "Jo, can I touch you? Is that all right?"

I nodded.

He stepped over and hugged me. Gently stroked the top of my head, my ear pushed against his chest. I could hear his heartbeat.

"You didn't have to do this," I said.

"I know this is a lot," he said, "and I wish we could've talked it out. But you're going to have to live with me."

"It's too much."

"I got you, okay?" He stroked my back. I relaxed into him. "You smell terrible. Terrible."

"We're going to have to burn these clothes." His hands felt so good.

"Angie called me. She said your dad . . ." He trailed off. I knew what he didn't want to say. My dad had refused to come.

"Thank you," I said.

"I know you would do the same for me," Preston said.

I nodded, but I didn't know if that was true. I couldn't imagine letting him live with me without a long conversation, more dates, admitting to him that he was in my phone as Party City, talking more about our future, kids, careers, let alone everything he had just agreed to. Our lives were tied together now. I took a step backward. His eyes were bright. He was smiling and sure. I took Preston's hand. Fit my fingers between his.

27.

Preston didn't drive me to his old apartment but instead to a small house on the city's west side. It was a neighborhood I had always loved: ancient trees reaching their hands to one another across the sidewalks and streets, big porches where families seemed to always be eating ice cream together and having conversations that would be remembered as the sepia-toned good old days, and a coffee shop I used to walk to when I was an undergrad and all the baristas gave me free refills while I spent hours trying to make everything I had heard in lectures and skimmed from textbooks fit into straight, followable lines.

"I thought it might be better if we lived somewhere new together," he said, his voice shy. His eyes were on the steering wheel. "We can always choose somewhere else, though, if that's better. It'll take some paperwork, but we could do it."

I knew he was underplaying the incredible amount of work it had taken for him to make this all happen, but I let it go. The leaves were orange and mauve in the golden autumn evening light. He told me the tree in the backyard was a mulberry. And even though mulberry trees were nightmares for allergies, the previous owners said the fruit was truly special. The house had belonged to an older couple who had decided to move to Florida rather than face another Michigan winter. Preston and I held hands as we walked up to our new home. Everything between us felt scrubbed new. I noticed the size of his hand, and the way he used his thumb to rub the back of my hand made me step closer to him.

On one corner of the concrete porch were the initials I + F. The screen door needed to be replaced, but the white door behind it looked like a gorgeous tooth. It was so much warmer down here than it had been in the Upper Peninsula, and it felt so good. Inside, all the hardwood floors creaked and yawned and said hello. All the walls were hideous beige and muted espressos, with one yellow snow outlier in the kitchen. But with each step I took, my heartbeat was saying, "This is home."

"I love it," I said and meant it.

We kissed for the first time since being reunited. His mouth warm and soft against mine. When we stopped, our arms remained linked around each other. Then he paused and said, "I can smell you again. I think I got used to it in the car, but, I'm sorry." When I got out of the shower, his gym bag was waiting for me outside the door. I pulled on a pair of too-big basketball shorts and a sweatshirt that was just right and went downstairs and talked paint colors, what needed to be fixed, what we wanted our home to feel like. Being fresh from the shower, wearing his clothes, trying to plan what a life could be like in that house all made me feel safe. He kept holding my hand. I didn't think of Linden and the island. I was swept away by the effort he was making for me. I thought more about the guilt I felt in having kept him distant from me for so long.

Looking back at this, I still can't feel anything other than the wide-mouthed giddiness of seeing someone working so hard to make me feel loved. Sometimes, I try to chip away at the moment. I think about how Preston did all those things without asking me. His agreeing to take me in, the house, the way he persuaded my boss to let me keep my job. He did all this without me. And how could that ever lead to a true partnership if one person made all the big decisions and the other was left to respond, Well, there's nothing I can do at this point but say okay?

I'm an adult. I know that even if relationships could somehow begin on the magical best of terms—every decision measured and considered in tandem with one another, feelings and thoughts equally shared, great sex, a mutual respect for boundaries and a willingness to build healthy ones—there's no guarantee that a couple would stay that way or even survive. I know only something like 0.01 percent of relationships in the history of people have somehow begun in the way that I think is best. And everyone's definition of best varies because the term and our ideas of love are subjective.

But all of those things didn't wipe away the fact that Preston had chosen all of this; I could only nod my head in agreement.

I was the one who knew exactly what would happen to me if things fell apart between us, how little protection I had. For him, if things fell apart, he could easily find someone new. Men were rarely blamed for witchcraft; they were always victims of seduction and perfidy. It was simultaneous and overwhelming—the amount of gratitude and disempowerment I felt when I thought of the life Preston had snapped together for us. Was this how my mother felt every day before she left?

"I know this is a lot all at once," Preston said, pushing me back into the moment. It made me feel better to see that he too was feeling weird about the sudden momentum of togetherness we were experiencing. After a year of literally fucking around, there were new negotiations, new things to learn. We hadn't ever said we were in love (or that we weren't in love). But here was our house glowing with the candlelight heat, and here we could start something new together.

We ate takeout on the floor. I waited for him to ask me where I'd been, what had happened to me during the days I was missing. But instead he kept putting more food on my plate. He put a hand on my shoulder. Sometimes gently rubbed my neck as if I were a cat who had scrambled in the door at the smell of food. He told me a convoluted story about work drama I couldn't follow but appreciated how ordinary it was, how it only gave me room to give advice, or to laugh, or to judge. We kissed slowly and the tenderness of how he was touching me made me want to cry.

"Are you okay?" he asked while putting more eggplant on his plate.

"No," I said and bit into an eggroll.

After a few days, even though Preston encouraged me to continue using my sick time, I went back to work. It was better to rip this Band-Aid off than build up a big sticky mess about how people were going to treat me. Over email the night before, my boss had made me promise to work for only a few hours in the morning. When I got there, she was waiting outside my office. She held both my hands and looked deeply into my eyes. I willed myself not to blink. I couldn't tell if the gesture was supposed to be comforting for me or for her. She searched my face for, what? The mark of evil? An unnatural red glow, a 666 in my left pupil, the Devil's face smiling back at her? But she saw only boring, slightly bloodshot brown eyes looking back at her. I squirmed under her touch.

"To be honest, Jo, I can't believe they're going to let you continue on here. If I were your case manager, I would assume all of this would be too tempting."

"I'm not a witch." I smiled while I said it, but a malicious part of me wanted to bake a loaf of bread with her name on it, hang it somewhere, and let it begin to molder.

She smiled but didn't mean it, tried to make her tone light. "I'll be keeping an eye on you." Her hands stayed on my wrists, squeezed for a moment, and then, finally, she let go.

At the staff meeting, her eyes kept coming back to me even though I had nothing to contribute. I took notes and looked at everyone who was speaking, even though it was an ordinary weekly check-in. Everyone knew I had been gone. They had gotten an email about the situation a few days before and had been encouraged to report me to the Bureau of Witchcraft if I acted in strange or menacing ways. I had worked there long enough to know everything would be repeated in emails, but I felt certain it was in my best interest to be extra engaged and put on a performance that showed how much this work meant to me. The only person who didn't at some point watch me during the staff meeting was a new intern who was staring at her cell phone underneath the table.

The museum was different to me now. I went to the exhibit of Blood Moon's work. I had missed the opening party for the donors. One of my co-workers told me that several board members had hated it, thinking it glorified modern witchcraft.

"What does that even mean?" I asked.

My co-worker laughed. She turned and shook her head at the television showing the video of the woman eating the terracotta pot. "How is that making witchcraft look sexy and fun?"

"Some people only want art that shows it's absolutely miserable to not be a rich, white man," I said.

"Look at you, returning to work with some hot takes."

"Tell me I'm wrong," I laughed. When my co-worker laughed too, my shoulders eased.

Most of the exhibit was just as I had thought, only art. But there were a few things: the bright red glass bubble, the staircase with thirteen steps, a small doll I hadn't noticed before I left that had the heartbeat of magic. When I was near these pieces, I could hear each one exhaling more and more of itself into the air. I put my hand on the stairs and felt the gentlest heartbeat, slow and steady, but it had never been there before. I kept my face down, didn't want anyone to ask what I was thinking. The stairs would make someone who was exposed enough to them feel saturated with longing. A tinged-red world, a heightening obsession with the color from the large glass circle.

The doll sat in an Eames lounge chair, its slack cotton body positioned in what was supposed to approximate relaxation. The placards on the wall next to it explained it was a meditation on sleep, on being consumed by the need for objects, on what it meant to be a woman who was only a vessel for other people's dreams. I reached out a tentative finger, touched its woven yarn braids gently. A curse pulsed within its threads: a nightmare in which you're the only one who knows you're a fish and you're trying to convince everyone around you that you are not a person, you are a trout. A milkshake filled with glass you know you shouldn't drink but you keep drinking. You are in charge of throwing three simultaneous open houses for needy eighteen-year-olds. Each teen is enraged that everyone has given them a gift of a laundry hamper filled with stinky potato salad.

There was nothing I could do about the curses. Linden had talked to me about dissolving spells in general: sometimes it took large groups of witches. Healing damage caused by spells involved specially prepared remedies, meditation, and sometimes years. Thinking her name made me wish she was by my side. She was the only friend I had now that knew everything about me. I couldn't tell Angie about the island or my mother because it would put her at risk, and I refused to do that. I wanted to take Linden through the museum, to see what she thought about the art, what she could tell me about the mummy in the basement. I wanted to see her eyes crinkle up with inspiration while looking at the cursed boots. I wanted to hear her tell me about our history. I let out a breath. I wanted to kiss her in one of the stalls of the women's bathroom, one of the few places where I would know we wouldn't be caught on camera and forced to watch the footage with my boss. They couldn't fire me for being queer—although every other year it felt like I was writing desperate letters and going to marches and sending money to make sure that right, the simple I-deserve-to-be-employed right, wasn't taken away from me.

All I wanted to do was live like everybody else. I didn't want to worry all the time because people just didn't like that I was different.

*   *   *

That evening, Angie came over to my new house with Preston with some of my stuff. She hugged me.

"I thought I would never see you again," she said.

"I'm okay, I'm okay."

She looked exhausted: dark circles beneath her eyes, a line on her forehead I had never seen before.

"I wish you could come home," Angie said.

"I don't. I want you to be safe. I'm sure they investigated you when everything happened."

"Only questions. Nothing more."

I nodded.

"My mom got so scared, though, that she made me agree to go on three dates through the matchmaking site."

We sat down on the floor together. Preston's couch would be delivered in the morning. He was in the kitchen making dinner and listening to softboy hip hop. Lyrics about yearning pushed up against icy production.

"A site for dating?"

"No. Marriage." Angie leaned her head against the wall. It still smelled like fresh paint. "She wants me married by the end of January."

"But how?"

She explained to me that her mother had found a service that in addition to "love marriages" would also discreetly pair up gay men and women. Michigan mostly left gay men alone, but some states still had laws on the books that equated homosexuality with witchcraft. It seemed the only safe way to be a gay man in most states was to be white with blond hair and to wear boat shoes and say things like "I keep my private life private." At the most recent protest I'd gone to, we put up pictures of every gay man who had been tried for witchcraft in the previous five years. Only three of the 279 tried in Michigan had been white. All three had been poor.

Angie was talking about signing a contract for a "marriage of understanding." Each of you could have other relationships, the man could not initiate divorce for a full five years, and you would work together to find palatable solutions if you wanted kids. Angie was going on three dates next week. Two of the three men were gay men who preferred for many reasons to not be out. The other was a straight guy who wanted companionship but identified as ace. She would date them all week one; do another round of dates with them two weeks from then, unless any of them was so heinous she could not bear to watch them slurp down another bowl of soup; and then, hopefully, choose one to keep dating for another month. If that month went well, engagement.

"I'm so sorry," I said.

"No, I'm sorry."

I shook my head.

"No," Angie said, "I mean, I told the police the last time I saw you, you were getting on a boat. Once they found out it was about your mother, well, they stopped treating it like a mental health crisis or like a potential abduction."

"It's not your fault. I should've known anything I did that had to do with her would be investigated."

I took Angie's hand. I looked up at the ceiling and continued talking. "Somewhere, there is a place where we could just be. No suspicions. We could marry who we want, when we want. We could fly rather than sink through life."

"New Zealand?"

We laughed, and then both of us pulled out our phones and looked at all the steps it would take to immigrate.

28.

"How long have you been together?" the monitor asked me. I looked around his office. Gray desk, an oversized black laptop, and white walls. A long black scuff on the white tiled floor. The decorations in it were a poster about what to do if you felt like you had been enchanted and a framed black-and-white photograph of a moose walking down a highway. The monitor seemed mostly bored, although he kept jiggling his knee in a way where he would hit the edge of his desk, wince, stop, and start again.

"Seriously, for two weeks. Before that, we were casual for about a year."

The monitor looked to Preston for confirmation. He nodded yes. I crossed my arms over my chest.

If you thought you had been enchanted, one recommendation was to drink warm water mixed with apple cider vinegar and lemon while waiting for members of the Bureau of Witchcraft to show up. It was supposed to make you vomit out any curses in your bloodstream. Did you feel not like yourself? Shivery? Did you hear someone's voice telling you what to do? Another flyer on the monitor's desk advised, drink a solution of salt, holy water if you could get it, lemons, and cayenne pepper to break the curse on your mind. I wondered how many people were accused of witchcraft for people's dumb mistakes and then reminded myself that false accusations also had financial penalties for the accusers.

"Josephine, do you feel tempted toward evil?"

"What is evil?"

"Do you ever think about killing Preston? Do you hear voices? Do you feel like causing harm to others?"

I crossed my arms even tighter. I wanted to say maybe these were the questions that should be asked of people before they buy guns. I also looked at Preston. He was giving me a look that conveyed that he too thought this was very stupid, but it was better to get it done quickly. "No."

"Do you hear your mother's voice? Does she ever appear to you?"

She could, but she won't, I thought. "No," I said aloud.

The monitor asked Preston if I had seduced him, offered him powers, or the chance to commune with a great evil to get him to be in a relationship with me.

He smiled for a moment. I could tell he was thinking about me offering to let him meet my best friend, Satan, for drinks, thinking of making a joke. I squeezed his hand. Do it, I thought. He shook his head, made his face blank and voice earnest. "Honestly, if anyone's being taken advantage of, it's Josephine. She's an independent person. I know it's hard for her to rely on other people."

"You didn't answer my question," the monitor said. He wore clear-rimmed glasses and had a circular scar on his left cheek that looked like the remains of one monumental zit from twenty-five years ago. I realized I had seen him once on Tinder. His profile was midlife cringe about finding someone "with whom" to enjoy cabernet sauvignon, actual champagne from France, serious books, and to see the world. No kids. In a photo of him with a dog he was making the same slightly constipated expression he was making at Preston. It was not a cute face.

"No, she has not promised me any cool wizard powers, seduced me with a magic vagina, or invited me to a party at Satan's house."

I looked at my feet and tried not to smile. His voice when it was sarcastic had a tone that almost always made me laugh, even when it was aimed at me.

"If you two aren't going to take this seriously," the monitor said, "I'm going to fine you each a thousand dollars. Continued attitude issues can result in the two of you being separated. Come on, guys. This can be easy." He talked in the tone of an exasperated high school basketball coach.

Preston reached for my hand. I clasped his. I had told him what had happened to me after I had been found, and he had said, "That's fucking sick." He had done that cis man thing where he was sure if we talked to the right people, if we filed complaints, talked to a lawyer, we could challenge the system from within. So many men think if they can just talk and maybe lightly joke with the right man, they can fix almost anything. Then a few days later, he had said, "I think I reacted the wrong way when you told me what happened to you."

"You did," I said, and we left it there.

"Sorry," I said to the monitor, "we're both just nervous and have bad coping mechanisms."

"I'm sorry, too," Preston said, but his voice was bordering on insincere.

The monitor opened a file. He told me my boss had said I was committed to the workplace but not in a way she found menacing or suspect. She said I was kind and driven and was clearly trying not to stray. No one had gotten suspiciously sick or had acted in a way that she felt could be traced to me. All my co-workers felt either neutral, unafraid, or safe around me. I could continue to return to the office at this time.

Our neighbors—surveyed without being told who they were being surveyed about—had said the neighborhood felt mostly normal. One woman claimed to have heard an owl hooting again and again, directly over her bed. A man said he had felt eyes were watching him from the ceiling. Another had a rash that wouldn't go away but maybe it was from eating cheese. The monitor took me through each claim, asking me if I had consorted with the owl or summoned it to annoy my neighbor. Did I know the man in the house three doors down? Was I attracted to him? Was I willing my spirit to watch him in bed, to watch him undress? In general, though, my neighbors were mostly unwilling to answer the surveys sent to their addresses. The Bureau would continue to assess my presence in the neighborhood.

The only image I had of the man three doors down was of him yelling at his house, "If you don't order a pizza right now, I'll die." It might've been a joke, but the way he yelled it hadn't sounded like a joke. Preston and I sometimes texted that to each other when we couldn't figure out what to eat for dinner.

"No, I do not will my spirit into his home. I don't think about him at all."

"Did you point or gesture at your neighbor and cause that rash?"

I thought of all the people I wished I had cursed. The man I'd gone on a date with who had grabbed my ass in front of people to look cool, and when I had pushed him off, he had berated me for making him look bad. The kids in high school who had consistently been racist to me. The girl I had dated for three months who had cheated on me with her art history TA. She was just "getting tutoring," it was normal to get texts from your tutor. The boys I had known in high school who had yelled "Hey, Witch Tits" at me whenever I was walking alone. My mom. My dad when he lectured me about being the right kind of woman. My dad now, still MIA except for a 5 a.m. text that read he was praying for me. I didn't know how to answer the text. Showed it to Preston and he rolled his eyes. My grandma on my dad's side. My boss whenever I saw her bumper sticker. All those people deserved rashes. I felt sure in those moments if I had the ability to point at them and make them itch for an hour, I would be a much happier person.

"No, I don't think about that person at all. And I don't have magic abilities."

The monitor took his glasses off. He stared at me with his small, heavy-lidded eyes. On his Tinder profile—I realized the reason why I remembered it—he had included an emoji of a champagne bottle. I had shown it to Angie and we had spent a while trying to figure out if he was referencing a weird sex thing or the size of his penis or just his love of champagne. It was why someone so un-extraordinary had stayed with me. I couldn't remember his name. But I could see the text—Actual champagne from France—and feel the look on my face at this annoying expression.

Preston squeezed my fingers. The monitor looked at me for a long time. His face was cold, and I could see he liked making me look him in the eyes. He was thinking deeply about punishing me, making sure we wouldn't come into his office again without feeling afraid. This man didn't care if I was a witch. What he cared about was making us, me, respect him.

I sat up straight and let go of Preston's hand.

"I'm not a witch," I said and for a moment, even I believed it. "And I'm sorry that you have to go through this trouble."

He put his glasses back on, leaned back in his seat. He handed Preston a pamphlet about how to know when you are a witch's sex slave. He handed me one about being a pure woman and told us he would see us in two weeks.

29.

There was the black cupboard where Preston took fresh white paint and wrote J + P on the inside. Every day our coffee cups saw J + P. I would sometimes run my hands over the letters and then feel embarrassed by how sentimental I felt for something I was still in the middle of. He had said I love you while we were painting the kitchen, turning it white instead of the rude yellow it had been when we moved in. I had surprised myself by saying it back easily and not agonizing over whether I felt it.

There was our rug patterned with cranes where he unbuttoned my shirt so slowly that I yelled "Hurry up, please," and we stopped to laugh at how my voice sounded, at the off-kilter politeness. And how after sex on that rug, he dabbed Neosporin and placed Band-Aids on my knees, my elbows, my ass. All the places where the friction of us versus the plush rug created burns and wounds that ached for days.

There was our kitchen table where we sat with friends drinking, and he kept a hand on my knee. We kept turning toward each other to see if the other was laughing, and yes, we were laughing at all the same things that our beautiful drunk friends were saying.

My dad once said to me the best foundation for a home and for a relationship was laughter. If you could laugh together any-time, anywhere, it was possible for it to last forever. At the time, I thought that was musty and impractical. But there were nights when I would lie awake and instead of worrying, think about his advice. The way his eyes were shiny as he told it to me. I could not remember my parents laughing together much.

When I came back from the island, my dad texted me to say he was praying for me. Two weeks later, he texted again to say he was happy I was fine, but he thought it was in both of our best interests to have some time apart. And that I should start going to church.

There was the bed where I said Yes, where I said How could this be getting better, where even my mouth got so wet from what Preston was doing to me I felt like all my teeth were going to fall out onto the pillow.

There was the bed where I lay awake at night and felt a restlessness that pushed my eyes open. I would watch the darkness of our bedroom ceiling, and my brain would tilt again toward the fact that everything I had was because of him. The house, the ability to go to work, having my own money, being able to send unmonitored emails, to even live in this city. I would turn and look at his dark hair, his soft lips dry with dreams, and I would remind myself Preston was good to me. That I thought he was funny and kind. I loved him. It was impractical and stupid for me to resent everything I had was because of him. I turned and shook my head.

There was the pink-and-green blanket I would pull over my head and think if I were given three wishes, I would long to be a simple person. I wanted to be someone who only wanted to be in love, who didn't think about what affected that love. Some girls I went to high school with seemed so blissfully average. They were still with their high school or college sweethearts. They had kids and worked as schoolteachers or administrative assistants or were fitness instructors. They shared memes about living, laughing, and rosé. And if it weren't a wholesome meme, they were sharing updates on their wide-eyed kids who were all somehow geniuses or needed people to buy a bunch of candy bars or wrapping paper so they could have music classes that would lead to them being the geniuses they were meant to be. I knew nothing was ever as good as it looked on social media, that often it was just a way to construct the lives people wanted to be living, each like, each click helping to build another day or year of the Me someone wished they were. But I couldn't help sometimes lying awake at night wondering how much easier my life might be if I wanted those things. And even more, I wanted to be someone who, when she got those things, could be content in them. I didn't want to lie awake at night and wonder Do I love you? or Do I have to love you to keep the life you gave me?

If I toured the house I grew up in, I could point at so many places—the living room couch, my bedroom, the kitchen sink, the front steps—where I thought or said, "I'm never getting married."

There was the tiny laundry room where we fought over the right way to use the machine. Permanent Press does not mean you can just dump in everything. Stop using scented detergent, it makes me feel sick. The dryer settings need to be changed for jeans or I'll have none left.

There was the black-tiled shower where Preston washed my hair and said, "I've always loved your hair. It's so curly and dramatic." He was careful to not get soap in my eyes. Massaged my scalp and said, "Beautiful, beautiful." He soaped my back and my breasts and kissed me hard on the mouth.

There was the white stove where, while I scrambled eggs, I wondered if I should tell him the truth about magic, the island, my mother, the things I had seen and done. The thought sloshed around inside me whenever I made something normal and ordinary like breakfast: Is it possible for him to love me if he doesn't know the truth about me? I wanted him to see me fly into the air.

I wanted to kiss him while we both held lumps of charcoal. When we surfaced for air, we would both be holding diamonds. I wanted him to feel the giddiness that comes from doing something extraordinary and knowing you can do it again.

There was the dinner table where my case manager told me I was being exemplary. He was so excited and proud of me. We had become polite after the uncomfortable first meeting. Even if evil had looked me in the face, I was building a new, untainted life. Preston and I looked at our plates. We kept the case manager's glasses filled with wine and water. We lied and said I had made dinner. He talked on and on. His forearms were so hairy they could've been two animals emerging from his torso.

There was our yellow front door where we handed out Halloween candy. The kids were dressed as cartoon characters we had never heard of that a few tried to explain in their spooky, high voices—cats, birds, and clunky robots made from cardboard. Their parents were dressed as tired or a little drunk. Preston and I wore matching skeleton pajamas. "We look like we're one of those terrible Instagram couples," he said and then kissed me. "That might be the grossest thing you ever said to me," I said and kissed him back. On the island, I would've been meditating and wearing a long black dress. I would've chosen someone else in the community, in secret, to pray for and give offerings to their ancestors. That morning, the museum had brought a mummified witch up to the lobby for people to pay their respects to. We were alone. Her skin still brown, her gray hair and fingernails ever longer. She opened her eyes. They were brown and the youngest thing about her. "May the new year be sweet to you, little sister," she said in a voice like a slowed-down cricket. I put my hand to the glass, and she turned her mouth into a hideous grin, then shut her eyes and went still again. None of the children were dressed as witches or ghosts. A few with obnoxious parents were dressed as saints. They refused candy and tried to hand me pamphlets with small shaking hands. Even those kids were cruelly adorable. Preston didn't ask me if I wanted kids. That night, watching them say thank you, watching them give me their best meows and arfs, I thought, Okay, okay.

There was the new couch where I was a little drunk when I told him, "I never want to get married, I've never wanted to get married, it's not a you thing, it's an everything thing." And he said, "Wait, are you breaking up with me?" I said, "And what are you going to do with your life if we break up?" And I waited for him to say something terrible, but I ended up more grossed out by myself, because a small part of me was disappointed that all he did was wait with a patient expression for me to keep talking. Asked me what he could do to help me feel good in this relationship.

There was the old leather couch we threw in the basement and went downstairs once to fuck on for nostalgia's sake.

There was the pillow where I covered my face and wondered if I had been so distant, so unwilling to know him before all this because I had seen enough to know it was very possible to love him.

There was the notebook I wrote joke ideas in when I couldn't sleep. I started earnestly writing about my life, trying to figure out why I couldn't conform. I wrote my first spell in that notebook. A way to infuse a whisper into a living tree, one only another witch could hear. Sometimes, I wrote about the spells I had seen in the museum and tried to reverse engineer them. The more time I spent around in the exhibits, the more I could hear beyond their heartbeats. I could sometimes hear words spoken hesitantly as if a person were thinking aloud, the sound of materials being gathered, or the scratching of a pen.

I kept trying to figure my way into a joke. What is the difference between having a husband and clinical depression? Both want you to give up your friends, lie in bed, and don't let you eat enough. The punch line of having a penis felt too obvious, but I wondered if I said it the right way, found the right framing, could it work? Or was the joke too dark?

There was the scratched-up counter where I opened the mail, tore into an envelope and found the bracelet Linden had made for me, which had been deemed officially not-magical and re-turned. I slipped it back on my wrist. When it touched my skin again, just like the art at work, I felt a small magical breath. When I was at work and felt my boss's eyes on me, I would hold on to the bracelet and feel a little less alone. Sometimes, it would feel like Linden was sitting next to me, ready to tell me everything floating through her big, beautiful brain.

There was the bed where Preston told me about how his dream job was to have his own wine shop. One of those small stores filled with interesting bottles where everyone who worked there looked happy because they all loved wine, and people came in just to browse and read the advice about how a particular wine tasted and what should be paired with it. I could see him standing in a cute shop, being knowledgeable but not intimidating. "You should do it," I said to him. "Let's find a way."

The backyard I avoided in early November because it was filled with crows. They kept calling to me, "We know you understand us. Witch, witch, witch. Come and have a conversation with us." They were disappointed by my bad manners. Sometimes I whispered to them, but they yelled back, "Speak up, speak up."

There was the porch where Preston turned to me and asked me if I wanted to start talking about getting married. It was December and we were cupping hot chocolates from the coffee shop down the street and watching snow fall. We could go to counseling, we could work out a prenup, we could talk about all the ways to do it that would help me feel safe. "Both of my parents have abandoned me now," I said. "Emotionally and physically." "I know," he said. Preston's voice was calm. "And it's awful." A therapist I went to briefly in my earlier twenties had said when sessions were working, the whole family was sometimes present. I wondered if, from what we had discussed, she had known my parents better than I did, ever will. Why couldn't I accept they had both chosen absence? I was twenty-eight years old. How could they keep surprising me? Maybe if I accepted them as who they are, it wouldn't hurt so much the next time they disappointed me.

There was the bathroom sink where I brushed my teeth, paused when I saw my phone alive with new messages. It was Angie texting to say she was getting married in two months. She wasn't ready to talk about it. I had to come to the ceremony, and I had to make it fun.

There was the basement where Preston and I stored our attempts at making his grandmother's kimchi and my grandfather's beer recipes. "Everything they wrote down was off," he complained. We kept trying.

There was the uncomfortable chair I sat in when his annoying friends came over and drank all the good whisky. I thought about the pink door in the sky—its scream like two cats fighting for keeps—and I longed suddenly to open it. I stood up and poured myself another drink.

There was the wood floor where I lay spread out supine after hurting my back. I had pulled it getting out of the bathtub. Only the floor felt good—the bed a little too soft, the couch's velvet easy to slip off. I should've stayed on the island, I let myself think. I didn't let it happen again.

In every room of that house, I told myself, If you keep acting normal, you can have a life.

In every room I told myself I had so many things other people were desperate for, so shut up and lean in to being happy.

In every room I wished my parents would tell me how to be the kind of person they could love, that they could like, that they could always be there for, because I was so tired of feeling not good enough.

30.

One day an envelope came in the mail that was crumpled as if the mailman had known it wasn't worth the time he had spent delivering it. I recognized my father's handwriting immediately. There was no return address, the stamp was upside down. I examined the stamp closely. It was a green-white-and-red Christmas tree. Upside down, it looked like an expensive umbrella. I considered throwing the letter away and trying to call him again.

"Just open it, Jo," Preston said when he saw me fussing with it on the couch. He put down the two coffee mugs.

"You read it," I said.

He took the envelope from me and opened it. Inside was a piece of neatly folded computer paper. The letter was typed and then signed. It looked impersonal, like maybe it was a Christmas newsletter. I tried to imagine what my dad could've written: "I grew a foot-long zucchini. Work is work. My daughter might be a witch. All my love to you and yours."

Preston shook his head. Some of his hair was sticking up in the back and I reached over and smoothed it down.

"You don't have to," he said.

I took it from him.

My dad wrote:

Josephine, it has become clear to me that the biggest mistake I made in my life was marrying your mother. The pain and grief

and hate she has tracked through my door through her actions
and words still linger and have now infected you. You are my
daughter and I love you, but I can't bear to see you following
her path. I have been talking to my pastor and your uncles, and
they have made me think about all the ways I failed you. You
could have had a good life, been a good wife, a good mother,
if I had taken a stronger look into your life and your morals. I
should have made you go to church. I should have warned you
against alcohol and other sins. There were so many times when
I said nothing. I am sorry I failed you so completely. When you
are ready to be married, to recommit yourself to good, I will be
waiting for you with open arms. I love you.

He had signed off as "Dad" in his small prickly cursive.

I read it again. A third time. I wanted to make a joke. When I re-read the line about him talking to my uncles, I wanted to call him.

"Are you pissed or sad or both?" Preston asked.

"Tired."

"You don't have to go to Angie's thing."

"Yes I do." I yawned. I put the letter on the coffee table. Preston was watching me. I couldn't meet his eyes for more than a glance. They were so kind and encouraging me to talk that I knew if I looked for too long, I would start crying because he so clearly wanted to take care of me. "I'm the maid of honor."

"I could come."

"No one wants you to go wedding dress shopping."

Preston took my hand. "Let me at least make you dinner. What-ever you want."

"I know you're trying to take care of me. And I really appreciate it. But I need to process this."

He opened his mouth. Shut it. Preston squeezed my hand and let it go. "Okay," he said.

*　*　*

Later, outside Once Upon a Yes: Bridal and Prom, my monitor was waiting for me. He was wearing a black duster and black sunglasses, and it took all my willpower to remind him we were dress shopping, not having a gunfight inside the matrix.

"Josephine, before you go in, a reminder."

Snow was lightly falling. It brushed against my nose and eyelids. He took off his sunglasses and his eyes were wolf-blue.

"No hand gestures. No chanting. No sacrifices. No encouraging any of these nice women toward evil."

"I understand one thousand percent." It was too cold and I was too tired to even address the ridiculousness of the possibility of anyone finding something to sacrifice in a dress shop.

"You may proceed."

The inside of the store was warm and smelled like a floral cleaning spray. Angie, her mom, and two of her cousins were already looking at the dresses. Lace and tulle and satin and beads. A bottle of champagne was open, and Angie pressed a glass into my hand even before I could take off my mittens. I drank it all in one long gulp before my monitor could say something.

"Looks like someone's ready to party," Mrs. Williams said. She did not look happy to see me, but her voice was light. "Let's cheers."

Angie poured me a much smaller glass, poured another one for my monitor, who surprised me by taking it and clinking it to mine. "Cheers," he said in a hoarse voice.

The monitor set up shop in a small chair in the corner. Took a wedding magazine and opened it on his lap.

A saleswoman approached us. Her hair was dyed bright red, and she was wearing a pink T-shirt with the text I <3 Love printed across her chest. "So, girls, what is the vibe of this wedding?"

"I'm twenty-eight and this ship is going down," Angie said.

Her mother pursed her lips. "I was thinking winter fantasy. White fur, long dresses, maybe a crown made out of greenery, bright blue shoes that will pop against any snow."

I nodded enthusiastically; I wanted her mom to like me again. "Sleigh rides. Lanterns. Antique candelabras on every table."

"A mid-ceremony yeti attack," Angie said, "or maybe the reception could be Donner Party themed. Everything looks like human arms and feet, even the cake."

I laughed. The riffing we used to do was burbling up in me. All the blizzard-based disasters I could think of would have been hilarious wedding themes.

The monitor looked at me and shook his head. I stopped laughing.

"This is a special day," Mrs. Williams said. "Let's take it seriously."

Both of Angie's cousins were looking at their phones and not paying attention. Mrs. Williams was watching the monitor. She handed Angie an expansive dress that would make her look like a cupcake and beckoned me over, led me to a wall of bridesmaid dresses. Ice blue to off white to storm gray. She shoved a mint green one in my hands and hissed under her breath, "You should know better."

"We both know," I whispered back, "that she doesn't want to get married. If she wants to have fun, let her have fun."

"Try this on," she said loudly.

"You promised no green or yellow," said one of the cousins.

"This isn't about you," Mrs. Williams snapped.

I went into the dressing room and tried on the dress. It was a size too big and drooped off me. The combination of the color and the overhead fluorescent lights made me look jaundiced. The fabric was uncomfortable and scratchy on my shoulders. I tried to think of two nice things to say about it and I could only come up with, "I look tall."

"Let me see," Angie called.

I came out, clutching the bodice to me.

"It's beautiful," Mrs. Williams said. "The other girls could wear emerald."

"If you make me wear green," the cousin said, "I won't pose for any of the pictures."

The saleswoman went on a long tangent about feeling our excitement, how it was the most special day of a woman's life to get married, how it was the one day when everything could be exactly what our lives should be. The monitor was nodding in firm agreement. "It's one of life's best pleasures," he said, "to see a happy bride."

Angie's engagement ring was three diamonds with a silver band. It didn't look like anything she would have chosen.

We went to three more stores. I rode with my monitor, while everyone else rode in Mrs. Williams's car. I kept offering to leave, but Angie insisted I stay. She tried on so many dresses: long lace sleeves, a long revealing V-neck back, and so many shades of white everyone else claimed to be able to see—fresh snow, ghost, antique, contemporary—but all I could see was white, white, white.

The only dress she liked was blush pink and silk. It made her look like she should be wearing a large diamond necklace, sipping a martini, and flirting with someone at a candlelit dinner party.

"I love it," I said.

Even Mrs. Williams nodded and said, "Yes, that's you."

Finally, Angie looked at ease.

"I'm sorry, but all brides should wear white," the monitor said.

Mrs. Williams turned to look at him. Her face softened from annoyance to capitulating. "It is tradition," she said.

Angie looked exhausted and irritated. "Who do you think you are?" Angie asked as she stepped toward him. He looked at me. "What makes you think anyone wants to hear your opinion?"

"She's had too much to drink," I said quickly.

Angie's mother grabbed her wrist and whispered something to her.

"We're going to go," I said. I grabbed my coat, gathered my mittens, and headed toward the door. The monitor followed me out. And so did Mrs. Williams.

"Jo, wait."

I finished putting my coat on and turned to her. My breath was dramatic smoke in the winter air. The sun was setting, and night was running in.

Her voice shook as she spoke. "I want to preface this by saying I love you. And I've always appreciated what a good friend you've been to Angie over the years. But I want you to think deeply about whether you should come to the wedding. Your circumstances. You know."

"I understand," I said. It wasn't a lie. Angie had no idea what it was like to truly be in trouble. To have a situation that couldn't be unraveled with a smile or a quip or a wide-eyed "I'm sorry, sir." That old envy loud and howling inside me. I wanted to go in and yell at Angie about how she didn't understand anything. I wanted to thank her for doing what I couldn't.

Instead, I got into my monitor's car. He turned on a talk radio station where a man told a rambling story about how his first wife had tempted him to evil: gambling, smoking, saying lascivious things to waitresses and women in grocery stores. She had been poisoning him.

"Sometimes, I wonder what God was even thinking when he created women," the host said.

"Amen," my monitor said and turned it up a little louder.

31.

I was making myself a cup of tea when I saw a woman standing on the sidewalk looking at our home. The snow and the moon made everything bright. I had to look a second, a third time, before I allowed myself to believe she was there. Linden.

It was a cold night filled with the breathless feeling of an incoming inch of snow. My breath made its own flurries as I walked out toward her. "You're here," I said, and the sound carried down the street in the evening chill. "How are you here?"

Linden was taller than I remembered her being. She was dressed like she had been on the day I first met her: black jeans, black shirt, black boots, bright red lips. The new addition was a short leather jacket with fringe that should have been ridiculous, but I liked her and couldn't help but think it was absolutely right for her. Her hair was buzzed all the way down, so it was only the slightest hint of hair on her scalp.

She stepped toward me and we paused on the sidewalk, my porch light keeping her mostly visible. Preston was inside on the phone talking to his grandmother. Linden and I smiled, tried to negotiate how to greet each other and ended up awkwardly leaning in to a half-hug that turned into a full, real one. "How long has it been for you?" she asked me.

"Three months," I said.

"It's been six months there. Almost spring again." Then, "You smell different. Have you been feeling sad?"

"I'm wearing perfume."

Linden's eyes were on mine. She ignored my answer. "Are you safe?"

"I don't know," I said. We were still holding on to each other's arms as we spoke. "They're watching me for any signs of witchcraft. We shouldn't be out here. I can't be alone with any other women without a man supervising me."

"It must be serious; you're not joking at all." Linden tightened her grip on me. For a moment, when she touched me, all the magic that had been building inside me felt alive. I looked at my hands and they were turning into green glass. There was a mixture of crackles and the tone of a glass being rubbed with fingers dipped into water. I gasped. My face too was changing, even my teeth and hair. In my face, the change was excruciating. Like when you're at the dentist and they start drilling but you haven't been anesthetized enough and you have to mumble not ready, it hurts. Porch lights were reflecting off me, extra bright. I could see my bones and the veins in my hands through the green glass. I knew Linden was seeing my eyes rolling around, my brain suddenly made visible, my tongue still soft and staying flat so it wouldn't hit against the hard new me, all through a layer of my new translucent face.

"Calm down," Linden said. She took a small jar out of her pocket, rubbed an essence on my hands that smelled like rotting animal corpse and lavender. "You're safe, you're okay."

I turned back into flesh. It felt like putting on a sweatshirt fresh from the dryer. I was sweating with the effort. The return to flesh took all my willpower not to faint. I was worried I would shatter if I fell.

"This happens sometimes. We see each other after a long time without magic and our bodies just melt down for a few minutes."

I covered my eyes with my hands. Felt nauseated by the quick slide from flesh to glass and back again. I rubbed the top of my head and reminded myself I was lucky the transformation was quick, impermanent. My entire life could have been glass.

My neighbors' lights were all off. A few windows had the blue shine of someone watching television and probably having one last glass of wine to help them fall asleep. I hoped no one had seen. They probably would've assumed the flash of light was a car's headlights. I let go of Linden, pulled my vape pen out of my coat pocket and took a pull. I offered it to her. She waved it off.

"Can he be trusted?" Linden pointed at the house.

"I think so." I nodded. "I do. I trust him."

"Why do you sound surprised?"

I told her because I couldn't remember the last time I had said that about a man. A friend from work had found out her husband was cheating on her by telling other women he and his wife were separated, hooking up with them, and then, when the fling was over for him, saying he was sorry, but he and his wife were giving it another chance. Two women had messaged her on social media about it after seeing her post pictures revealing her pregnancy. The work friend had eaten carrot stick after carrot stick while saying, "I could slam his head into the fucking dryer, but what can I do? I'm pregnant. No one is going to want to marry a woman pregnant with another man's baby." I had handed her a yogurt because I couldn't think of anything helpful or nice to say. What I had thought is, maybe if her husband had died in a fire or of cancer, yes. But she was right, not many men would want to raise a living scumbag's baby.

"I missed you," Linden said.

She told me her spell had finally worked. On the island she had built her nine-sided house with the help of eight other witches. It needed herbs, magnets, and it had to be placed north. It was working though. Strawberries still were not aging inside it. A calico kitten lived there now and had grown at most a week's worth since. They were going to test it on people soon.

"Should we walk?" Linden asked.

I looked around again. It was cold, and the neighborhood was still mostly holiday empty. I wanted to feel even briefly that my life was entirely my own.

I took her arm. While we clomped down the street in our boots, I told her I'd been thinking a lot about spells, how many of them were about community. What resonated with me beyond the teenager reaction of magic is so, so cool was that we could only safely have magic with one another. I wanted to build a path made from salt and nutmeg and mint that would help anyone flee to safety. It would need stones from all over the world. Hundreds of people would have to work together to make it, to say the incantations for it. But if it worked, people using it couldn't be seen by those trying to harm them as long as they stayed on the path. It could connect different ways to the places where witches lived. I thought maybe if such a path existed, it would be possible to slowly but surely change the world.

"You would need to do it under an eclipse," Linden said. "And we would have to find a way to light it and keep it secure."

We brainstormed more as we walked. At one point, Linden paused and wrote into her notebook. She kept saying, "This is so ambitious," in a way I knew meant her brain was whirring. Few things made me feel happier to be alive than having an idea, telling it to a friend I respected, and having them instantly take it seriously. The more things we said to each other, the bigger and more tangible the path became in my imagination. It would also be beautiful. Pinks and silvers and greens and whites surrounded by floating golden lights. Linden said it would be the kind of thing that would attract friendly spirits. And I could imagine them above it, a cloud of smeared faces urging their descendants to keep going.

She made me feel like I was home again.

We went into the coffee shop. It was mostly empty except for a few students biting their nails and studying and what looked like an awkward break-up. I bought myself a steamer, but Linden insisted on trying a red-eye. As they made our drinks, I watched her look around the shop: the blue espresso machine, the blond-wood seats, the art by kids from the Boys and Girls Club that people were bidding on for a fund-raiser, the rug-pattern couch surrounded by discarded newspapers. It was so warm inside after the freezer of outdoors that all of me felt fogged from the change of temperature.

"I know coffee shops are probably super ordinary to you, but I love them," Linden said. "Every single one smells good, they're loud, and they almost always have a good vibe."

"They make a drink here that's espresso plus cardamom soda."

She looked greedy for it and I asked her how long she had been in town. I hoped the question sounded relaxed.

"Since this morning." Linden told me she had eaten a steak alone at a restaurant for lunch. It had tasted great; she had loved the experience of eating alone somewhere nice and daydreaming. A woman had told her she was jealous of her for being able to eat alone and that had been the most depressing thing Linden had heard in a while. Then she'd gotten a little sick from the richness of the meat and had drunk a lot of water and fallen asleep until about an hour ago. I had so many questions—about what she was doing for money, where she was staying, what she was thinking. Our drinks were called. When I came back with them, Linden was tilting her head a little bit.

"You haven't asked me about her yet."

I dropped the to-go top I had been trying to put on my drink, picked it up, started trying again to put it on.

"What else are you going to do here?" I asked her.

"Don't you want to know how she's doing?"

"No, not really." We could both tell I was lying.

"But she's your mother."

I shrugged. "That's a fact that is simultaneously true and false."

"I thought the path was in honor of her."

"She only helped herself," I said. "I get it, but I don't want to be that way."

"Okay," Linden said. She took a sip of her red-eye. "It's so bad. It's so good. Both the drink and being out here."

From what she had seen of America, everything was simultaneously right and wrong. Like with witches. We still thought of them as something taboo, criminal, bad, but there was a weird space where because of capitalism, they were still everywhere because they made money. It seemed to her that capitalism allowed anything to exist as long as someone could exploit it for money and power. And those things seemed to make room only for loneliness when it came to most people.

"A lot of people know this," I said. "We can articulate it. We can make arguments about it. What you're saying isn't new or wrong."

She frowned a little. Drank more.

We went back to the street, started back toward my house.

"I don't feel comfortable talking about elsewhere," I said, "but when you grow up somewhere and spend your entire life worrying that one day someone will say that you're a witch, that you'll die in poverty or your life will be harder because no man will marry you, or because it feels like every day someone with power is doing something to take things from you for no good reason really except for them keeping their power, it's hard to build a community. You can't even think about changing anything because by the time you're a woman in your twenties, unless you're very lucky, you most likely are only thinking about how to survive."

It was snowing again. The flakes brushed my cheeks, caught in my eyelashes. I took a long gulp of my steamer. Honey and milk. My heart was beating fast from everything I was saying and thinking. For the past hour, I had said all the thoughts that had been building inside me for months. I wanted to go into my house and cry alone in the bathtub to let all the emotions out, feel feet-after-a-babyfoot-treatment smooth.

We linked arms again. The snowflakes were large and looked like moths under the streetlamps.

"Why did you come back here?" Linden said.

"Because for me, it was the right thing to do. I feel a lot of things about the decision, but I don't regret it."

In the distance a cop car was flashing red and blue. An older woman who kept her hair dyed bronze, the one with the peaches-and-cream complexion who regularly flushed to boiled red when she was out in the sun, was talking to two men. Bill and Bill.

"Linden, you have to go."

"What? Why?"

They were here for me.

32.

My neighbor had seen the transformation. Caught some seconds of it on her phone camera. Another video of me walking away, arm in arm with Linden. If I had renounced Linden, ran back into my house, I might have been able to claim she had bewitched me. But it was clear that I was doing magic and was comfortable with it.

Preston was on the front porch being interviewed. He said, "Jo, Jo, are you okay?"

"He's been enchanted," one of the Bills muttered.

A few of my neighbors caught wind of what was happening. They came out as I was being silver-cuffed and offered testimony. The crows were extra loud when I was around. A white man I didn't even recognize said that once I had given him a dirty look when he said hello to me. Immediately, he had come down with a fever that lasted three days. The neighbor who had filmed everything said she had thought this was a dream at the time, but now, she was certain I had flown past her window on the last full moon. Praise Satan, I had sung.

"Preston, stay away," I called as they led me to their car.

I knew he too would be in trouble. In the car, one of the Bills sat by me while the other continued talking to Preston. I told him I was a witch. I had bewitched Preston by making him drink a love spell. Nothing he said or did was his fault.

"No, you didn't," Bill said.

"He didn't know."

Preston ran to the car. He was wearing no coat and only the

thick Batman socks that were so uncool, so contrary to how he used to try to impress me. One toe had a darned hole in it because he just couldn't get rid of them.

"We're getting married," he said. "I take responsibility."

"I love you," I said. It was one of the few times when I didn't say it as a response. I immediately wished I had said it more often.

One of the neighbors was asking Bill if it was possible I had cursed her grandmother to death. She had been ninety-three, had some mild health issues, sure, but the doctor had said she could live to a hundred. And that grandma had died in her sleep on the neighbor's couch closest to our house. It was my fault. Another woman was saying I had given her kid dyslexia. A man said I had forced him to download the worst pornography about a butt detective and that had ruined his most recent relationship.

"Please," I said to Preston.

"Where are you taking her?" He kept knocking and knocking on the window. The Bill who was in the car with me got out. He told Preston to calm down or he could be fined or even charged.

I was going to be tortured again. I knew it. There wouldn't even have to be a trial. I covered my face. I thought about how years ago, I had protested the burnings of witches. How can we say we're a culture of life if we still allow people to be put to death? I felt certain no one would feel sorry for me. There was clear evidence I was exactly what they said I was: a witch.

It was so cold. Preston's nose was running. His eyes were on me. The witches on the island would have told me now was the time to transform. Become a bird, Josephine. Make yourself into a mouse. I couldn't bring myself to do it. What if I was stuck that way forever? That isn't worse than burning, a small voice said. And besides, I was in this car. If I became a mouse, I would be easier to kill. As a bird, I could maybe tear at someone and flap my wings and scare them into letting me out the door. But the Bills had guns. They wouldn't hesitate to shoot me out of the sky. I didn't know why, but it felt better to me to potentially die as a woman than to be shot out of the air.

"Preston," I spoke as loudly as I could. "I need you to call my dad. There's nothing you can do for me tonight. Please. I'm sorry. Please."

His eyes were shiny, white and black in the darkness. They were beautiful. He pressed his hand against the glass. I looked up at him. Nodded, mouthed, I'm okay, I'm okay. I couldn't tell if he could see me. After what felt like too long—I kept waiting for him to be arrested or reprimanded—he took a step back.

33.

They told my friends and family there would be a trial in a few months. They told me there would be a burning at the end of the week. I had done magic; I had cavorted with another witch; and they were still investigating all the claims my neighbors made. It had spread beyond the dead grandmother and speaking to animals, the dyslexia, the porn, to claims about illnesses, bats in attics, cars and refrigerators that kept breaking, a Black man dressed all in black I had summoned to seduce wives and end marriages. There was no way to prove I hadn't done all the things they claimed. I was not entitled to a lawyer. In cases where a witch has been verified, a lawyer couldn't do anything. The only way to stop my magic was to kill me.

For the first four days, I spent twenty hours a day alone in my cell. I spent two separate hours outside the cell, also alone. There was an hour and a half for questions, which almost felt like a relief after all the silence, and a half-hour when a woman wearing headphones sprayed me with holy water infused with garlic and muttered "ugly little witch" under her breath.

Angie visited and tried to joke at first. "You could've just told me you didn't want to go to my wedding. You didn't have to do all this."

We were being supervised by three people. One was a man wearing headphones in case I decided to start popping off curses. The others were two women holding assault rifles and wearing face masks that made them look like baseball umpires. The meeting space was small enough that if one of them fired the gun, all five of us would have been taken out. The walls were white, the chairs were silver, and it smelled like sage and garlic.

"You know me," I said. "I'm a drama queen."

Angie's skin was fake tanned and a little orange. It was hilarious, but I told her she looked great. Her hair had a blowout. On Friday night, I would die. On Saturday morning, she would get married. They would adopt a kid or get a surrogate in two years according to their contract. I wanted to tell her goodbye. There wasn't a point though. It would only make her feel bad. She couldn't do anything. Why spend this last time telling her they were going to kill me rather than have a trial? Why let her spend this week trying desperately to save me, when she couldn't? We had known each other for so long.

"I'm sorry I'm going to miss it. You're my best friend. I wanted to be there for you."

She paused and pursed her lips. Angie looked at all three guards. Touching between two women was strictly prohibited.

"Don't," I said.

"If our videos are cleared of witchcraft, post them online," I said after a few minutes. "I have nothing to lose anymore. We wrote all those jokes. We should believe in ourselves."

"I'm going to see you again, right?"

"If they let you."

"Oh, my god, did you kill that grandma?" Angie asked, trying to joke again. Then she shook her head at herself. "I'm sorry. It's not funny at all."

"I mean it's a little funny. She was, what, ninety-three? A leaf falling from a tree and hitting her in the face probably could've killed her. A spicy dinner or a slightly old clam could've killed her. But they think just because my house was on their street."

Finally, she laughed. It was a relief to hear it again.

"You know," Angie continued, "a woman in Illinois was accused of something similar to you a few years ago. She ended up agreeing to pay something like ten thousand dollars in fines and live far away from all major populations. Didn't even have to go to trial."

"Was she Black?"

Angie sighed. "No."

My dad had scheduled a time to visit but didn't come. I sat with my arms crossed wearing the black scrubs they'd given me. I looked at the no-shoelaces black sneakers. Pretended my fingernails were extra-interesting because I didn't want to make eye contact with any of the guards.

The part of me that did not want to die holding grudges tried to find ways to understand this was for the best. I wasn't entirely sure if I could lie so easily to him as I could to Angie. I wanted her to feel good and to always think of our last visit together in a positive way. With him, I didn't care how he thought of our last time together. All I could think about was his silence and distance since I had returned. The letter he had sent. It made me feel sixteen years old again, drinking a whole bottle of wine in the bathtub, thinking about whether or not I should die while he fell asleep in front of the television like he did every night. We had both been depressed, but I was the child. I sat with that thought for a while, thought again about his mental health. How withdrawn he was, the way he slept on the couch whenever he could, and the ways people spoke about him. I didn't know if I could forgive him, but I tried to see him as a person who deserved my compassion. My hands covered my eyes.

Someone touched my shoulder and I looked up, hoping it was him. The guard with the headphones on was offering me a box of tissues. I took two and thanked him profusely. Anytime someone made the effort to treat me like a person, the gratitude poured from my mouth. I didn't even have it in me to be embarrassed by the earnestness in my voice. The other guards were giving me an it's-just-a-tissue look.

* * *

Preston showed up wearing a suit, his hair a little disheveled, as if he had spent too long deciding how it should look and then messed it up.

"You look like a hot lawyer on TV," I said.

He smiled but didn't laugh as he would've at home. I was aware of his feet and his hands and his lips. Even his eyebrows made me want to stand up and hug him. There were dark circles under his eyes, and it was clear he hadn't been sleeping or eating well. I kept my hands bunched into fists, didn't allow myself to lean forward in my seat.

We sat and looked at each other. I could see every thought shifting across his face. Preston was glad to see me. He thought I hadn't been sleeping or eating well, either. He was worried about me. He loved me.

"My dad didn't come," I said.

Preston rolled his eyes. "I know he's your dad, but he's such a little punk."

I laughed. The sound of it made him relax a smidge.

"How are you?" we asked each other at the same time.

"Cursed," I said.

"Bad joke," he said.

I paused. This would be so much easier, I thought, if I could hold his hand.

If the situation had been different and I had known this was going to be the last time we ever saw each other, I would've put in effort: deep-conditioned my hair and paid special attention to the edges. I would've done a face mask, put essences on my skin, worked to make it glow with health. I would've thought on and off for at least a day about what to wear. I wanted to be the most beautiful, carefree, memorable version of myself. I could feel the tangle growing at the nape of my neck, the same place it always started if I wasn't meticulous in my grooming. A zit loomed painful on my chin.

"Do you want me to try to say something to your dad?" he asked.

"Tell him." I shook my head. "You don't have to tell him anything. But if you end up talking to him, I guess, tell him I missed him and I hope to see him soon."

"I probably would've said 'tell him to fuck off.'"

"I'm working on being generous to other people."

"Are you going to come out of here as a suspiciously good person? One of those people who is all warm and kind because under the mask there's a deep terrible void?" His hair fell across his forehead and he brushed it back.

"Yes, exactly that. You better get ready." I shook my hands loose. I forced them down at my sides. Preston was looking at me— tenderness in his eyes, smiling because I was near. I thought if I had been more willing to see him, more available sooner, we could've had so much more time. I let out a big, shaky breath.

"Do you love that woman you were with in the video?" he asked. Preston was no longer looking at me but past me toward the white walls.

"What?"

"When you transformed."

"No, I know who you're talking about. I just didn't expect the question."

"Do you?"

"A little." There was no point in lying. "Linden is a person who I think I'm always going to be a little in love with. I feel like I can be anyone when I'm around her. But I didn't cheat on you that night. She and I have kissed before, but that was before you and I were serious. And she's hot in a way that I've always been attracted to."

He nodded but still didn't look at me.

"I know it hurts your feelings, but I want everything to be open between us. And I'm really attracted to you, too."

"Jo, I—"

"I'm a witch," I said.

"No, you're not."

"I am."

He crossed his arms. "They'll never let you leave if you keep saying that."

I opened my mouth, stopped myself from saying, They're burning me tomorrow. Preston cleared his throat but didn't say anything.

"If things are going to work for us, I want to be completely honest with you." I shut my eyes. "Is there anything you think I should know?"

"It used to really hurt my feelings," he said, "the way you treated me when we started hooking up. I've always liked you, wanted you to want more. I did some dumb shit, tried to act casual because I thought that's what you wanted. And I've loved the last few months with you. They were what I always wanted, but sometimes I wondered if they were happening only because finally, finally, you needed me." His voice was even as he spoke. I could hear all the times he had thought these things and considered saying them in how unemotional he was being. "Did the last months happen only because you needed someone, and I was there?"

"No. I don't think so. No. I think I never realized how much you actually cared about me until you showed up for me. It wasn't." I wished I could sound less emotional. My voice was getting high and wavery. "I wish I had been able to be more available."

We were both crying. I didn't tell him I had sat with the tangle of it, needing and wanting and loving, and didn't know if it was ever possible to be fully certain if I loved him as long as my safety was based on him.

"I'm sorry I can't hug you," I said.

"Someday," he said.

34.

Once, there was a witch named Josephine who was the daughter of a witch who flew away into the night. She was the great-great-great-great-great-grandniece of a witch who survived a burning, who flew away from the burning pillar and plunged her burnt feet into the sea, making a fog that lasted a week.

Once, there was a witch named Josephine who transformed into glass at the wrong time and was caught on camera. She was accused of many things she hadn't done, but while they were preparing her for death, Josephine wished that she had done those things because at least the whole process would've felt a little less spurious.

Once, there were men who loved to see punishment. They were elected officials, businessmen, community pillars, and every kind of man in between. They loved anything that would balkanize everyone they considered beneath them. If everyone was busy fighting for their rights, fighting each other, and the men stayed together, they would always get to be in charge of everything.

When I say men, this isn't to say there weren't women like that, too. Gender expression has never guaranteed solidarity, especially among people who are trying to survive.

On a cold winter night, a group of these people bundled themselves in their wool overcoats and drab gray scarves. They went to a small beach not open to the public and sat in uncomfortable beach chairs. A few tried to make "jokes" like, "If this was Jamaica, I would've gotten served three cocktails already!" Even though the jokes made no sense, they were used to people politely chuckling because they were the kind of people who other people treated gently. Some chatted about the case. One man sat tense and berated himself for not advocating for this poor woman. He thought burnings were disgusting and outdated and cruel. All deaths by the state were, but his political party believed that it was part of this country's great traditions and should not go away. He liked going to his office and he liked going to D.C., and he liked going to nice dinners where people asked him in soft tones to think deeply about how many jobs, how much money could flow into his great state of Michigan if he voted against this bill or voted for that one or maybe found a way to sponsor this. The man loved feeling important more than being right.

The witch Josephine was prepared for death. She ate a dinner of garlic knots and oversized pizza from the pizza place she always went to when she was drunk. They had told her she didn't have to be cheap about this, it was a time-honored tradition for prisoners to eat steaks or lobsters or homemade pastas, but she had said, "I might as well be honest." Then she changed into a long black dress, a pointy hat, and shoes with ugly buckles that she rolled her eyes at while putting them on. A guard injected her with a sedative. She did not cry. She did not leave a last will or testimony. To one guard she said, "This makes me feel like I'm getting my wisdom teeth pulled again."

"May God have mercy on your soul."

Then she was led out to the beach and tied to a pillar. Birch logs soaked in kerosene were placed around and against the pillar in neat triangles. Newspapers were crumpled and put between the logs. A low murmur of conversation continued. The only personal effect the witch wore was a small bracelet from a friend; everything else was provided by the state.

A chaplain said a prayer to her no one else could hear. He raised a cross and said loudly, "Do you renounce the Devil? Do you forsake the dark magic boiling in your soul?"

The witch did not respond because already she was feeling soft-slipper-brained from the sedative.

An officer of the Michigan Bureau of Witchcraft read out the charges. This took a while, and a few people were astonished by the depth of her depravity. A few wondered where the proof was for all these accusations. They had looked at the records and seen a video where the woman in front of them seemed shocked and frightened by what had happened to her. But they couldn't think of anything they could do except maybe donate to an advocacy group anonymously. Most people were watching the witch's face, they were smelling the kerosene and the cold lake, and they welcomed the coming fire because at least they would be warm again.

A match was struck. The people in attendance applauded as the logs burned orange and smoke began to drift. Some immediately covered their noses. They had been to burnings before. Smelled burnt flesh and hair, and while they loved the spectacle, they did not want to experience that again. Some people put in earplugs, assuming that as the burning progressed, the witch, even sedated, would scream and plead. None of them was allowed to have a cell phone.

This is the story of the witch who refused to burn.

Some people said that there was power in her blood, a gift from her ancestors that meant she could endure the flames. Some said it was from the bracelet given to her by another witch. That the bracelet was enchanted by three witches, it was woven with cattails and dune grass and seaweed. When the flames touched it, water leaked farther and farther out, putting out the flames that tried to take her. The witch said even though her mind wanted to sleep, her body was alive with the desire to live, and that manifested as magic.

I could feel myself burning, Josephine said, and I told myself I was a glacier. I thanked all the icebergs that had been on the Earth, apologized to those left. This land, who I was, all of it in some part was because of them. They had carved the Great Lakes, they had made Michigan, those things had made me. I asked for their protection.

I saw the door I had seen so many times in the sky. Pink and gray. It was silent this time, and slowly, as I felt the logs' heat, my robe burn, even the edges of my hair, it opened in front of me. Out of it came the sound of women singing, their voices harmonizing. I didn't recognize the song, but it made me even in this, the worst of moments, feel moved. It grew louder and louder. All the voices. Birds joined in, squalling and singing trills. When I needed it most, somehow, they were there. I thought among all that sound I could hear Linden. I could hear my mother. Inside I felt like I had drunk something too cold; it knocked the breath out of me. I told all of me to become the strongest ice the world has ever seen. And my lungs and heart and intestines and tongue obeyed. My skin followed. Steam was rising everywhere between me and the flames. The flames had already destroyed the robes and bonds. People were backing away. I wanted to live. I had never in my entire life wanted something so badly. A fog drifted up from the lake. A bird called to me, "Gratitude."

When I felt ready, I soared up into the air. Snow and hail fell around me as I went up into the clouds. Someone fired a gun up into the night, but the bullet was nowhere near me. I flew for a mile, fast and sure, reacting only with adrenaline. And when I felt safe enough to stop, I paused, far down the shore, and sank my feet into the cold lake. Watched the steam rise and the fog grow.

35.

I flew straight to Angie's old house. I knew she would be there. She was in her childhood bedroom with the ratty old loveseat next to the window, the posters of female soccer players still bold and exuberant on her walls. Angie was drinking a beer and looking at her phone when I tapped on her window.

She dropped the beer when she saw me. I think she swore, but the windows were closed against the January cold. I didn't feel the wind or ice. I wondered if there would always be a layer of permafrost inside me. It didn't matter. I was alive.

Angie let me in. Her wedding dress was slumped on a hanger in the closet. She handed me a blanket. Asked if anyone had seen me.

"The storm is too bad," I said.

"Have you always been able to fly?" Angie asked.

"It's not safe to do magic alone," I said, "but I was already going to die if I didn't do something."

Then she was hugging me and she was crying and I was overwhelmed. I couldn't cry, but I held her until we both felt ready to speak.

"I couldn't leave you without saying goodbye," I said.

She blew her nose. Stuffed the used tissue into her robe pocket. I had seen her in that robe so many times, writing, pacing at night when she couldn't sleep. I realized this plaid blue-and-white robe was what I often pictured her in. The fake tan had become a little less supernaturally orange.

"I know you've made a lot of plans," I said. "But you could come with me to the island."

We had stayed up late so many times in this bedroom. We had come out to each other while watching an episode of a sexy spy show. We had talked about college and our parents. We had started writing together, sitting next to each other on that loveseat. Fifty jokes about what it's like to be a high school girl. None of them good, some were stupid, some were offensive, but we laughed together for hours while writing them. It felt right that if we were never going to see each other again, our time together ended in this same place.

I told her my mother was on the island, still alive. That it was a place where people could go and live the lives they wanted. It wasn't perfect. The sky bled sometimes. There were monsters.

"But we could both be free."

Angie paused and clasped her hands together. Her fingernails were painted white with little rhinestones pasted on the tips. They were ridiculous and clearly her mother's idea. "I already knew your mother was alive."

She sat up and walked over to her bed. Angie reached under the bed and pulled out a box. Inside were two dolls that looked like us. Their hair was made of reeds and dune grass. They smelled of rosemary, like my mother's hut.

36.

It's a June day with soft blue skies filled with bright white clouds when we start building the path. We will have to dig up the soil, place rocks and herbs and even notes of encouragement that will go beneath the special cement. A layer of feathers from living and dead birds. Another layer of cement. The path will appear only to those who need it. We don't know if it will work, but we know we need to try.

We turn to each other with our shovels, we lift out dirt, pebbles, worms. We say the words, "You will be safe here" and lay down the first layer of stone and shells. The sun looks down hot, and I think of all the people across the world who need this path and dig out another footstep. And I see you.

It's a moment when you're trying to find something, anything, anyone to keep the world at bay, to make it stop pinning down your arms and legs and gnawing at your throat. You take your coat, look around at your home for one last time, and shut the door. You drive for miles and miles, until you hear through the bumps and tire sounds your own name being called. Warm. Welcoming. How long has it been since someone spoke your name with tenderness and not irritation or boredom or anger or threats? At the edge of the woods, some place dark that usually you might be cautious of, especially alone, especially at night, there's a light.

The path is silver and white and pink and green. It could almost be made from candy, the colors are so vivid. It shouldn't be real. You leave your car. Lights and engine still on, you walk toward it. Your name is louder and louder, called with more sweetness, more trust, the closer you come. It's the path talking. Telling you people will be waiting with food and blankets. It will be a place to start again. To be free. You start walking.

Acknowledgments

Four years ago, I told my agent, Dan Conaway, I wanted to write about witches. I don't think he'll remember this now but his immediate response was, "If anyone can make them feel new, it's you." I don't entirely agree with that—I want to read so many witch books—but the immediate compliment kept me writing this book. And in general, I feel really lucky to have an agent who pushes me like Dan does. And thank you to the rest of the staff at Writers House, but especially Chaim Lipskar, Peggy Boulos Smith, and Lauren Carsley. I also need to thank my agent at WME, Sanjana Seelam, for her dedicated efforts toward making this book get into the right hands.

Thank you to everyone at Amistad, but especially Rakesh Satyal, Judith Curr, and Paul Olsewski. Rakesh, there's a lot of wonderful things I could say about you but let me get to the point: working with you on this has made me a better writer. And thank you to Maya Alpert, Brieana Garcia, and Tara Parsons. And to all the HarperCollins sales reps: I didn't get a chance to thank you for your hard work on *Lakewood* after it came out, but I still think about how much you all have done and keep doing for my career. Thank you.

And speaking of *Lakewood*, there are so many people who did so much for that book in that time after the book is printed and out in the world. Daniel Goldin at Boswell Books, everyone at Source Booksellers in Detroit, Kelsey Ronan and the Room Project out of Detroit, Hilary Leichtner, C Pam Zhang (you made lockdown book release still feel special with tiramisu), Maisy Card, Phong Nguyen, Cathy Bowman, East City Bookshop, Women & Children First, Katie who basically became a walking-talking Megan Giddings pop-up bookstore/younger sister, Steffan Triplett whose writing about my work made me push myself, Anne Valente, Kelli Jo Ford, Matt Bell, Megha Majumdar, Alexandra Chang, Ladee Hubbard, Juan Martinez, Marisa Siegel, Jami Attenberg, Kelly Link, and every person who went out of their way to feature my book on their social media, invited me to events or put my name forward for things, people who had me on their podcasts, put me on lists, wrote about *Lakewood* in thoughtful criticism, or sent me a letter letting me know how much they enjoyed it. *Lakewood* could've easily disappeared during everything that happened in the spring of 2020, and it's really because of so, so many people—and I'm sorry if I didn't list you here—who made it visible.

Back to *The Women Could Fly* gratitude! I need to thank the anonymous witch who made and sent me a spirit chime for my office. Thank you to Rishi, Naomi, and Travis at Hillman Grad. I hate being complimented; I needed the compliments to keep writing. Angel Pean who made Josephine come to life in the audiobook. Dr. Robin Silbergleid and my students at Michigan State University. Romayne Rubinas Dorsey for all the walks and for all the times we've spent telling dogs how good they are. Lisa Locascio Nighthawk and all my grad students at Antioch. Audra Puchalski for sending me zines and talking plants. Katie Penguin who kept hyping me up as only a longtime friend turned librarian could. Aaron. Paul Asta and Scott Fenton; we've been friends for almost a decade now, and I still want to impress you both with my writing. Nadxi Nieto who in just forty-five minutes made me understand the island. Dustin Wycliffe for giving me free, surprise inspiration. Laura, if I don't see you in the next year, I will explode. Hartley,

Nazar, Gary, and Doctor for sitting on me and making me work. My parents, Jeff and Karen, my sisters Jennifer and Katie, and my niece, Miss Amelia. Marie, Miguel, Nick, and Levi. Thank you to Ava, my massage therapist who said, "this book is killing your neck," and kept fighting off all the death I was doing to it. Thank you to Lance Cleland who read a chunk of this novel before it was unfinished and made me a part of the Tin House family. Thank you to my workshop at Tin House for making me fall back in love with novels right when I was feeling like I was too tired to keep going.

Thank you to wine, bonfires, nightguards, road opener oil and mugwort ointment. Thank you, Bob, for your little black cabin in the woods where I wrote several chapters of this book. Thank you to everyone who let me vent or worry to them the past two years. Thank you to late night rain and storms that kept me company when I was writing, instead of sleeping. Bees, figs, walks with friends.

One of the few uncomplicated good things that happened during the start of the pandemic, was my brother, Jeff Giddings, came to stay with us. During that time, he started his doctoral degree in AAADS, and thus became my research assistant for Black Studies, especially about transformations, utopias, and how we build new communities. I'm grateful that you put so many books and ideas on my radar. I'm lucky that you're my brother and my friend.

Finally, thank you, Jon. You've taken my author photos twice now and find a way to not make me look someone who's always thinking, "yikes." I'm a complicated person who wants to talk about everything all the time and you take my hands every time and lean in. I love you. Thank you for always believing in me.

About the Author

Megan Giddings is an assistant professor at the University of Minnesota. Her first novel, *Lakewood*, was one of *New York* magazine's top ten books of 2020, an NPR Best Book of 2020, a Michigan Notable Book for 2021, a finalist for two NAACP Image Awards, and was a finalist for a *Los Angeles Times* Book Prize in the Ray Bradbury Science Fiction, Fantasy, and Speculative category. Megan's writing has received funding and support from the Barbara Deming Foundation and Hedgebrook. She lives in the Midwest.